"I want the truth," he said softly. "Which you never told me. Not last night. And not before."

"The truth?" Claire repeated. Hearing the tone of accusation, she thought of the long lie Griff had lived this past year. Whatever he meant, he didn't have much room to chide her about truth. "The truth about what?"

"Just why do they think I'd be willing to do anything in order to get your daughter back?"

His voice was soft. And reasonable. But she didn't like what she heard there, underlying those surface qualities.

"What do they want you to do?" she asked.

"She's mine, isn't she, Claire?" he asked, ignoring her question. "That's why these people are so certain they can call the tune, and I'll have to dance to it. She's my daughter. And you never told me."

Dear Reader,

The most frequently asked question an author hears is, "Where do you get your ideas?" For this trilogy, that spark was wondering what would happen to our secret warriors now that the Cold War has ended.

What if a highly specialized black ops team is considered by the CIA to be obsolete in today's New World order? What if the men who had spent their lives carrying out incredibly dangerous missions around the globe are now an embarrassment to their own government? What if the agency that created them wants to destroy their identities, so that even if the operations they took part in come to light, they could never be traced back to their superiors?

In this trilogy, three men, all members of the CIA's elite External Security Team, are in such a position. Their identities destroyed, but with all the deadly skills they have been taught still intact, these men embark on private missions that will test not only their expertise in dealing with danger, but also their hearts. And the skills they once used to guard their country will now be employed to protect those they love.

Please watch for all the stories in this new MEN OF MYSTERY series from Harlequin Intrigue: *The Bride's Protector* (April 1999), *The Stranger She Knew* (May 1999), and *Her Baby, His Secret* (June 1999). Enjoy!

Love,

Gayle Wilson

Her Baby, His Secret
Gayle Wilson

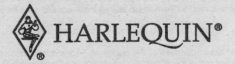

TORONTO • NEW YORK • LONDON
AMSTERDAM • PARIS • SYDNEY • HAMBURG
STOCKHOLM • ATHENS • TOKYO • MILAN • MADRID
PRAGUE • WARSAW • BUDAPEST • AUCKLAND

For my friend Shirley—
another dedication to add to your collection—
with my love and great affection

ISBN 0-373-22517-2

HER BABY, HIS SECRET

Visit us at www.romance.net

Printed in U.S.A.

CAST OF CHARACTERS

Claire Heywood—Someone has stolen her baby...and the ransom they want isn't something within her power to give them.

Griff Cabot—The daughter he never knew he had has brought him back from the dead. But are her kidnappers asking the impossible?

Carl Steiner—Griff's replacement in the CIA. Is he friend or foe? Or simply a man trying to do a thankless job?

Jake Holt—The team's computer expert. It's up to Jake to provide them with the information they'll need to carry out their final mission.

Jordan Cross—He owes Claire Heywood for more than one favor.

Hawk—Griff Cabot's closest friend. But does Lucas Hawkins have an agenda of his own?

Monty Gardner—Claire's grandfather and a former director of the CIA.

Prologue

It was always night in the dream. And she was running. It felt as if she were running away from someone, but she knew that couldn't be right. At least at some point in the sequence she knew that.

Running. And the maze of rose bushes that surrounded her tore at her arms and her face as she ran. The light ahead was so dim and distant, but she knew she had to reach it in order to be safe. If she could only reach the light…

And then the house would materialize in front of her, looming up out of the gray netherworld of the dream. She always stopped when that happened, her feet suddenly reluctant, her passage through the maze and the darkness slowed by an unbearable pressure she didn't understand.

If she could only reach the house… She knew that she'd be safe there, and yet invariably her footsteps slowed until she was walking, the sound of her shoes on the gravel path disturbing the soft, surrounding stillness of the night.

She would climb the steps, and as she neared the door, the scent of roses from the maze she had escaped would pervade the air. She knew that their fragrance meant something, but she could never decide exactly what, or how she felt about it. Her emotions about the roses were as confus-

ing, as nebulous and unformed, as her reluctance to approach the door.

She always raised her hand to knock, but the sound she made, if there were one, was muffled by the darkness and the now-overpowering scent of the roses. Then the door silently opened anyway. And behind the man who stood within its frame was the light she had been running toward.

It was only after she put her cold, trembling fingers into the hand he held out to her that she could see his face, materializing before her, just as the house always did. His eyes were dark and compassionate, and although she expected him to, he never seemed to judge what she had done.

As soon as she looked into his eyes, all the doubt and reluctance vanished. Spiraled away in the darkness, to leave only the feel of his hand. Warm and so strong. Strong enough to pull her out of the maze in which she had been lost, and into the light. Strong enough to keep her safe.

Then he was leading her up the staircase, although she could never remember crossing the threshold. And because she knew so well what lay at the top of the stairs they were climbing, anticipation increased with each step.

Ascending together. Hand in hand. Somewhere in her heart she knew that this was the way it was supposed to be, and that this place was where she was supposed to be.

She didn't understand how she could have gotten so lost. So lost in the maze. In the clawing pain of its thorns. She had been so alone.

Never again, she thought. Not as long as she held on to his hand. Then, even as the thought formed, it was all gone. His hand. The staircase. The house.

And once more she was running through the maze, in the cold, dark sickness of her grief and despair, toward a light she knew she would never be able to reach again.

Chapter One

Claire Heywood opened her eyes slowly, climbing out of sleep as if it were a pit. Too little sleep, she diagnosed groggily, automatically analyzing the weak winter sunlight that was filtering into the room.

It was too early to think about getting up, but there had been something... She listened to the dawn stillness that surrounded her, waiting for whatever had disturbed it to be repeated. When it wasn't, her eyelids dropped downward again, her body returning to that blessed state of relaxation possible only when she knew everything was right within her small world.

Nothing alarming had intruded into its safe and well-kept familiarity. Nothing was here that shouldn't be. Only the accustomed quietness of the exclusive Georgetown neighborhood where she lived. Peaceful, apparently, even on New Year's Day.

Because of the holiday, Claire had been up much later than usual last night. At least later than was now the norm. She had let her sister goad her into attending one of the embassy parties. Of course, no one could provoke Claire like Maddy could. In her anger over her sister's repeated accusations that she was turning into a hermit, Claire had also agreed to the oh-so-eligible escort her sister's husband had casually suggested.

The two of them had ridden over to the embassy with Maddy and Charles, but still, Claire acknowledged, there was no way around the awkward reality. She had had a blind date, more commonly known now as a fix-up. And even if she argued that last night hadn't technically been a date, it was still as near to one as she had come in a long time.

And in all honesty, the experience had been relatively painless. And relatively meaningless as well, of course.

Claire rolled restlessly onto her side, pushing her pillow into a more comfortable shape under her cheek. For some reason, despite the lateness of the hour when she'd gone to bed, she didn't seem able to slip back into sleep this morning, as much as she wanted to.

Too much champagne? she wondered. A little hung over? She must have been the slightest bit tipsy when she'd gotten home last night. Giddy enough to let John Amerson kiss her at the door, she remembered with a pang of remorse and embarrassment. She hadn't meant for that to happen, but in all honesty she couldn't say that the kiss had been unpleasant. Actually, there had been nothing about the whole evening that had been unpleasant.

She opened her eyes again, studying the familiar pattern of light that the rising sun, reflecting off the carpet of her bedroom, threw against the wall. White wool had not been a practical choice for carpeting, she supposed. When she had decorated the house, however, not only had practicality not been a priority, it had not even been much of a consideration.

Now, of course, it was both. Another aspect of her life that had drastically changed in the course of the last year. More than enough changes, she thought, her lips tightening reflexively.

She lay, watching the spill of sunshine and willing her mind to disengage from that familiar litany of regret. There was nothing she could do about any of it. Nothing she could change. And of course, there were a great many things about the last twelve months that she wouldn't change, even if she could.

Her lips relaxed into a smile, envisioning the room next door. Its occupant was apparently still sleeping, cuddled under the heavy warmth of the quilt her Great-grandmother Heywood had hand-stitched to celebrate her birth. It would be stretched tightly over a small, rounded bottom that at this time of the morning was usually sticking straight up in the air.

And that air, Claire realized, despite the normal efficiency of the central heating unit, was decidedly chilly. She pulled the covers up over her exposed shoulder, trying to relax again into the peaceful cocoon of oblivion. Trying not to think about last night. Or about New Year's Eves past. Trying not to think about anything.

After a few minutes devoted to that fruitless endeavor, she determinedly directed her thoughts back to the nursery next door. Gardner was a distraction from regret that almost always worked, except on those rare occasions when Claire let herself acknowledge how much her daughter looked like her father.

But this wasn't going to be one of those times, she decided doggedly. Not after last night. Her first date, she thought again, almost amused by the phrase.

Maddy, as usual, had been right. It *hadn't* killed her to go out with John Amerson. Her lips tilted at the memory of her sister's familiar arguments. And Maddy would, of course, be calling this morning for a report.

"Yes, I survived. Yes, he seems to be very nice." A firm *"It's none of your business"* to the rest.

And for herself? she wondered. An acknowledgment, maybe, that although he wasn't Griff...

But then, no one else ever will be Griff, she thought. *And*

*here I am, right back where I was determined not to be.
Especially not today, the beginning of a brand-new year.*

Disgusted, she pushed the covers off and sat up on the
side of the bed. If she wasn't going back to sleep, she might
as well get up and get some work done before Gardner
woke and began demanding attention.

The whole wonderful day lay before them. A rare one
that they could spend totally together. Claire had a couple
of things to take care of, but she didn't have to go into the
office, of course. She had given the nanny the long holiday
weekend off, so it would be just the two of them.

She slid her feet into her mules, standing up and stretching out the kinks. Her watch confirmed her guess that it
was early—only a little after six. Considering the time
she'd crawled into bed last night, it was no wonder she was
feeling rocky. *Not* the champagne, she decided. Just lack
of sleep.

Shivering, she crossed the expanse of thick white carpet,
rubbing her palms up and down the sleeves of her pajamas.
Maybe the baby-sitter had turned down the heat last night
and forgotten to mention it before she left.

Claire always kept the house warm because of the baby.
Mrs. Crutchen, the nanny, was cold-natured, so she never
complained, but maybe Beth, being younger, had decided
it was too hot. In any case, Claire was glad she'd gotten
up. If Gardner had managed to kick her covers off, she was
probably freezing her sweet little tush by now.

Claire opened the nursery door and was met by a damp
coldness that sent a frisson of alarm through her. If her
room had seemed chilled, then this one…

The damn window was open, she realized, hurrying
across to pull down the sash and lock it. Why in the world
would Beth, the most reliable sitter in existence, despite her
age, leave the window open in the baby's room? It made
no sense. Not in the dead of winter. Not in this freezing

cold. It was a miracle that Gardner wasn't screaming her head off....

Claire's gaze automatically found the crib. There was no rounded bulge of baby bottom visible. Gardner had probably retreated from the cold, burrowing deeper into the warmth of the covers.

Claire took the three or four steps that separated her from the baby bed and looked in. That was when her heart stopped, congealed by a cold that owed nothing to the temperature of the room. In spite of the evidence of her eyes, she frantically pulled the covers back, flinging them to the end of the bed. And then she jerked them up, ripping them loose from the mattress and throwing them to the floor.

Which didn't change the harsh reality. There was no baby in the crib. Knees trembling, Claire bent, crawling under the bed, as if she thought her six-month-old daughter might suddenly have mastered the art of climbing out over the rails.

Still on her hands and knees, she picked up the wadded quilt and sheet, knowing immediately by their weight that there was nothing else in the pile. When she had physically confirmed that face by pawing through them again, she dropped them, her eyes searching every corner of the room.

Shock and disbelief clashed with acceptance of the unacceptable, so her mind sought another explanation. Any other explanation. Maybe Beth had taken Gardner home with her for some reason. But Claire had seen the sitter out last night, locking the door behind her. And there had been no one else in the house. No one...

Her gaze flew again to the window. Which had been open on this bitterly cold night. A window that shouldn't have been left open, unless...

No note, she told herself, scrambling up and running her hands over the mattress. She picked up the sheet and quilt again, shaking them, almost relieved when nothing fell out.

She examined the top of the chest and then the changing table, but there was nothing on either of them.

If someone had taken the baby, she assured herself, they would have left a note. So Gardner had to be here. She *had* to be here.

Claire ran across to the closet and opened the door, as if she believed Gardner might be playing some macabre game of hide and seek. With trembling fingers, Claire pushed aside the hangers that held exquisite, doll-size dresses, her mind denying what her heart had already been forced to acknowledge.

The closet, too, was empty. As empty as the room. As empty as her life had been before her daughter had been born. *Gardner,* Claire thought, the images of the short months since her birth flying through her head like a video tape on fast forward.

But if someone had taken her daughter, then surely... Surely, dear God, they would have told her what to do to get her back. They would have told her where to go. What they wanted. They wouldn't take her baby and leave nothing behind, not even a threat, a demand for ransom, a stereotypical warning about not calling in the authorities. Surely they hadn't taken her baby and left her nothing.

And yet, as she stood trembling in the center of the room, surrounded by its joyfully chosen furnishings and toys, Claire Heywood realized that that was exactly what they had done. Someone had opened the nursery window last night and had taken Gardner away from her. And had given her no idea of what she should do to get her back.

"MY NIECE," he said, smiling as he carefully placed the sleeping baby into her arms. "I'm afraid my sister is having some...problems," he said hesitantly. "Nothing serious, I think, but caring for Karen right now is proving to be...difficult. A little...more than she's up to handling at the moment. I think that's not uncommon for first-time mothers,'' he added, his eyes seeking her assurance that that was so.

Poor man, Rose Connor thought, holding the baby he had given her cuddled against her ample bosom. *He sounds as if he's afraid I'm going to judge. And Rose Connor judges no one. I've enough sins on me own head.*

"Oh, not uncommon at all," she said aloud, eagerly turning back the blanket in which the baby was wrapped to look down at her face. She seemed to be sleeping very soundly, but then it was morning nap time.

"This is my number in case you need to get in touch with me. You can leave a message if I'm out, and I'll return your call as soon as possible. The pediatrician's number is there as well, but...I'm afraid I would prefer that you call me first."

"Of course," Rose said. "Unless it's an emergency," she added.

Rose always made an effort to follow her employers' instructions, strange as some of them seemed to be, but she wouldn't do anything that might compromise her ability to give the care her babies needed. She made no promises on that.

"She's a healthy little thing. I doubt you'll have any problems you yourself aren't capable of handling. You come very highly recommended, Ms. Connor."

"Just Rose," she corrected, still examining her new charge.

This one certainly appeared to be well taken care of, Rose decided. Whatever problems that poor girl might be having, they hadn't affected the baby. What she had told her new employer was certainly true. She herself had, of course, worked on more than one case where a new mother's emotions created problems. The stresses of modern living, she supposed. Not having a granny or an aunt nearby who could help out.

When those baby blues struck, it was always wise to have someone else step in and take over care of the baby. If only temporarily. *If* the parents could afford it. As these apparently could. Or at least the child's uncle apparently could, she amended.

"She's a real little darling," she said, smiling down unthinkingly, as if the sleeping baby might be reassured by her face or her tone.

After all, Rose was a stranger. And this sweetheart would miss her mother. They always did, even when they were as young as this one.

"She's a good little girl," Mr. Kimbrough said softly. "I'm sure you won't have any trouble."

"Don't you worry your head none, sir, about this dear rosebud," Rose said, her warm heart already engaged by the baby in her arms. "I'll take good care of her, I will. I'll keep her right as rain, I promise you," she said.

The soft lilt of her native Ireland always came back a bit more strongly when she held a baby. Maybe that was because of the memories of her own mother's gentle hands and voice. Maybe that was why Rose had chosen to do this. To care for other people's children.

She had never had any of her own, of course. No man had ever asked Rose Connor to marry him, but her broad, homely face and her softly rounded figure didn't frighten the little ones. They didn't care, bless them, how you looked, as long as you saw to it that they were fed and warm and dry. And as long as you held them when they cried. As long as you loved them. And she always did. No matter how long or how little a time they were in her care, she always loved them as if they were her very own darlings.

Smiling, she touched the soft cheek with her blunt forefinger, delighting in the smoothness of the skin. Savoring again the sweet aroma of baby powder. She would give that poor woman credit. No matter how bad she was feeling, she had taken care of this one.

And so would she, Rose thought, turning away from the man who had brought the baby. He had already been forgotten as she laid the little girl into the crib, smoothing its freshly laundered sheets and soft blankets with her fingers. She looked down on the sleeping baby with a satisfaction that verged on possessiveness.

And so she missed *his* smile. Satisfaction as well, perhaps, but for entirely different reasons. And Rose Connor was intuitive enough that she might even have been bothered by that smile, had she seen it.

It was probably just as well that her total attention was on the baby who had just been given into her very capable hands. Probably just as well for her peace of mind.

"LET'S GO OVER IT AGAIN, Ms. Heywood," the detective said patiently.

His round face was perspiring, and the top of his damp head gleamed bone-white through the strands of thinning hair he'd combed across it. He had patted at his forehead with a folded handkerchief a couple of times in the course of the interview, but so far he hadn't complained about the heat.

Claire had turned the thermostat up after she'd made the phone calls. She was still shaking, however, despite the rising temperature. And the small internal clock that had begun ticking inside her head as soon as she discovered Gardner was missing had turned into a jackhammer. Almost blinding in its intensity, the pain of the headache made it hard to think. Hard to talk. Hard to hope.

"I got home around two," she said, wondering how many times he would want to hear this. And wondering when her grandfather would arrive. That had been the first call she had made, of course, and he had been the one who had told her that she had to notify the police.

"And the baby-sitter was here?" the detective asked, referring to the notebook where he had carefully written everything down the first time she'd told her story.

She nodded, her eyes moving back to the staircase. She wished she weren't sitting where she could see the stairs and the parade of people who had climbed them in the last half hour. The detectives first and then the crime scene technicians, carrying the boxes and cases that held their equipment.

To all of them, this was just another case. Annoying, perhaps, because they had been called out on a holiday. Interesting, maybe, because her face or her name might be familiar. But still, just another job. And for her... For Claire, this was her baby. Her life. Her heart.

"You paid the sitter," Detective Minger continued, his calm voice interrupting that loss of control, "and then you let her out the front and locked the door."

"I turned off the lights down here, and I went upstairs," Claire said, trying to gather her thoughts as she pulled her gaze back to his face.

Which seemed devoid of suspicion. Whatever else they thought, apparently the police had decided that she hadn't had anything to do with her daughter's disappearance. She wondered if she should thank her minor celebrity for that conclusion.

"But you didn't check the back?" he asked, referring briefly to his notes again before he looked up, waiting, lips pursed as if in thought. As if he didn't already know the answer to this.

"There was no reason to," she said.

That was exactly what she had told him before. Beth wouldn't have unlocked the back door. Claire knew that.

The teenager wasn't careless, and despite the much vaunted safety of the neighborhood, it would be a rare teenage girl who would want to be alone in a big, empty house at night with the doors unlocked. Not given the state of the world these days.

"And when you went upstairs…?"

Claire swallowed, feeling the despair build again despite her attempt to hold on to her rationality, at least until she had told them every detail, as many times as they wanted to hear it. Only then would she be free to collapse in self-reproach.

Perhaps there was no logical reason for the overwhelming sense of guilt she felt. No reason to believe that if she had done something differently, this might not have happened. She hadn't, and it had. And there was nothing she could do about that now. Nothing but help the police as much as she could. Nothing but answer whatever they wanted to ask, as many times as they needed to hear it. Nothing but tell them the absolute truth, and then pray they could find her daughter.

"I stopped at Gardner's door and listened," she admitted.

She hadn't gone in. She had had her hand on the knob, but for some reason—the lateness of the hour, the peaceful silence emanating from the closed door, or the fact that her feet hurt—for some unknown reason, she hadn't turned the handle.

She hadn't looked in on her sleeping daughter. Something she had done hundreds of times in the past, but not last night. Not the one night out of those hundreds when it might really have made a difference.

"But you didn't look into the room," Minger continued.

There was no trace of condemnation in his voice. Of course, it didn't matter what he thought. Not about this. Ultimately it only mattered what *she* believed.

If she had turned that knob, could she possibly have prevented what had happened? Or if her daughter had already been taken, how many hours might she have won back from the cold, empty darkness? Hours during which the searchers might have found a fresh trail or a clue. Might have found something.

"I went to bed," she said simply, unwilling to elaborate on her guilt.

She had undressed, slipping out of her shoes first and then throwing her clothes over the chair in her room, too tired to think about hanging them up. She hadn't even removed her makeup. It hadn't seemed important. Nothing had seemed as important as crawling between the welcoming smoothness of the cold sheets and relaxing.

Maybe even a little tipsy, she thought again, hating herself. *Sleeping off the effects of those two glasses of New Year's Eve champagne while someone took my baby.*

"And you heard nothing until you woke up this morning…at 6:10?" Minger asked, referring to his notes for the time she'd given him.

"Nothing," she confirmed simply.

Of course, she wasn't sure that she had heard anything this morning, either. Although that had been the implication of his question, she didn't bother to correct him.

"And you don't know what awakened you?"

"Maybe the cold. The cold from the window in the baby's room," she suggested. She couldn't be certain about that, but there had been nothing else that she could swear to.

"When you went into the room, the window was open, and the baby was gone."

"That's right," she whispered.

"Is it possible, Ms. Heywood, that for…some reason the baby's father might have decided *he* should take custody of your daughter?"

Claire knew that what he was suggesting was the most familiar scenario that played out with missing children, one the police would probably feel obligated to investigate. Only this time, of course...

"Gardner's father is dead," she said.

Nothing more. No other explanation. She had never made any. Not even to Maddy, who had certainly demanded one. Only to her grandfather had she admitted the truth. And it was also to him, of course, that she had turned this morning.

The silence that fell after her clipped statement was awkward. She wondered if Minger believed her. Not that it mattered, not unless the thought that Gardner's father might have had something to do with the kidnapping slowed down their investigation.

"And you say you found no note," Minger continued, apparently willing, at least for now, to drop the possibility that this was a noncustodial-parent snatch. "Nothing that would give you any indication as to why someone had taken your daughter."

Taken your daughter. With his words, the nightmare images she had fought invaded her head. Wondering if they were taking care of her. If she was warm. If she'd been fed this morning. She was used to having her breakfast before now, and if they didn't know that...

Claire took a breath, again denying the devastating worry. Denying it at least until she had done this job. Until she had done everything she could do to help them find Gardner.

"I didn't find anything," she said. "Do you suppose it's possible the note might have blown outside?" she asked, the thought sudden. "I mean, with that window wide-open..."

As she made the suggestion, she felt a spurt of hope, one that she tried to control because it made no sense. They wouldn't be that careless. Whoever had gone to all this trouble wouldn't leave a message where it might blow away.

Minger, however, methodically made a notation on his pad. "I'll have them look. You haven't been outside?" he asked, his eyes coming back up to examine hers.

"This morning?"

He nodded.

"You think there might be prints?" she asked instead of answering, realizing where he was heading with that question.

"Anything's possible. If they *did* get into the room through that window, then there ought to be some evidence of that outside. If not footprints, then impressions made by the ladder they used. Something. At least we'll hope so."

She nodded, although she wasn't sure what those things would tell them that might be useful in finding Gardner. There might be evidence outside that could eventually be used in court. She understood that, of course, but evidence of that kind wasn't what was important right now.

"Any idea why your alarm didn't go off?" he asked.

Surprised, she looked up at him, wondering why they hadn't checked that for themselves.

"I assumed it had been cut. Tampered with in some way."

Minger shook his head. "We checked. As far as we can tell, it should be working. When they opened that window, the system should have gone off here and at the security office. Apparently, it didn't."

"But…how could that happen?" Claire asked. If anything, the system had been too sensitive. So why last night, when it would have made such a difference…

"We don't know. It's something else we'll be looking into. We're also in the process of questioning your neighbors, at least those close enough that there's a chance they might have heard or seen something. We've already set up your phone to record incoming calls, of course,'' Minger said. ''And an extra line to handle our calls or any you might need to make.'' He had begun to unfold his bulk out the chair as he talked.

''How likely would it be that someone might have seen something?'' Claire asked. ''I mean…it was the middle of the night.''

Claire suddenly wished for a neighbor who was a busybody or an insomniac. As far as she knew, however, she had neither. So she didn't hold out much hope that the cops' strategy in canvassing the neighborhood would yield anything useful.

''It was New Year's Eve,'' Minger reminded her. ''Somebody might still have been up. Or coming in from a party. Besides, we don't know that it was the middle of the night when your daughter was taken,'' the detective said. He folded his notebook and stuck it into his inside coat pocket, his lips pursing again. ''Your sitter put the baby to bed a little after ten. Apparently nobody saw or heard anything out of the ordinary after that.''

''Beth says she didn't hear anything, either?'' Claire asked, knowing, because he had told her, that they had already talked to the teenage sitter, who lived only a couple of houses down the street.

''Not a sound. No noise of a ladder being put against the house, although that's on the other side from where she was watching TV. No alarm. And not a peep out of the baby, although the monitor was on down here. Would that be unusual, Ms. Heywood? For the baby not to wake up after she was put down, I mean?''

Gardner had begun sleeping through the night—at least most of it—early on. Sometimes she awoke if she were out of sorts or teething, but the fact that she hadn't cried after

Beth put her to bed wasn't all that surprising. Or that helpful, Claire supposed.

"Not really," she said.

Minger nodded, holding her gaze. "Well," he said, drawing the syllable out as an obvious indication he was through with the questions. "You think of anything else, you be sure and let us know."

"What are you going to be doing in the meantime?" she asked.

Surely he wasn't leaving. Surely there was more to what the police needed than this? More than to ask her some questions, dust the nursery for prints and examine the flower beds. Surely to God there was something else they all ought to be doing.

"Asking questions," he said. "Running a match on anything they find upstairs. Checking this one against the details of other kidnappings we have on file. And waiting," he added after a moment. "Waiting for somebody to get in touch with you."

"But you think they will?" Claire asked, seeking his reassurance.

He looked around the room, evaluating. "Most kidnappings that aren't parental are carried out for profit. In this case, your family, both sides, are pretty well known in this town. It wouldn't be hard for somebody to dig out enough information about you to carry this off. They'll be in touch, Ms. Heywood. My take on this is that somebody figures to hold you up for a nice, tidy sum in ransom."

"Then…you think that means they'll take care of her?" she asked.

She was aware that that didn't always happen. Things could go wrong. There was the Lindbergh baby, for example. But if all these people wanted was money…

"They got no reason not to," he said softly. "And a lot of reasons to. At least that's what we're hoping for."

"How long?" she asked. "How long before I'll hear something?"

He shrugged, thick shoulders rising and holding a second, lifting the ill-fitting suit coat with them. "The sooner the better for them. It won't be long," he said reassuringly.

The last was meant to be kind, she supposed, but the impression she was getting was that the cops were willing to play the waiting game, maybe because they didn't know what else to do at this point. She wasn't willing. Not with Gardner as the stakes.

Claire didn't get up and escort him out when he walked past her chair. She wasn't sure if he would be going out the front door or back upstairs, but she was certain that *she* was going to stay right here, near the phone. After all, he had said it wouldn't be long before she'd hear something.

"Are you by any chance working on a story right now, Ms. Heywood?" the detective asked.

She turned in surprise at the question, looking at him over her shoulder. Minger was standing in the archway that led into the front hall. His face was bland, only polite inquiry in his eyes, but as it had when she'd opened the nursery door and felt the unexpected cold, a shiver of apprehension slipped along her spine.

"I'm a lawyer, Detective Minger. I'm not really a journalist," she said. "The networks sometimes ask me to do analyses of their political stories. Those that have legal overtones."

"Guess there are a lot of them," he said, his lips moving into a smile. "I see you on TV sometimes," he said. "I just wondered if you were working on something right now."

"I'm not working on anything," she said, but Claire understood what he was getting at. And it frightened her. The possibility that this might not be about money at all but about...anger? Retaliation? Something personal.

Mentally she reviewed the features she had done in the last six months. Although there was always the chance that someone who had been touched on in one of her analyses might be unhinged enough to do something like this, it seemed unlikely, as most of them were highly respected figures on the national scene. People she knew personally. And who knew her or her family.

Politics in this town were many things to many people, but seldom did they involve violence. The only things that she could think of that she had been involved in lately that might possibly be connected to anything violent...

Had to do with the members of Griff's team, she realized.

She didn't know how that sudden thought was reflected in her face, but it must have been. An involuntary widening of her eyes, perhaps. A hesitation in her breathing. There must have been some reaction, obvious enough that Detective Minger hadn't missed it.

"You think of something, Ms. Heywood?" he asked softly. "Something we ought to know about?"

Slowly she shook her head. Even if it were possible that Gardner's disappearance might in some incredible way be connected to what she had done for Jordan Cross or for the man they called Hawk, Minger wouldn't be the one to deal with it. She understood that. Minger wouldn't get to first base with any inquiries he tried to make concerning Griff Cabot's External Security Team.

"No," she said softly. "I can't think of anything else I can tell you, Detective Minger."

He nodded, still holding her eyes. He knew she was lying. Apparently Minger was better at his job than she had given him credit for. For a second she thought about telling him the truth, afraid that if she didn't, he would draw his own conclusions about what she was hiding.

She resisted the impulse because she knew she had been right before. The things she had gotten involved with in helping the CIA agents who had once worked for Griff Cabot couldn't be handled by the cops.

And she wasn't exactly sure who might be able to inquire about them within the dark and dirty bowels of the agency itself. Perhaps her grandfather, although the people he had been associated with there were, like himself, long retired from the intelligence agency.

And Claire herself probably wouldn't get any further within the CIA than Minger could. Not unless she could contact Jordan or Hawk directly. Again, as she had earlier, she felt a surge of hope at that thought.

There would be no one better to find Gardner than the men of Griff's team. There was no one with more expertise at tracking someone down, as Hawk had proved in finding Griff's assassin. No one more experienced at putting the pieces of a puzzle together, as Jordan Cross had done in coming up with the location of the millions that had been stolen from the Mafia.

And they both owed her. *Quid pro quo*, she thought. They owed her. And, of course, they owed Griff Cabot even more.

With her daughter missing, Claire knew that she would call due every favor she had ever been owed by anyone in this town. With these men, however, she also knew that wouldn't be necessary. All she would have to say to them was that Griff Cabot's daughter was missing. And that she needed their help to get her back.

Chapter Two

"And what the hell makes you think someone within the agency had anything to do with what happened?" Carl Steiner asked angrily. "You have to know better than that, damn it. You have to know *us* better than that."

When Griff Cabot didn't answer, Steiner shook his head in disgust. After a few seconds he closed his eyes, rubbing his forefinger tiredly up and down the bridge of his narrow nose, as if his week had already been too long, and this at the end of it was too hard to deal with.

And then Carl had driven out to the wilds of southern Pennsylvania, fighting the holiday weekend traffic, Griff remembered. He supposed he should be grateful for the swift response to his message. However, he was having a tough time evoking gratitude for anything right now.

His leg hurt like a son of a bitch. And he was furious. Steiner had certainly known him long enough to read that fury, although Griff was working hard at presenting his case calmly and rationally, just as he would have done when making any professional argument. After he had allowed the echoes of Carl's anger to fade into silence, he again ticked off the points he had already made in his original message to the director.

"One of my men is fingered for an assassination he didn't carry out. As a result, he almost ends up on the most wanted list. Another is set down in the middle of a deal that's an open invitation for somebody to murder him, in a very slow and extremely painful way. Those things happen within weeks of each other and within a few months of my agency-engineered death. So I find all these incidents to be just a little too coincidental, Carl. Those kinds of things don't happen by chance. Not in our world.''

Griff watched as Steiner's lips tightened, but thankfully Carl resisted reminding him that it wasn't exactly ''our'' world any longer. When he had agreed to go along with the story they had put out after he'd been injured in the terrorist attack at Langley, Griff hadn't believed they would use his ''death'' as an excuse to cut his people loose. Or that if they then got into trouble, the agency would refuse to help them.

''Normally I'd agree,'' Steiner said, his voice carefully moderated to sound calm and reasonable. ''However, in those two particular cases—''

''Spare me the crap, Carl,'' Griff said succinctly.

He pushed up out of the chair he was sitting in, the one *behind* the desk, of course. Assuming that position of power hadn't really been intentional, however. It was simply force of habit.

For too many years Griff Cabot had been the one in charge. The one people reported to. Now he was on the outside looking in, having to depend on old friendships to get to the bottom of what had been happening to his team. And he found he didn't like that position worth a damn.

He limped across the library, leaning on a silver-headed cane. Griff Cabot had hated all the restrictions his injuries had imposed, but most of all, he had hated this damn cane, a constant reminder that he was no longer the man he had once been. So he had worked particularly hard on being able to get along without using it. Most of the time he succeeded.

Today, however, he'd had another poking and prodding session with the surgeons, who had spent the afternoon putting him through their tests and congratulating themselves on their latest handiwork. The combination of that and the cold rain he'd been out in most of the day had had its effect. As a result, he had been forced to acknowledge that if he wanted to be mobile during Carl's visit, then the hated cane was his only option.

It seemed to him to be a symbol of everything that had happened. The attack. The agency's reaction to his injuries. Their lingering effects. The sooner he accepted those, one of the doctors had told him this afternoon, the quicker he would make peace with his limitations.

Screw them. Screw them all, Griff thought, looking out the window at the rain-drenched garden below.

Not that it was much of a garden. Not at this time of year. In the winter downpour it looked exactly like what it was—cold and gray and dead. Just like him.

His eyes flicked upward, expecting to catch the reflection of his guest in the glass, which had been darkened into near opaqueness by the twilight outside. Instead he found his own image, distorted by the streaks of rain. He could see enough to know, however, that he didn't like what he was looking at.

His body canted slightly to the side because of the cane. His hair was too long by his own once impeccable standards. And the eyes reflected in the glass appeared to be without color. *Cold and gray and dead* echoed again in his head. He watched his jaw tighten in frustration, and he forced it to relax.

He turned around to face his visitor, propping his left hip on the deep ledge of the windowsill and leaning gratefully against the glass behind him. Standing probably hadn't been such a hot idea, he acknowledged.

He realized gratefully that his leg was protesting a little

less, now that some of his weight was borne by the ledge. He hadn't taken anything for the pain, but he knew he would have to eventually. *If* he intended to sleep tonight.

And to him that would be another triumph for the terrorist bastard whose bullets had shattered his leg. Another small defeat in a battle he had fought every day of the past year.

"I know you're concerned about your people," Carl said quietly.

Griff looked up to find Steiner watching him, compassion evident in his eyes. He hid the emotion as soon as he realized Griff was looking at him, but the fact that it had been there angered Cabot anew. He wasn't even sure whether the cause of that pity was his injury or the concern for his men Carl had just referred to.

"But I can assure you," Steiner added, "and the director has asked me to give you his assurance as well, that those were totally unrelated and coincidental events. They had nothing to do with the team or with operations."

"They've both been retired. Two of the best people we had, Carl, and you let them go."

"Their choice. They *chose* to leave. And we gave them all the help we could to successfully make that transition. All the help they would accept from us."

"Things just…went wrong?" Griff asked, his voice as low as Steiner's, but edged with sarcasm.

"In Hawkins' case he tried to help a woman. Chivalrous perhaps, but foolhardy as well, given his profession. And it put him in the wrong place at the wrong time. You'd have to admit that when we saw Hawk on camera at the scene of a political assassination, we had a right to be a little…shall we say wary? Even suspicious?"

"Not unless you sent him there," Griff argued. He stretched his aching leg out in front of him, using the cane to push himself farther back onto the deep sill of the window.

"We didn't send him to Baghdad, either," Steiner reminded him.

Griff supposed he should have known Hawk would undertake that mission, but he hadn't been in any condition to make that assessment at the time. Even if he had been, Griff suspected he wouldn't have attempted to dissuade Hawk. After all, five people had died in the terrorist attack for which Hawk's mission had been payback. But the sixth...

Like Mark Twain, he thought, *the reports of my death have been greatly exaggerated.* The firm line of Cabot's mouth moved slightly in amusement. "That was personal," he said softly. *Because Hawk was my friend. And because I was his.*

"We had no way of knowing that the other wasn't personal as well. When we saw Hawk on the videos, we assumed al-Ahmad had some connection to the terrorists responsible for the Langley massacre. We couldn't afford to have an agent operating on his own agenda, not on an international level. Not as volatile as the region is. You know that. You would have been the first to rein Hawkins in."

He would have been, too. Griff would never have allowed a member of the team to make that kind of decision. Not even someone like Hawk, whom he trusted implicitly.

Steiner's explanation made sense. And from everything Griff had been able to discover about her, Tyler Stewart had really been an innocent pawn in that assassination. Griff knew he was one of the few people who could believe Hawk was romantic enough to have done what Steiner claimed he had—played knight errant to protect a woman.

"But that doesn't explain why you let Stewart out of protective custody," Griff said.

"Obviously," Steiner said, his own anger creeping out

again from under the surface calm he had imposed, "we let her go because we thought it was over. When Holt confirmed what we'd been told about the assassination being an extremist plot, we didn't see the need to protect Ms. Stewart any longer. We were wrong, but what happened as a result of that error didn't impact on Hawk. He was never a target for retaliation. Not by us."

"And what happened to Jordan?" Griff asked. "Are you trying to tell me that was *another* coincidence?"

"After the fiasco at the airport, Cross needed a new face," Steiner said simply.

His voice, however, reflected his displeasure with what had occurred in Mississippi that day. Again Griff couldn't blame him. Any time an agent was exposed, the organization suffered, especially if it were someone whose responsibilities were as sensitive as Jordan's had once been.

"And so the agency gave him one that belonged to a man who was the target of a Mafia manhunt," Griff said softly.

He was careful to keep any accusation out of his tone. Antagonizing Carl wouldn't be smart, since Steiner was one of the few people within the CIA who knew Cabot hadn't died in that attack on headquarters. One of the few people he could still talk to about the operations of the agency whose missions had occupied more than half his life.

Griff admitted that he missed being in on policy decisions and on the day-to-day running of the intelligence unit once known as the External Security Team. His job had encompassed a lot of diverse and fascinating activities during the dozen years the team had been in existence.

Now he had been put out to pasture, and the men he had trained were slowly being reassigned or dismissed or, like him, forcibly retired. Griff didn't have a right to object to that process, he supposed. Not when he got down to the bottom line, which was that he *had* agreed go along with their announcement of his death.

He had done that because he had known the director was probably correct in what he'd suggested. That *was* the safest way to protect Griff from the possibility that someone might try to retaliate for the team's past operations. At the time, the agency had viewed the terrorist attack at Langley as just such a retaliation.

Griff's life had already been a shambles. Given the extent of his injuries, it had been evident that his professional life was over. And then, considering what had happened between him and Claire... He took a deep breath, remembering.

At the time, it had seemed like the simplest thing to do. Maybe it had been just following the path of least resistance. Allowing them to "retire" him with a gravestone rather than a gold watch as his monument. After all, they all knew there weren't that many special operatives who lived long enough to collect on the watch, anyway.

And there had been increasing pressure within the agency to do away with his particular branch of the Special Operations Group. The External Security Team had been Griff Cabot's brainchild, although the concept behind it certainly wasn't new. Just more politically unacceptable with each passing year.

However, despite the strictures and limitations now in place on CIA operations, there was still occasionally a need for the so-called quiet option. The need to do away with a dangerous madman whose continuing existence threatened the security of the nation. That was one of the primary jobs of Cabot's group.

One of the last assignments the team had undertaken under his direction had been to find a Russian gangster who had somehow acquired a handful of suitcase nukes. To find him, to take him out and then retrieve the weapons.

With the collapse of the Soviet Union, a lot more nuclear devices were showing up on the international black market. Most of the world couldn't begin to conceive of the kind of terrorism that would engender. It would soon be able to, however, and Griff wondered who would be around then with the mandate the team had once had. A team that, with his retirement, was slowly being destroyed.

Griff hadn't realized, of course, the implications his "death" would have for his people. And although he would certainly have argued against standing down the team, whether the agency's agenda where his men were concerned was smart or not was not really the question.

Mothballing them was one thing. Getting rid of agents who knew too much was another. From the outside looking in, Griff Cabot had begun to suspect that was what was being done, especially in Jordan Cross's case. And Griff wasn't about to let them get away with that.

"You know how it works, Griff," Steiner argued. "We don't make the decision as to whose face someone gets. The surgeons do that, based on existing facial structure, coloring, whatever. Why the hell would anyone want to expose Cross to something like what happened to him?"

"I don't know," Griff said. "I've been trying to decide that since I found out what was happening."

"And frankly, I'd like to know exactly *how* you found out," Steiner said quietly. For the first time there was a hint of challenge in his eyes. Of personal affront.

Again Griff didn't respond, but he didn't allow his gaze to drop. It was a legitimate demand. One he certainly would have made had he been in Carl's position, probably a lot more forcefully. That didn't mean, however, that he intended to answer it.

"If you're in touch with someone in the agency, then that's a breach of security," Steiner continued. "You know that. If you were still in charge of the division, you wouldn't put up with it, and you know that as well.''

Carl was right, of course. He wouldn't have.

''I can't allow it either, Griff. No matter how well intentioned you are—and I believe that, by the way—I can't allow you to interfere with the functioning of the division.''

''I was not aware that I've interfered with anything,'' Griff said. ''Are you?''

Steiner's eyes assessed him before he answered, his voice softer now. ''For a lot of the members of your team, their primary loyalty was never to the agency. Or even to their country. It was to you. That's a dangerous situation, Griff, and we both know it.''

''Is that why I was retired?'' Griff asked. He could hear the bitterness in his question.

''You were retired because you could no longer function as the head of a vitally important intelligence division. At the time, no one was willing to predict that you would *ever* be able to function in that position again. The DCI made the decision that was in the agency's best interests. He always will. That's the director's responsibility. And you felt that way, too. At the time,'' Steiner reminded him.

''And now you think I've changed my mind. Is that it?''

''I don't know. You tell me, Griff. Are you drumming up a conspiracy because you miss it? Because you miss the team? The excitement? The thrill of the chase?''

''Which effectively reduces what I did for the past ten years to some macho bull-crap exercise in self-aggrandizement.''

Steiner's snort of laughter relaxed the tension his previous questions had created. ''Yeah? Well, there are a lot of people who think that about all of us in the agency. It wasn't a personal accusation.''

''I want my people taken care of,'' Griff said softly.

"We're trying," Carl said. "They are sometimes…shall we say, difficult to protect."

"Difficult to control," Griff suggested, again fighting an urge to smile.

"I told you. Their loyalty was personal."

"Is that what this is about? Getting rid of them because they were *my* men?"

"As far as I can ascertain—and believe me, I've tried—no one is trying to get rid of *them*. The team itself is a different story. You're aware of the current thinking about its function."

"Yeah, I'm aware," Griff said mockingly. "Suddenly everybody in the world loves one another. No more bad guys. No more madmen."

Steiner looked down at his hands, which were lying, totally relaxed, in his lap. Night was falling outside, and the room had darkened. Griff supposed that as a good host he should turn on some lights, but there was something about the dimness that invited confidences.

Griff Cabot's position meant he had been well trained in all the psychological tricks. In getting people to do what he wanted. In bringing out the best they had to offer in any situation. And sometimes in pulling things out of them that they didn't want to reveal. It was always easier to be truthful about painful things in the darkness.

When Carl looked up again, Griff's eyes were on his face. Carl didn't look away. It was obvious to Griff that Steiner was assessing him as well, maybe assessing his motives, even across the distance that separated them.

"A lot of people think the members of your team *are* the bad guys," Carl said.

"Not a lot of people," Griff said, fighting the familiar rush of rage at the old argument. "*Most* people don't think about what we do. *Most* people don't care."

"The ones now making the decisions do," Carl said.

Again, neither of them said anything for several long seconds. The era of intelligence in which Griff Cabot and his team had functioned was over. They both knew it. One of them didn't want to accept it. Which didn't change anything.

Finally, Steiner stood up. The raindrops that had glistened in his dark hair hadn't completely dried, but it was obvious he believed he had said everything he had come here to say.

And it was obvious that this had been a warning as well, Griff thought. A warning sent by those in charge, and deliberately, it had been delivered by a friend. They had hoped, apparently, that the message would have more effect coming from Carl, who *was* his friend. As well as his successor.

"If you're having second thoughts about your retirement, I'd advise you to keep them to yourself," Steiner said, almost as if he had just read his mind.

He walked across the room, however, and held out his hand. Cabot could see, despite the low lighting, that the skin under Steiner's eyes was dark with fatigue, discolored like old bruises, and the lines in his face were deeper than they had been twelve months ago. Of course, it was the end of a long, hard week. The end of a long hard year, Griff amended.

Griff remembered what that felt like. Suddenly, unexpectedly, he envied his successor those days of turmoil and hard decisions. Maybe Steiner was right. Maybe his anxiety and anger were simply the result of being so far out of the loop. Out of the seat of power he had occupied for so long. After a moment Griff leaned his cane against his thigh and took the outstretched hand.

"My advice is to keep any future accusations to yourself as well," Steiner added softly. "The days of running the world to suit ourselves are over. It's a new ball game."

"With new players," Griff said. "Is that what you're suggesting?"

"With new players," Steiner repeated. "New rules. And like them or not, we'll have to learn to play by them."

"I won't," Griff said.

Steiner took a breath, and his lips flattened again. Then they relaxed into a smile. "Get a hobby, Griff. Something besides this. Besides living in the past. If your men are as smart as I think they are, they'll do the same. But don't be looking over your shoulder. Nobody from the agency is after them. Or you. Boredom's not an excuse for paranoia."

Griff Cabot's eyes narrowed at the last comment, but after a second, he laughed, the sound of it again breaking the tension that had grown with the darkness. Then he nodded, releasing his friend's hand.

"Thanks for coming all the way up here," he said.

"I didn't mind. I know what you meant to the agency. I don't want to see you do anything to destroy the memory of what you accomplished there."

"I appreciate that," Griff said.

"And I know the way out," Steiner said. "So don't even offer."

It was the closest Carl had come to referring to his injuries, and Griff appreciated his sensitivity. Maybe Carl was even right about the other, he thought, as he watched his guest open the door to the study and then close it softly behind him. Maybe Griff *had* read too much into a couple of unrelated incidents simply because he didn't have enough to do. Or enough to think about.

Hawk and Jordan Cross were certainly capable of taking care of themselves. Even in intelligence work, he acknowledged, there had always been the occasional chance mishap. Now, like a bored old maid with a new pair of binoculars, he had created himself some excitement. Imagined a mystery.

Old maid, he thought again, the phrase especially unpleasant. Maybe *hermit* was a better choice of words. But that life-style wasn't really necessary. His isolation had been a matter of choice. Probably an unhealthy one, he admitted.

He hadn't gone the route they had chosen for Jordan. His face had never been that well known, not outside the inner circle of the intelligence community. He was not a public figure, so a change in appearance hadn't been considered necessary.

The other had been easily accomplished. A change of location. A new identity. He had done that countless times for other people. Now the agency had done it for him.

He stood up, wincing at the resultant protest from his leg, and walked away from the window. Looking out at the rain was almost as depressing as the isolation. Despite the subject of their conversation, he had enjoyed Steiner's brief visit. Someone to talk to. Someone who...

He blocked the thought, knowing from long experience that thinking about Claire wasn't something he could afford to do tonight. And after all, it had been quite a leap from Carl Steiner and the team to that other lost relationship.

He supposed it was the holiday. Holidays always seemed a time for nostalgia. For remembering.

Grateful he didn't have to hide his discomfort anymore, he eased carefully down into the chair behind the desk, looking at the blank computer screen. Carl's question about how he had known what was happening to his men had been legitimate. He had just been headed in the wrong direction. Steiner had been right, however, about the ethics of what Griff had been doing.

Old spies don't die, he thought, paraphrasing badly. They just lose their integrity. But of course, most people thought that was an oxymoron to begin with. Spies and integrity. The CIA and ethics.

He swiveled the chair away from the temptation of the keyboard. He supposed he should have been expecting Jake Holt, the team's systems expert, to show up out here, instead of Steiner. Jake had taught him all he knew about getting information out of the system, even how to get in and out without leaving footprints. At least, Griff amended, without leaving a trail that would be obvious to anyone except the Jake Holts of the world.

And if Jake had found his footprints, he was probably going crazy trying to figure out who had left them, Griff imagined. Which meant that at least Jake had something to do. "Get a hobby," Steiner had advised.

And screw you, too, Griff thought.

He savagely punched the remote button, and the TV screen across the room blinked into life. It was almost time for the evening news. He could watch what was happening around the world just like everyone else. No longer a player, but an observer. That message had come through loud and clear.

Despite the pictures flickering across the screen, his mind began wandering again, mulling over the recent conversation. Then something the announcer said connected, and suddenly Griff's entire concentration was engaged by the picture on the TV.

The house they were showing was familiar. Too damned familiar. His finger found the volume control, his eyes never leaving the visuals marching across the screen as the announcer talked.

Images of a woman now. The same woman in a variety of settings and backgrounds. In different groups. Or looking straight into the camera. Talking. In one scene she was standing outside the Supreme Court building, the wind whipping strands of blond hair out of the neat chignon into which it had been confined.

With a gesture so familiar it closed his throat, she lifted

a slender hand to brush a tendril away from the oval perfection of her face. *Claire,* he thought, unable to draw another breath as he watched. Claire.

And finally, when the words the reporter was intoning managed to break through the spell Claire Heywood had cast over him since the first time he had seen her, Griff began to realize what had happened. And why the face of the woman he loved, a woman who believed, along with the rest of the world, that he was dead, was once more appearing on his television screen.

As soon as he had, Griff Cabot picked up the phone on his desk and, without hesitation, without considering the wisdom of what he was doing or its possible effects, punched in the number Carl Steiner had just warned him never to call again.

Chapter Three

"Because according to the agency, those men you asked me to find don't exist," Claire's grandfather said. "Apparently, they never have," he added softly.

"But...that's not true," Claire said, feeling despair seep in. It dampened the hope that had been created by the thought of being able to put the nightmare of her daughter's kidnapping into Hawk's and Jordan Cross's capable hands. "I met them. I talked to them. They worked for Griff."

"If they did, there's no record of it now."

"He told me they were going to do that," she said, remembering the meeting she had helped Jordan arrange when the man called Hawk had been targeted by his own employer.

"They were going to do what?" her grandfather asked, obviously puzzled by the reference he couldn't possibly understand.

"Destroy the records. At least...destroy the ones on Hawk."

"Cabot told you that? Even if that were true, it sounds like something that wouldn't be discussed outside the agency."

"Not Griff. A man called Steiner. An assistant deputy director. He told Hawk that when he got through, there wouldn't be anything left there with his name on it. Not a pay voucher. Not a memo. Nothing.''

"It seems he was right," her grandfather said, his eyes bleak.

Tonight he looked every one of his seventy-eight years, Claire realized, and that was something she had never thought before. Montgomery Gardner's slender, erect figure, with its almost military bearing, never seemed to change with the passage of the years. To Claire, he had never seemed to age, appearing no different than he had been in her earliest memories of him.

Although his hair was white and the lines in his beloved face were deeply drawn, she had never thought of him as an old man. Not until now. Tonight his shoulders were slumped, his normal confidence subdued.

But she didn't know how she would have managed today had he not come to help. Her parents had been spending the holidays in Europe. Although they had begun scrambling to get a flight home as soon as she had gotten in touch with them, they hadn't yet been successful because of the holiday traffic. And she wasn't sure when they would finally arrive.

But she could bear even that, Claire had thought when her father called to tell her. She had been reared in her father's highly liberal ideology, but her sternly conservative grandfather had always been the calm, stable rock in her world. He had seemed prepared to fill that role again when he had opened the front door this morning, full of plans and suggestions.

Now, however, despite everything they had done, they were no closer to a solution to Gardner's disappearance than they had been then. And her grandfather appeared almost defeated. As despairing as she was.

It hurt her to see how much this had shaken him. And it

frightened her even more to realize that the clever and ruthless Monty Gardner was afraid. Afraid for Gardner.

All day Claire had fought the images. Pushed them from her head because she couldn't stand to have them there. Images of her baby. Would there be someone to comfort her when she cried? If she were cold or hungry? Did she miss her mother?

And yet Claire had been forced to acknowledge that there was nothing she could do about any of those. She was powerless to change a thing about Gardner's situation. So she had fiercely concentrated on doing everything she could to get her back from the people who had taken her. Whoever they were. Whatever they wanted. And Hawk and Jordan Cross had been her best hope—the one she had clung to throughout the afternoon.

"So…what can we do now?" she asked her grandfather.

The idea that they might be able to appeal to Steiner for the information they needed had crossed her mind. But remembering the cold fury in his eyes the day Hawk had tried to bargain for Tyler Stewart's life, Claire believed he wouldn't tell her anything. The agency had made its decision where Lucas Hawkins was concerned. Apparently they had done the same thing with Jordan, as well.

"I've requested that the DCI put me in touch with any members of Cabot's team who are still working for the agency, but frankly…"

Her grandfather's lips tightened. He shook his head slowly, revealing his frustration with his contacts within the intelligence community, about whom he had been so hopeful this morning.

"You don't think he will," Claire suggested softly. "Not even for you."

"As far as they're concerned, this is a private matter, Claire. Something that has nothing to do with the agency, of course. The people Griff Cabot worked with aren't detectives who can be called in to solve the odd crime or two. I suppose I should have known better than to ask him. I would probably have done the same thing—given a polite brush-off to someone asking a personal favor that has nothing to do with the mission of the agency.''

She knew that was over thirty years of intelligence work speaking. And a desire to be fair. It had nothing to do with his love for her or her daughter. Her grandfather would do anything to get Gardner back, but apparently he, too, had no idea where else to turn. And despite Detective Minger's assurance this morning, no one had called demanding ransom. Or demanding anything else.

This had been the longest day of her life, Claire thought. Every minute had been a battle to contain her frustration and control her growing terror, at least enough to be able to function, enough to think, enough to give information to all the people who had asked for it. Now, as night fell, she had no more idea of who had taken her baby or why than she had had this morning when she'd opened the door of that empty nursery.

Since he'd arrived, her grandfather had spent hours on the phone line the police had set up. And he was the one who had urged her to call the FBI. To talk to the media. To issue a plea to the public for their help in finding Gardner.

Maddy and Charles had agreed with that idea. After all, they had argued, her celebrity might be a blessing in this situation, despite the fact that Claire had chosen to keep her daughter out of the spotlight.

Only her family and closest friends even knew of Gardner's existence. That had been fairly easy to accomplish, since Claire had been out of the country during all but the earliest stages of her pregnancy. She had always tried to keep her private life separate from her professional one, and up until now, she believed she had been successful.

But maybe, she had been forced to acknowledge, she had been wrong about that.

So she had gone over and over each case she had worked on. And she had thought through every on-the-air pronouncement she had ever made. Reviewed mentally every political story on which she had commented.

Since she wasn't a criminal lawyer, the odds of a client or someone connected with a client having had anything to do with Gardner's kidnapping seemed so small as to be inconsequential. As for the bits and pieces she had done in front of the camera, there was nothing in the fairly dry political commentary that seemed threatening or dangerous. Nothing that should provoke this kind of outrage. And she was again right back to where she had been this morning.

"Griff's people would help me find her if they knew," she said.

She was still as certain of that as she had been when she'd suggested to her grandfather that they should try to contact Hawk and Jordan. But if they couldn't reach them, the only hope she had was that they would see the TV interview she had done this afternoon and contact her. It seemed the one remaining chance to solicit their help.

She tried to think of anyone else they might appeal to. If only she knew what had triggered this. If only she understood the seemingly senseless motivation in taking a six-month-old baby. If it had not been done for money—

The shrill of the phone interrupted those circling thoughts. Her eyes lifted quickly to meet her grandfather's, which had widened in shock at the unexpected sound. She found the same sense of expectation she felt reflected in his face.

But when it rang again, she realized that this was the extra line the police had set up, and not her regular number, where any call from the kidnappers could be expected to come in. Her hand still shaking from that first mistaken impression, she finally picked up the receiver.

"Claire Heywood," she said.

"I have a message for you, Ms. Heywood."

"A message?" she questioned, trying to think if she had ever heard this disembodied voice before, trying to place the caller. No one had this number, unless her grandfather had given it to whomever he had talked to today. She certainly hadn't. Except to her father, whose voice she would have known immediately.

"From a friend," he said.

A message from a friend? None of whom had this number? From a man whose voice she didn't recognize?

Her pulse began to race, as her mind discarded those possibilities. And as it did, the thought that this might finally be word from whoever had taken Gardner began to grow in her heart.

Please God, let this be what we've waited for, she prayed, motioning to her grandfather that she needed something to write on. "All right," Claire said into the receiver when she was sure he understood her gestures.

Then she brought her entire consciousness to bear on listening and remembering—tone, accent, word patterns. It was almost an intellectual exercise, deliberately undertaken because the rest of it was too important—waiting for those words she so desperately needed to hear in order to set her world back on its axis.

"He wants you to meet him in the rose garden," the voice on the other end of the line stated.

Her grandfather had placed a notebook and pen beside the phone. Claire had picked up the pen, automatically turning the pad to face her. It reminded her of Minger's meticulous note-taking this morning, of how careful he had been. And she must be just that careful, too.

But when her caller said those words, her hand hesitated

over the paper. For a moment all she could think of was the one at the White House, but of course that couldn't be right.

"The Rose Garden?" she repeated, her inflection questioning. If this was someone's idea of a prank...

A hint of laughter whispered across the distance. "He said to tell you not *that* one."

As if the caller had read her mind. *Not that one.*

"I'm afraid I don't understand," she said carefully, aware of the slow deflation of the hope that had blossomed with the ringing of the phone.

The rose garden? she repeated mentally, bewildered by the instructions. Her mind ran through every connotation that phrase might have. Every reference. And came up with nothing that made sense. This seemed too bizarre to be the real thing. Someone's idea of a cruel joke? Someone who had seen her on TV?

"He said you'd know. If you really think about it."

"Is this about my daughter?" she asked bluntly.

Cut to the chase, she had decided. Ignore the taunting suggestion that if she were only brighter she would be able to figure out what he meant.

"Indirectly," the man said softly. "But it *is* important, Ms. Heywood. I can tell you that."

"Then don't play games," Claire said sharply, all the anger she had hidden during the long day boiling up within her, surprising her by its intensity. "I don't have time for tricks. I want my daughter back. And I want her back *now*, damn it."

Her voice climbed as she made the demand. Her grandfather put his hand on her arm. Her eyes lifted to his again, reading in them a warning.

"Please," she added, struggling to modify her tone. "Please, just tell me what you want me to do."

"Go to the rose garden," the man repeated. "As soon as you can. He'll meet you there."

She thought she could read a hint of regret, even apology in his tone.

"He said surely you remember the rose," he added.

Then, unbelievably, the connection was broken. Claire gripped the dead phone, willing it back to life. He couldn't have hung up, she thought. If they had gone to the trouble to call, they would want to tell her something that made sense, and this didn't. The only roses...

Her racing thoughts slowed, hesitating over the word *rose*. "He said surely you remember the rose." Singular.

And she did, of course. Someone had sent her a rose after she had helped Jordan Cross. There had been a message then as well. Something to the effect of thank you for your help.

She had thought the flower must have come from Jordan. Or Hawk, although the gesture had seemed somehow out of character for him. Too romantic. Too soft for such a cold, hard man. Too...sentimental.

Of course, Griff had often sent her a single rose, and there was not a sentimental bone in his body. He'd been hard, pragmatic, brilliant, but hardly what most people would consider romantic.

Suddenly, the memory of the vast gardens at Griff's Maryland estate was in her head. The lovely hybrid tea roses there were his hobby. Their care, and his love for them, were something he'd learned from his grandmother, who had started that rose garden. At least the flowers were something he could control, Griff used to say, smiling.

Eventually, she had understood what he'd meant by that. So much of what he had to deal with was beyond his control. World situations. Politics. The inner workings of the agency itself.

Griff Cabot had had a rose garden. One that she had visited. One she remembered.

"Was that…?" Her grandfather hesitated.

The soft question faltered as she looked up at him, her attention once more brought back to the present. Her fingers released the pen, laying it carefully on the pad, blocking the painful and unwanted memories of Griff.

"I think that was one of the team," she said.

"Cabot's team?" he asked, obviously surprised.

He sounded as if he had thought they were mythical. Maybe the product of her imagination. Her desperation. What they did *was* a little unbelievable, but they themselves were very real. She had met them. At least two of them.

She nodded. "I think that was a message from Jordan Cross. Maybe…maybe he saw the interview. Or maybe the director *did* forward your request, despite your doubts."

"And this Cross is willing to meet you?"

She nodded again, thinking about the instructions she'd been given. Nothing else made sense. Griff's rose garden. That was someplace she certainly knew, and a clue that was a dead giveaway for anyone who *really* knew Griff. A connection. Even more of a connection if, as she suspected, Jordan had been the one who'd sent the rose after she had helped him. It all made sense because it fit.

"I have to go," she said, standing. "Will you stay here and take any calls?"

"I'll go with you," her grandfather said, starting to rise. "Maddy can answer the phone. Or Charles."

Her sister and her husband were in the kitchen trying to put together something for supper. Maddy had suggested that, glancing pointedly at their grandfather when Claire had said she wasn't hungry.

She hadn't been, of course, and no matter what Maddy said, the thought of sitting down to eat while Gardner was missing was unthinkable. Nauseating.

It would be much better to be doing something that might help find her. This was the only thing all day that had made sense to Claire. Secure the help of someone like Jordan Cross. Take advantage of the offer she thought had just been made.

"No," she said, putting her hand on her grandfather's shoulder to urge him not to get up.

They hadn't told her to come alone, but if this were Jordan, she thought he might object to her bringing someone like her grandfather, who still had ties to the agency he had once worked for. Especially if the director *hadn't* been the method by which Cross had learned she needed his help.

"I don't trust anyone else to answer the phone," she said, smiling at him. "Not Maddy. You know she'll be too nervous to get it right. And Charles...Charles isn't *really* family."

She said the last only for her grandfather's benefit, to convince him that he had to stay here. He had never approved of Maddy's choice of a husband, who held a minor position in the diplomatic corp. She knew Monty Gardner wouldn't want Charles in a position to make any decisions.

"I don't like the idea of you going by yourself," the old man argued. "You ought to at least notify Minger or the bureau. You can't be sure that this is—"

"I'm sure," she said, bending down to place a kiss on the top of his head, lightly touching the gleaming sweep of white hair with her fingers as well, a small caress.

She *was* sure. The more she thought about what the man on the phone had said, the more certain she was that this had to be one of Griff's agents. Certainly someone who knew Griff Cabot well enough to know about his hobby, an avocation that seemed so out of character for a man like him.

And apparently this was someone who was willing to

help. Offering her assistance would be "indirectly" connected to her daughter's kidnapping. The wording of that had been very careful. They didn't want to mislead her into believing they were the kidnappers, so they had chosen that telling phrase with which to answer her question. Maybe they had even thought out the wording before they'd placed the call.

But the voice hadn't been Jordan's. She would have recognized the soft Southern accent he had never quite lost. It had always reminded her of Griff's.

The voice on the phone hadn't. But it hadn't been Hawk either, she decided, replaying the conversation in her mind. A friend who had been asked to convey a message. Just exactly as he had said.

"You stay here," she urged her grandfather. "I'll call you as soon as I've talked to whoever this is. I promise I will."

"I don't like this, Claire," the old man argued. "You can't be sure this is one of Cabot's men. It could be anyone. Someone trying to lure you out of the house. Maybe even the people who took the baby."

"All the more reason then for me to go," she reminded him gently. "But it's not them, Grandfather. I *know* who this is. It has to be. Too many things fit. Things that only someone who knew Griff very well would know. And besides, I don't know anything else to do. Neither do you. This is a chance we can't afford to pass up. You know these people. Or at least you knew agents who were like them. If *they* can't find Gardner…"

She let the sentence trail, knowing that was the reality. Her grandfather would know it, too. But putting into words the possibility that they might *not* be able to find Gardner was unthinkable. Therefore, so was a rejection of this offer.

"Be careful," Monty Gardner said softly. He reached out and took her hand, squeezing it gently with his long aristocratic fingers. "Be very careful. I couldn't bear it if anything happened to you, my dear."

"I know," she said. "But nothing will happen to me, I promise you. These people are friends."

Who owe me something, she thought again, *and are apparently willing to acknowledge that debt. Quid pro quo.*

She freed her hand. Lifting the tips of her fingers to her lips, she touched them to his cheek in farewell. She wasn't afraid of what she might find at Griff's estate. She knew in her heart that whoever met her there would be someone who wanted to help her get Gardner back and put an end to this nightmare.

GRIFF HADN'T BEEN CERTAIN she would come, not until he saw the lights of the car approaching down the long curving drive that led up to the house. And when he did, the once familiar anticipation began to stir in the pit of his stomach.

Just the thought of seeing Claire again, even in these circumstances, had the power to rouse all the old feelings. Emotions he had spent the last year and a half denying. And so he denied them again, concentrating on why they were both here tonight. Together again...and yet farther apart than ever.

He had tried to picture Claire with a baby since he'd seen the news report of the kidnapping, but somehow the images wouldn't form. That was not the way he was accustomed to envisioning her. In his memories, she still moved, as he once had, in a world peopled by the powerful, the influential, the political. Somehow he couldn't quite reconcile the woman he had known so well with motherhood.

He had never even thought that she might want a child. They had never talked about having children. He had never considered the possibility. He supposed that if their relationship had gone further—

The distant slamming of a car door broke the stillness, and he knew that it would only be a moment or two before she made her way around the house and into the winter-devastated rose garden. Asking her to meet him here had been a ridiculous idea. He had known that since he'd lowered himself more than an hour ago onto the cold, damp concrete slab of the garden bench.

It was a frigid January night, and like a fool he had suggested an outdoor meeting. Somehow, his memories of Claire had interfered with all the realities of the present. This garden was somewhere he knew she would remember. A place she would associate with him. That had been a warning of sorts. An attempt to prepare her for what she would find here.

When he arrived, however, he had realized at once that this garden was as cold and dead as the one he had looked out on only a couple of hours ago in Pennsylvania. He had known that if Claire did come in response to the message Jake Holt had delivered for him, she would drive. And the chopper he'd hired would, of course, get him here long before she arrived.

It had. Long enough that the chill had crept into his bones as he waited. Along with the dread. Dread of the meeting he had been eager to set up when he'd first called Jake.

Griff could hear her steps on the loose gravel of the path, and he felt his heart rate accelerate. He couldn't be sure how she would react to seeing him again. Not given the things she had said to him the last time they'd argued. And not given the fact that as far as she knew, he was dead.

He had tried to tell her that he was not. The message he'd sent with the rose, thanking Claire for helping his men, had been a pretext for reestablishing contact. He had even understood his motives at the time.

But of course, there had been no response. Either she

had not understood the gesture, not understood the single bloodred rose was from him, or…she had chosen to ignore it. And now he knew that even if she *had* suspected the flower was from him, she had already become involved in a relationship with someone else. A man by whom she had had a child.

"Jordan?" she called softly, her voice hesitant, a little breathless, full of anxiety or fear.

He had known Claire Heywood in many moods. Fear had never been one of them. But then never before had someone kidnapped her baby. He was still having a hard time coming to grips with the senseless cruelty of that.

It was not that he wasn't intimately acquainted with the depravity human beings were capable of inflicting on one another. With his background, he was well aware of their endless brutalities. But things like this happened to other people. Not to those he loved.

The word reverberated inside his head, echoing through all the memories. He didn't bother to deny it. He had loved Claire Heywood almost from the beginning. Almost from the first time he had seen her.

And, he acknowledged, he still did. What other reason would there be for his being here tonight? Alone in a cold, dark garden, waiting with incredible anticipation for a woman who might believe he was dead. A woman who was, in any event, involved with another man.

"Jordan?" she called again.

Griff hadn't realized how near she was. He had been lost in the past, something that was always dangerous when there was a job to be done. In this case their shared past was incredibly painful, as well.

No matter what she had said to him before, no matter if she had chosen to ignore the rose he had sent, he knew that having to confront him tonight would be another blow on top of the kidnapping. Especially if she hadn't realized from that gesture that he was alive. This meeting would be something else for her to deal with on a terrifying and terrible day.

This was a mistake, he realized belatedly. A stupid and cruel error of judgment, although neither of those had been his intent. He should have contacted Jordan and asked him to help Claire find the baby. It was obvious that was who she had come here expecting to meet.

Instead, he had rushed in to play rescuer as soon as he had seen her on TV. And he had not once considered that he was not in any position to undertake that role.

He could no longer call on the resources of the agency, at least not officially. Only on his people, the few who were still working there. Who were still loyal to him. People like Jake, he acknowledged, remembering the shock in Holt's voice when he'd identified himself and asked for his help.

"Jordan?" Claire said again, more softly this time. She sounded more focused. No longer searching.

He realized she was standing at the top of the steps that led up to the gazebo where he was sitting. There was enough moonlight, in spite of the drifting pattern of broken clouds, to outline her figure against the lesser blackness of the night. He knew that she had seen him, but he also knew he would be no more than a shadowed hulk across the wide floor of the gazebo.

"If you're not Jordan," she said finally, "then…who are you? Why did you bring me here?"

"I want to help you," Griff said softly.

He wondered if she would recognize his voice. She had heard it a thousand times whispering from the darkness. Despite his determination to reveal nothing of what he was feeling, he had been aware of a telltale breathlessness in his response, which had changed the normal timbre of his tone. The strength of her effect on his emotions had always been incredible. His physical responses to Claire Heywood had been stronger than to any other woman he had ever known.

She took another step, moving nearer. He knew that she still wouldn't be able to distinguish his features. Not in this light. He even thought about asking her not to come any closer.

Then he could stay hidden in the darkness. He could offer to help and never reveal that the man she had been told was dead was really alive. And not reveal that he was still as caught in the spell of love and desire she had woven about him as he had always been.

Perhaps she couldn't make the leap of logic it would require to recognize his voice if she still believed he was dead. Dead and buried for more than a year. It *should* be inconceivable to her then that he could be sitting in the gazebo of his own rose garden.

He had lied to people on occasion. Everyone had, he supposed, but especially in the position he had once occupied. It went with the constraints and requirements of his job. But he had never lied to Claire.

Sometimes, after it was over between them, he'd wished that he had. At least lied about what he did. What the team did. And especially what he believed about the necessity of those actions. Instead, he had finally told her the truth, because he'd thought he could do no less. Because he'd thought he owed her that truth.

Eventually he would have to do that now. No matter how difficult that might be. For her. And for him.

"Do you know something about Gardner's disappearance?" she asked.

A logical question. He wished to hell he did. But the truth was... The truth was that until tonight he hadn't known of the existence of Claire's child. That knowledge had hurt, making him burn with a jealousy he had no right to feel. Burn even after all this time.

"I'm sorry. That's *not* why I asked you to come," he said.

"Then…why? How did you know about the rose? Are you the one who sent it?"

In the darkness, Griff Cabot's lips moved, tilting into the slight, enigmatic smile Claire would certainly have recognized. If she had been able to see it.

"I sent you the rose," he said.

"Because of what I did for Hawk and Jordan?"

"Partly."

"I don't understand," she said.

"It was intended to be…a message as well."

A single bloodred rose, like those which grew here. That one had been a hothouse variety because of the season. He had chosen it himself that same evening, and then he had sent it to her, the dew still beading its silken petals.

Because he had wanted her to know he was alive. And because of what he had felt when he'd found out she had been helping his men. Men who carried out the missions she had once professed to despise. If Claire's feelings had changed enough to allow her to do that—

"What kind of message?" she asked, interrupting that thought.

She took another step, the wooden boards creaking under her weight. Coming here tonight had taken courage. That was something Claire had in abundance.

Of course, what she had done before had taken courage as well. Almost eighteen months ago, at the same time she had made him promise that he would never try to see her again, she had openly confessed how she felt. She had told him how much she loved him. And needed him.

She herself had broken the agreement they'd made. Only once. As he had broken it in sending her the rose.

Broken it only once. Before tonight.

"Who are you?" she asked again.

Before he could answer, however, she raised her hand, bringing up the flashlight she had carried from her car. She turned it on, directing it toward the darkness where he was hidden. And unerringly, its beam found his face.

Chapter Four

For an endless moment Claire couldn't breathe. Couldn't think. Couldn't move. Couldn't have done any of those things had her very life depended on it.

Griff's eyes had narrowed against the intensity of the light, and he lifted his hand, placing it protectively, palm outward, before his face. At the same time he lowered his head, effectively hiding the features she had once known as well as she knew her own. More intimately than her own, perhaps, because they had appeared so often in her mind's eye.

As they did now. They had been captured like an image on film, burned on her retinas, frozen to stillness by the cold, piercing finger of the flashlight's beam. That first image played over and over in her head, blocking questions. Blocking reaction. Blocking thought.

"Turn it off, Claire," Griff said quietly.

How had she not recognized his voice? she wondered, hearing it now. Knowing it. Knowing it instantly.

Because he's dead, of course. Griff Cabot was dead. She had grieved for him. Every day of this endless year, she had grieved for him. Grieved for the all the foolish, meaningless things she had once said to him. And now...

"Turn it off," he said again, this time in a tone of command. The voice of a man accustomed to being obeyed.

Why shouldn't it be? Everyone obeyed him. They always had. Just as they listened to his opinions and respected them. Everyone, it seemed, except Claire Heywood.

Now, however, her finger pushed the switch in unthinking obedience. The powerful light blinked out, disappearing as suddenly as it had appeared.

As suddenly as he had once disappeared, she thought. *Dead.* They had told her he was dead.

"I'm sorry," Griff said softly. "I did try to warn you."

I'm sorry. She couldn't fit the understated simplicity of that apology into the scope of her pain. *I'm sorry?*

Sorry they had told her he was dead? she wondered. Sorry he had brought her here to find out in this brutal way that he was not? Or sorry he had done this whole despicable...thing to her? Or had let the agency—

The thought was so sudden, she gasped a little with its impact. Almost too great a shock after the last.

The CIA had given Jordan Cross a new face after the incident at the airport in Mississippi, because his picture—his face—had been spread out under the banners of a thousand newspapers. Had they done it again after Kathleen Sorrel had turned over the Mafia's money? That had been only a couple of weeks ago. But maybe...

"Jordan?" she asked, pushing the question past the hard constriction of her throat. "Is that you?"

The man in the shadows laughed, the sound deep and soft, but *known.* Familiar. So familiar.

"You seem to have some sort of fixation with Jordan Cross. I think I might be jealous, Claire. If things were...different."

His voice. Griff's voice. And despite her shock, its sound flowed through all the places in her mind and body that had once known his touch. Known him so intimately that there could be no longer any doubt about who was sitting in the darkness of the old gazebo. No longer any room at all in her heart for doubt.

Tears stung her eyes, still widened with the shock of what the flashlight had revealed. They had now adjusted to the moon-touched darkness enough to be able to watch as he slowly lowered the hand he had raised.

Griff Cabot was alive. This was not someone pretending to be Griff. Not a figment of her imagination, brought on by the incredible stresses of this day. And not a phantom.

"Why?" she whispered, trying to understand. "Why did they tell me you were dead?"

And then, before he could possibly have answered the first, even if he had wanted to, the more important questions followed.

"How could you *let* them tell me that, Griff? How could you let me believe you were dead?"

"I wasn't in any condition to stop them," he said softly.

Condition? Because he really had been a victim of that massacre? she wondered. But if that part was true—

"And besides..." His words had interrupted that thought, but then he hesitated before he completed the sentence. "You and I had already made our agreement."

She knew at once what he meant, although she didn't know why he would bring that promise, *his* promise, into this discussion. Why he would think that had any bearing on what he had done.

"Our *agreement* never included lying to each other," she accused.

Her knees were weak, her palm clammy as her shaking hand clenched the heavy flashlight. Reaction to finding out that the man she loved, the man she believed had been killed more than a year ago, the man she had grieved for every day and every night of that year, was still alive. *Still alive.*

"Didn't it?" he asked calmly. "Somehow, I thought that

was *exactly* what our agreement was about. We pretend that how we felt about each other wasn't as important as..."
Again he hesitated, maybe reluctant to dredge up the old arguments. "As the other things in our lives," he finished. "Or wasn't that a lie as well, Claire?"

He was right, of course. It had taken her only a few days after his death to reach that conclusion. And for the rest of the time, from that day to this, she had been forced to live with the reality of what a falsehood it had been.

They had disagreed about politics. About their view of the world. About which solutions to its problems they valued. About what he and his team did.

Senseless arguments. Intellectual. Cerebral. But without any merit at all, without value, when she had lost him. When she *thought* she had lost him, she amended, because all along that, too, had been a lie. She still found it hard to believe Griff would let her think he was dead. That was larger and far more hurtful than whatever sin he was accusing her of.

Moral arrogance, she remembered. That had been one of the phrases he had thrown at her in their last, most bitter argument. Morally arrogant because she thought there were other ways to protect this country. Other ways to settle the problems of the world than those he had chosen, which were both violent and clandestine. And abhorrent to everything she just as vehemently believed in.

"What do you want?" she asked finally, almost numb from the battery of shock, pain and grief she had endured today. "Why did you bring me here?"

She had been forced to accept the fact that Griff Cabot was alive, but she didn't know what that meant. Or why he had, after all these months, decided to tell her the truth. To *show* her the truth in this way. At this particular time.

"I want to help you find your daughter," Griff said.
Your daughter. He had given the words no special em-

phasis, but they impacted in her mind. Not *our* daughter. And of course, Griff had had no hand in her upbringing. He had been alive, and yet he had never once acknowledged his daughter's existence. He hadn't done that even now.

"Why?" she asked.

She had no idea what answer she expected. *Because she's my daughter as well. Because I want her to be safe. Because I love you.* All the answers she thought he might give her echoed inside her head as she waited, not breathing, wondering which one of them he would say.

"Because I have the skills," he said.

None of the things she had been prepared to hear. *I have the skills.* The most mundane and rational of reasons. He did, of course. Resources she couldn't possibly match anywhere else in the world. His team. His contacts. His knowledge.

Which it seemed he was willing to use on his daughter's behalf. As long as she was safe, Griff had apparently been content to stay out of their lives. Content to live out the lie the CIA had created. But now...

Despite the way she felt about the things Griff Cabot once done for the CIA, she had always known that inside him was a solid core of decency and honor. That unshakeable belief was one of the things that had made the decision she had ultimately come to so difficult. And one reason she had never understood how he could do the jobs he did.

How could he issue orders for someone to be assassinated and close his mind to the reality of the human suffering that caused? How could he order a commando raid? How could he argue the virtue of the taking of one life to protect another?

To her that always sounded like the twisted statement someone had made during the Vietnam War—that the U.S. must bomb a particular village in order to save it. That was both senseless and destructive, as if violence could ever be defeated with more violence.

The old questions and arguments beat at her, as if she and Griff had made them only yesterday. Just as they had beat at her eighteen months ago when she had finally told Griff she couldn't see him anymore. That she didn't ever want to see him again.

That, too, had been a lie, of course, but at least she had known it was when she said it. She had even admitted to him the enormity of its untruth.

And that was the reason for the promise she had elicited from him. She knew how weak her will was when confronted with the reality of this man. Because she also knew how much she loved him.

So she had made him swear that he would never seek her out again. That he would never call or write her. Or come to her. Or ask her to come to him. Because if he did, she had known she wouldn't be able to resist—or deny him.

Griff had kept his word, of course. But he hadn't refused her the night *she* had come to *him.* The one night when the seemingly endless longing for the caress of his hand and the heated touch of his mouth against her body had drawn her here, unable to bear the loneliness and deprivation of living without him any longer.

Here to this house, she remembered, her gaze lifting, searching for and finding through the wooden filigree of the old gazebo the dark, familiar shape of the mansion. *She* had come to *him.*

And when he had opened the door and found her standing there, he had taken her cold, trembling fingers into his warm ones and drawn her inside. He had not released her hand, leading her through the silent house like a child. Or a blind man. Leading her up the wide curving staircase to his bedroom. So familiar, even in the sheltering night.

They hadn't spoken a word. The ghosts of the old arguments had not been released to haunt those hours. They had met almost as strangers, coming together physically in a deliberate denial of all the intellectual barriers that had kept them apart.

That night Gardner had been conceived. And Claire had not yet had a chance to tell Griff that before she had been informed of his death. She would have told him, of course. Eventually. At least it had comforted her through these long months to believe that she would have. Comforted her through those bleak, lonely months when she had believed he was dead. And now...

"Why would you *do* that?" she asked again, unable to move beyond the agony of what he had done. Unable to forgive him. "Why would you let them tell me that?"

He drew a breath, so deep the sound was audible in the stillness. And it was obvious when he answered that he understood what she was asking.

"It had *already* been done. And long before they did, what had been between us was over. Because *you* decided it should be. *You* decreed it was over, Claire. Because of who I am."

She shook her head slowly, trying to understand that reasoning. *What had been between us was already over.*

"That's not the same as *death*," she whispered.

It wasn't. Not the same as letting someone that you knew loved you believe you were dead. Nowhere near the same cruelty.

"It was to me," Griff said simply, his voice as low as hers, without any emotion she could read.

She examined the claim, trying to understand. And when she thought she did, she shook her head again. This time in denial.

"No," she said.

"No?" he questioned.

"I didn't tell you I was dead," she said.

''What was the difference in what you did, Claire? You wanted me out of your life. So what was the difference in the distance you created between us? In the separation?''

''You *know* the difference,'' she said, her anger that he would try to deny responsibility for what he had done building. ''You *have* to understand the difference.''

''What I knew was that you weren't here,'' he said simply.

''That's not *dead*,'' she accused, furious with what he was saying. With equating his supposed death with what she had done. She closed her eyes, hearing the growing stridency in her voice. No one but Griff could make her so angry. Or so confused.

Confused because as much as she wanted to deny it, there was some grain of logic in what he was saying. If they were never to see one another again, as she had demanded, then what *did* the cause of that separation matter? How could it matter what he had let them tell her?

''I'd like to help you find your baby,'' he said again, but only after he had let the painful silence lengthen unbearably. ''What have they asked you for?''

''Nothing,'' she said truthfully.

And with that word, the remembered despair of the long day broke through her anger. His question reminded her of why she was here. She couldn't believe that devastating reality had left her mind even for a moment. For a second.

Even now, Gardner might be frightened or cold or alone. And unless Claire found her soon… Her mind shied away from that word *unless.* She couldn't bear it, just as she couldn't bear the thought of what Gardner might be going through. She had fought those images all day, pushing them into a tightly locked corner of her mind. Fighting panic and despondency because they would cripple her at a time when she needed all her strength.

But she didn't feel strong right now. There had been too

much to deal with. Her emotions were shredded. Griff, whom she had thought was lost forever, was alive. And their baby... Their baby.

"There was no note. No phone call. No demand for ransom."

She made herself enumerate the list of negatives, feeling despair well up as she realized that she knew nothing more than she had known this morning when this had all begun. This morning when someone had destroyed her world.

"I thought when the phone rang tonight..." She stopped, wondering again who had called her. She had been certain it wasn't either of the agents she'd met. And it wasn't Griff. "Who called me?" she asked.

"Jake Holt," Griff said. "I contacted him because I thought he could help. Then I asked him to arrange for you to meet me here."

"You thought he could help how?" Claire asked carefully.

"He finds people," Griff said simply.

For the agency, Claire realized. Or for the team. Jake Holt was another member of Griff's External Security Team, she realized. Like the man they called Hawk, and Jordan Cross.

"And you think he can find Gardner?" she asked.

"It would help if she were using a credit card," Griff said softly.

His voice had been touched with the familiar sardonic amusement she had heard there so often before. She knew he used humor as a defense against the painful realities of his world, but of course this time those realities were too personal for this cool detachment. Or they should be. There should be nothing amusing about someone taking your child, even a child you didn't know.

"I don't understand," she said, her voice stiff, offended.

"I'm sorry," he said softly.

The unforgivable humor had been wiped totally from his deep voice. And she realized Griff could still read her every mood, every nuance of her tone.

"Jake uses the computers to find...patterns," he explained. "In purchases, phone calls, bank withdrawals. In a thousand different ways we leave footprints of our movements in the computer. We do it a hundred times a day without even thinking about it. Without ever being aware that if someone wants to find out about us, the computers that handle our every transaction offer a wealth of information."

"And he...this Jake...finds that information."

"Compiles it. Examines it. Sorts through it until he discovers a pattern. Something recognizable."

She thought about the process Griff had described, trying to see how Jake's expertise might be applied to her daughter's kidnapping.

"I don't understand how that will help," she said finally. "How will that help find Gardner?"

"I'm not sure. But that's always where we start any search. With Jake. With the computers."

"You think they aren't going to contact us," she said, fear making her voice flat.

That was the only explanation that made sense out of Griff using someone like Jake Holt. They would only need to do that if the kidnappers didn't issue any ransom demand.

"No," Griff said quickly. And reassuringly. "They'll call. They want something or they wouldn't have taken her. You'll hear from them. Making you wait is simply part of their strategy. Because they know the longer it goes on, the more eager you'll be to agree to whatever they ask. They'll be in touch. I promise you that, Claire."

The calm surety in Griff's voice comforted her, lessening the urge to hysteria she had hidden during this endless day.

Hours during which she had pretended to be rational and controlled. And she realized she had found his promise to be far more reassuring than Minger's professional opinion or her grandfather's earlier buoyancy.

Because, of course, this was Griff. If he told her everything would be all right, it would be. And if *he* told her he would get Gardner back, then he would.

"I knew your team could find her. I was trying to get in touch with Jordan," she said, remembering the hope that idea had given her. Almost as strong as the one Griff had just planted in her heart. "Or with Hawk. I thought that if anyone could find her, they could. Of course, I didn't know that you..."

Her voice faded. *I didn't know that you were alive.* Alive, she thought again, almost unable to deal with that on top of all that had happened.

"They're very good at what they do," Griff agreed.

They were his men. Accustomed to working under his orders. He had trained them. He didn't remind her of that. And, of course, he didn't need to.

"When Grandfather tried to locate them through the agency, he discovered all their records were destroyed. According to the CIA, those men never existed," she said, wondering if Griff had known what the agency had been doing.

"Because they have found them to be...difficult to control," he said.

She recognized the care he had taken in that choice of words. And underlying them, she heard amusement again. *Difficult to control.*

She knew from her grandfather that among some elements of the intelligence community, Griff himself had been considered difficult. But he had also been brilliant and insightful and incredibly successful, his operations so well planned and executed there were seldom problems for the agency to deal with. No collateral damage.

And so they had been willing to put up with him in exchange for what he could do. Even willing, it seemed, to put up with Griff's arrogance.

Moral arrogance. The phrase he had once used against her echoed in her head again, but in a different context. Griff wanted to help find their daughter. She had come here because she was desperate to contact someone who could. Even more easily than Jordan or Hawk, Griff would be able to do that. And he would have more reason to, of course.

"If you're wrong... If they don't call..." She took a deep breath and, setting aside her anger over the lie he had lived, she asked, "Will you find her for me? Will you find Gardner?"

Will you help me find your daughter? Will you return to me your child? The child you gave me. The child who was my only comfort in the long empty darkness of your death.

"Yes," he said.

No equivocation. A simple statement. A promise and a vow. And without questioning whether he could really do what he had just said he would, Claire found herself, as always, believing him.

WHEN GRIFF HAD ELICITED every detail, every piece of minutiae Claire knew—which were too damn few, he acknowledged—he had sent her home to wait for the contact from the kidnappers he'd promised. That would come eventually, he believed. And when it did, he wanted to be ready to move.

And if it didn't... Then he would call on those same people who had answered every call he had made on their strength and courage and intelligence during the past ten years. There were more than a dozen men who had worked on the special operations team known as External Security.

And he knew that any of them would respond to his plea for help.

Each of them had, however, very specialized skills, and he wasn't sure yet which of those he would need. That depended on the conditions the kidnappers demanded for the exchange. That was always the trickiest part, of course. And although it wasn't their usual mission, the team had handled a few of those kinds of negotiations in the past.

Once they had been sent to recover an operative whose cover had been blown. Once it had been to achieve the release of an MIA, by whatever means. Those situations had been too politically sensitive to be made public, but they'd been successful. So Griff had no doubt they could arrange this exchange.

Maybe Claire felt that the man she was involved with, the baby's father, wasn't equipped for this. Not many people were, which was why Griff had offered her his help. One of the reasons, he acknowledged.

He sat down behind his desk, propping the cane against the edge. It had been a long day and a longer night, and he could feel every minute of it aching along the damaged nerves and muscles of his leg.

He debated whether or not to try to contact Jake again, or whether to grab a few hours of sleep, whatever was left of the night. That was something they had all learned to do—sleep when they had the opportunity. When things weren't happening.

He glanced at his watch. It was almost 2:00 a.m. They needed to formulate a plan for what they would do if, worse case scenario, the kidnappers didn't contact Claire. For that he would need a clear head. And given the strains of this day, he knew he didn't have one.

He had already, during his first call, asked Jake to check for anything that looked suspicious in Claire Heywood's world. That reminded him that he needed to tell Jake about the malfunctioning security alarms. Griff had chosen the company that had installed Claire's system, and they were the best in the business. Whoever had rigged it to short-circuit last night had to be pretty sophisticated. That expertise might give them a starting point.

He glanced down at the keyboard of the computer, thinking about sending Jake an e-mail at home. It wouldn't be encrypted, but that shouldn't matter in this situation. After all, this wasn't agency business.

It took a second for his brain to register what he was seeing. A single piece of paper, folded once, lay on top of the keys. His name had been typed in all caps across it—GRIFFON CABOT—and he knew it hadn't been there earlier tonight when he had called Jake. Or when he had made the arrangements for the chopper. He would have seen it. Which meant...

Which meant that someone had put it there while he'd been gone. He had given his housekeeper the holiday weekend off, so it couldn't have been her. Maybe Carl had come back for some reason and, finding him gone, had left a message. After all, Steiner was one of the very few people who knew the man who lived in this house by that name.

Griff found a silver letter opener in the desk drawer and carefully inserted its point between the edges of the opening formed by the two sides of the folded sheet. He lifted the top half and read what was written there.

It was a message that changed everything he thought he knew about the kidnapping. Everything about his relationship with Claire Heywood. And if what was written on this piece of paper were true, then everything about his own life, as well.

Chapter Five

Poor dear, Rose Connor thought, listening to the sounds the baby she held was making. *Poor little darling.*

She pushed the rocking chair back and forth, her broad, bare toes barely making contact with the wooden floor. The soft creak of the chair was relaxing, and her eyelids drifted downward. When she realized what was happening, she jerked them up again, fighting the urge to sleep.

Only a little longer, she told herself, patting the small bottom held securely in the crook of her arm. The baby had gradually relaxed, the screams that had awakened Rose turning into soft sobs and then finally into small, hiccuping breaths. Now even those were fading, as the little girl's dark head rooted in the soft flesh of Rose's shoulder.

Almost asleep, Rose thought, her toes pushing rhythmically against the floor. *Almost…creak…asleep…creak…* The same steady rhythm of the human heart. Never forgotten.

And as soothing to her as to the dear ones she cared for. She smoothed thick, spatulate fingers over the tiny back, cherishing its regular lift and fall. Savoring this incredible moment of triumph. Of success.

She had always loved this feeling. She had begun caring for her brothers and sisters when she was just a wee bit of a thing herself. Her mother had so much to do to tend to them all during the day, and too little sleep at night.

So when the baby cried, Rose would slip out of bed, and moving through the darkness of the cottage on bare feet, she would hurry to the crib to comfort the newest addition to the family. Holding the infant against her narrow chest, she would croon the same wordless lullabies her mother had sung to her.

Just the two of them in the quiet world of night. She and a babe who needed her. Who responded to her touch. Who loved her. As near to heaven as Rose Connor expected to get here on earth.

Soon, she knew, she'd be able to put this one back into her crib. Then maybe the blessed sweetheart would be able to sleep out the rest of the night. And if she couldn't, poor little mite, then old Rose would come again and hold her.

Chase away the shadows. Soothe the nightmares and frighten away the bogeyman. Stand in for that sad little mother who must be missing the quiet joy and satisfaction of this closeness.

Poor little thing, Rose thought again, her toes pushing and then relaxing against the floor. And this time, it wasn't the baby that her warm heart pitied.

CLAIRE THOUGHT she had probably slept less than three hours. And those had been spent in a half-waking consciousness that something was very wrong. Listening with dread—for the phone, for a knock on the door or for any of the sounds she should have heard last night and had not.

When the doorbell did ring, a little before six, she was in the kitchen making coffee. It was something to do besides worry. And if the technicians and investigators who had passed in and out of the house yesterday came back today, she thought she should at least be able to offer them a cup of hot coffee.

She realized that whoever was at the door was in all probability simply the first in the long line of people who would ask her questions or take pictures or dust one more object in the nursery for nonexistent fingerprints. However, the adrenaline had kicked in so strongly with the sound of the bell that her hand was shaking as she hurried to turn off the alarms and open the front door, leaving its security chain in place.

Griff Cabot was standing on her doorstep. An obviously furious Griff Cabot. ''I saw your light,'' he said, the words bitten off. ''We need to talk.''

''Something's happened to her,'' Claire said, her sudden fear as paralyzing as when she had first discovered Gardner was missing. ''Oh, my God, Griff, something's happened to Gardner.''

Eyes wide, she watched his face change, the anger fading, or at least controlled, with his recognition of her terror.

''No,'' he said quickly. ''No, Claire, I promise you that isn't what this is about.''

That isn't what this is about. The words made no sense, since there was nothing else between them now. But she could see the truth of what he said in his eyes. And the same compassion that she always remembered from the dream. The compassion that had been there the night he had opened *his* door and found her outside.

''Do you swear that's the truth, Griff?'' she demanded, but she already knew it was, and her racing pulse began to slow.

''As far as I know, Gardner is safe. I swear to you.''

As far as I know. That's really all she could ask him for. So she nodded, and then slid the knob of the chain out of the slot and opened the door.

''I made coffee,'' she said. ''We can talk in the kitchen.''

He hesitated, lips compressed, before he stepped inside.

She noticed for the first time that he held a cane in his right hand. And then, as he limped past her, she realized why.

She let him lead the way. He knew the house, of course, but that wasn't the reason. He seemed totally in charge, in command. That was Griff's personality, but today that quality was even more pronounced. And, of course, that was exactly what she had asked him to do, she acknowledged. To take charge of whatever was going on. To get Gardner back.

When they reached the kitchen, the smell of freshly brewed coffee permeated the room. It was a comfortable aroma, familiar, making things seem almost normal. Even between the two of them.

"Sit down," she suggested. "I'll bring your coffee to the table."

She knew at once her unthinking offer had been a mistake. She would probably have said the same thing to any other guest, but she had never waited on Griff. She had never treated him as a guest in her home because he had been so much more.

And she knew by his face how he had interpreted what she'd said. Even she couldn't be certain that she *hadn't* made that offer, at least in part, because of the limp and the cane.

She would have felt free to ask about those had they still been the same two people they had been before. Had their relationship been the same. But it wasn't. So, despite what was in his eyes, she said nothing.

The awkward silence lasted only a few seconds before Griff obeyed, shrugging out of his overcoat and throwing it over one of the kitchen chairs before he eased down into another, leaning the cane carefully against the edge of the table. She watched his movements, and when she realized she was, she turned to the cabinet above the sink and took down two mugs, filling them with the fragrant Jamaican blend Griff had introduced her to. Something she still un-thinkingly bought because he had liked it.

She put one of the steaming cups in front of him and then sat down across the table, preparing to hear whatever had brought him out here so early this morning. Whatever had made him angry. She held her mug with cold fingers, savoring the warmth as she watched him lift his to take the first sip.

His eyes met hers over the rim of his cup, and the almost physical connection that had always been between them flared within her, igniting memory. And the slow-burning fuse of desire. Nothing had changed, she realized, in how she felt about Griff Cabot. The same way she had always felt. Since the very first time she had seen him, standing with her grandfather at some crowded Washington party.

She had thought he was the most attractive man in the room. Remarkably, nothing had changed about that initial assessment, even after she'd arranged to be introduced. It had never changed. To her, Griff Cabot would still be the most attractive man in any room.

Watching him complete the interrupted motion of his cup, which hid whatever had been in his eyes, she was forced to acknowledge, however, that he was different from the man he had been then. Some changes, like the limp, were terribly obvious. Others were more subtle. And she guessed there were some no one would ever be allowed to see.

The physical ones were the easiest to trace, of course. The coal-black hair threaded with gray. The deepened lines around the corners of the sensitive mouth she had known so well. Etched by pain? Or by the frustrations she knew he would feel over the limitations a damaged leg would impose on the man he was?

Remembering the limping journey down the hall, she realized for the first time that he had really been seriously injured in the attack at CIA headquarters. Last night, she had assumed the agency had used that act of terrorism as an excuse to further their own ends in some way. Now she recognized that the terrorist's bullets might actually have been the cause of the story they'd put out—that Griff was dead. And she remembered what he had said about being in no condition to stop them.

Of course, none of that explained why he hadn't contacted her later. When he was once more in control of his own destiny. Their destiny, she amended bitterly.

He was watching her, she realized, when she looked up from her coffee. The dark eyes were unreadable now. Lips unsmiling.

"I know what they want," he said.

It took a moment for the import of that to sink in.

"You know what the *kidnappers* want?"

"I received a ransom note last night," he said, his voice as hard as it had been when she'd opened the door.

That even made some kind of sense, she supposed. Their contacting Griff. After all, he was much better off financially than she was.

"How much?" she asked.

"You're not surprised the ransom demand was sent to me?" he asked instead. His eyes were cold. And so dark they were almost black.

"I don't..." She hesitated, again sensing, and yet not understanding, his anger. As soon as her words faltered, he spoke, filling the silence.

"*I* was," he said. "But then, I didn't know, of course."

"Didn't know what?" she asked, trying to understand what was wrong. This was what they had been waiting for, and yet Griff was acting as if... As if it wasn't good news that the kidnappers had contacted them.

His eyes held hers. Held them long enough that the blood began to pound in her temples.

"The truth," he said finally, his voice flat. "Something you apparently saw no reason to tell me," he accused softly. "Not last night. And not before."

"The *truth?*" she repeated. And hearing the tone of accusation, she thought of the long lie he had lived this past year. Whatever he meant, Griff didn't have much room to chide her about truth. "The truth about what?" she asked, truly bewildered.

Again the silence stretched, but angry now herself, she didn't allow her eyes to fall, and finally he spoke again.

"About why they think I'd be willing to do whatever they want in order to get *your* daughter back?"

His voice was soft. And reasonable. But she didn't like what she heard there, underlying those surface qualities. And she didn't understand the emphasis on the pronoun.

"What do they want you to do?" she asked.

"She's mine, isn't she, Claire?" he asked, ignoring her question. "Gardner is my daughter, and that's why these people are so certain they can call the tune, and I'll have to dance to it. She's my daughter. And you never told me."

Then, of course, it all fell into place. His anger. The tone of accusation. But if he hadn't known, then who the hell *did* he think had fathered Gardner? And how was she supposed to let him know about the baby when the agency had lied to her, telling her he was dead?

"My God, Griff, I thought you were dead. Or have you forgotten that?" she asked bitterly. "I don't do seances. Or maybe I was supposed to whisper that I was pregnant to your tombstone."

"And last night?" he asked.

"I thought you knew," she said truthfully. "I thought that's why you called. Why you offered to help."

He said nothing for a moment, but the coldness didn't leave his eyes. "I did the math," he said. "If she's six months old, as this morning's paper said, then you had to have known you were pregnant. *Before* Langley.''

Before Langley. A pleasant euphemism for what had happened to him. For the lie the CIA had told her. But he was right. She had known. Not long, but long enough to have picked up the phone and told Griff.

And she hadn't. The unexpected pregnancy had complicated everything. And it had all been too complicated to begin with. By their conflicting ideologies. Their matching stubbornness.

And by her stupidity, she admitted, remembering the sleepless nights of regret after his death. Regret that she hadn't told him about the baby. But of course, Griff was dead, and eventually she had forced herself to acknowledge that it was too late to change anything she had done.

"It happened that night?" he asked. He already knew the answer, of course. Since he said he had done the math, it was the only answer.

That night. The night she had come to him. Because she couldn't stay away any longer. The night she had dreamed about over and over again.

She hadn't intended to go to him, of course. Not even when she had left this house. But driving aimlessly through the fall darkness, she had found she couldn't resist any longer what she had wanted for the last three months. She couldn't deny herself another minute. Because she loved him. And she wanted him. Wanted to be with him.

"Yes," she admitted.

"I thought you were protected," he said.

After she had broken off their relationship, there had been no need for protection. She hadn't been involved with anyone else, and she had known she wouldn't be. When her prescription had run out, she hadn't even bothered to renew it.

And when he had taken her hand that night and drawn

her across the threshold, the fact that she hadn't never crossed her mind. Maybe, she admitted, because she didn't want it to. She had always heard there was no such thing as an unwanted pregnancy.

"I wasn't. Not...then," she admitted.

"You got pregnant that night," he said. "And you didn't tell me."

"There wasn't time," she said quickly. That was the same excuse she had offered herself after his death. There hadn't been time. "I intended to. But..."

She hesitated, knowing some part of that was a lie. There *had* been time. Only a few short weeks, but time nonetheless. She had still been trying to decide what to do when they'd informed her, through her grandfather, that Griff Cabot was dead.

There were some admissions, however, that were too painful to make. And ultimately, of course, she had made all the right decisions. The only one she had ever regretted was not to tell Griff as soon as she knew she was pregnant.

"I know what they want in exchange for the baby," Griff said, not even waiting to hear what excuse she might offer for what she'd done. "*If* you're interested."

"If I'm interested?" she repeated disbelievingly. "Of course I'm *interested,* Griff. This is my daughter."

"And mine. I might have been prepared for this if I'd known."

She wasn't sure if he meant prepared for the kidnapping or for whatever the kidnappers wanted him to do in exchange for Gardner's return. She knew from what he had already said that it wasn't money, but something they wanted Griff to *do.*

Give them information? Something classified? With that thought, her heart squeezed painfully because she wasn't sure Griff would ever commit treason. Not even to save the life of his child.

"Will you do what they want?" she asked.

It was a far more important question than those he had been asking. She waited for his answer, afraid the code of honor he had lived by so long would keep him from getting Gardner back.

"First, I think I need to hear you say it, Claire. I think your telling me is long overdue. Why should I do what they want?"

She didn't know why he thought this was necessary. A form of punishment, maybe? Or simply a need to hear her say it, as he'd claimed? But whatever his motives, she could think of no reason not to comply. Not when it was so important.

"Because Gardner is your daughter," she said, her voice low.

He nodded, holding her eyes.

"What do they want?" she asked again.

His lips moved into a semblance of his familiar smile. Unlike any other smile she had ever seen on Griff Cabot's face. Not in all the time she had known him. It was totally without humor. Without amusement. As cold and as empty as the nursery had been yesterday morning.

"They want me to kill someone," he said softly.

"*Kill* someone?" she repeated, after a stunned second or two of thinking that she couldn't have heard that right. She could hear her horror at the thought echoing through her question.

"An assassination. After all, I've arranged those before. Given the orders for them to be carried out. That's all they're asking, Claire. They just want me to arrange another assassination."

Bile surged into her throat as she realized he was serious. *Assassination.* This was part of what had driven them apart. There had been other things about his job that bothered her, of course, but this...

That had been the one thing she could never condone. Never forgive. Or accept. Not from the man she loved.

"As soon as it's done, they'll give Gardner back."

There was a silence, so deep she could hear her blood rushing through the veins in her ears.

"I assume," Griff added softly, "that you won't object to me paying their price."

The silence grew and expanded, and his eyes held hers, waiting for her response.

"Who?" Claire whispered instead, still fighting the sickness climbing into her throat.

This was a growing nightmare she couldn't escape. Instead, with each minute that had passed since she'd found that open window, it had grown worse, more frightening, more horrifying.

"The less you know about that the better," Griff said.

"I have a right to know."

She supposed she did. That didn't mean, however, that she really wanted to. Griff was right. The less she had to think about all this...

"And when you do?" Griff asked quietly.

She knew what he was really asking. Would she refuse to let him do what they demanded? Was she prepared to sacrifice her daughter's life for a principle? And she didn't have an answer for him.

"I have a right to know," she repeated stubbornly.

Griff took a breath, his lips flattening, his eyes still on hers, and then he said, "His name wouldn't mean anything to you."

"But it *does* mean something to you?"

"I know who he is."

"And you know why someone wants him dead?" she asked, knowing from his tone that he did.

"A lot of people probably want him dead," Griff said.

That was almost comforting, until she realized she was

falling into the same trap she had almost fallen into before. Long ago when they had argued—intellectually then—about this. It was a trap of logic that said it was all right to take someone's life if he were engaged in actions that were reprehensible. Threatening to others. Or inhumane.

"Are you going to do it?" she asked, because she believed she had read that in his eyes as well. And then she waited, bracing herself for the questions he had only implied before.

Do you want me to? Do you want your daughter back badly enough to tell me to do what they've asked? Even if doing it is something you have always condemned, no matter the justification.

Moral arrogance. Did she want Griff to get Gardner back like this? At this cost? Yesterday she would have said she would do anything to get her baby back. And she would have thought she was speaking the truth.

"Let me handle it, Claire," he said, his eyes almost as soft now as his voice. "I'll stay in touch."

Dear God, she wanted to let him handle it. How could she weigh her daughter's life against everything she had ever believed? Against everything she had been taught?

Her daughter's life. And all the precious images of Gardner's short existence ran through her head. Suddenly, Claire wanted to tell Griff how much his daughter looked like him. How her minute chin could tilt at exactly the same angle his sometimes did. If he were being challenged. In the heat of argument. And how Gardner's eyes, as dark and beautiful as Griff's, would sometimes study Claire's face as intently as his were now.

She wanted to say all those things to him. She wanted to tell him about their daughter, so that he would love her as much as she did. So that *he* would make this decision. So that he would do what they had told him to do, no matter what she said. No matter what she had once argued. No matter what she said she believed was morally right.

But instead, the confusion of too many conflicting emotions made her strike out at Griff instead. Just exactly, she would realize later, as she had always done.

"I *should* leave it to you," she said bitterly. "After all, this is your fault. You're the one who brought these people here. Into Gardner's life. Into mine. This is *your* filth, Griff. This whole nightmare is the result of how you chose to live your life. I damn well hope you're satisfied with the results."

She saw his eyes change. There had been compassion in them when he'd told her to let him handle it. That was replaced slowly by pain, an agony so unbearable it was visible. And then his entire face hardened, accepting that unforgivable blow.

He didn't say another word. He pushed up from the table, picking up his coat and the cane. Then he turned, limping back down the hallway to the front door.

She listened, unmoving, as the uneven footsteps faded. It was not until she heard the slam of the front door that she remembered to breathe. And then, using the heels of her hands, to wipe away the tears.

She had no right to blame Griff for what had happened to Gardner. This was simply the inevitable intrusion of the world he had warned her about. A world that lay in wait just beyond the confines of the safe and protected one in which she had grown up. The one she had arranged for her daughter.

Maybe what had happened to Gardner *had* originated in his world, but she knew Griff had done everything in his power to protect her from it. She had once thought he was too obsessive about keeping their relationship private. Too secretive.

This was, of course, what he'd feared. That she would

be used against him in this way. A victim of the violence he knew so well. Instead of threatening her, they had used his daughter. A daughter he had never known and couldn't possibly love as much as she did.

So in her fear, she had struck out at Griff, just as she had done before. And struck out at him because she knew in her heart she wanted him to do anything to get Gardner back. God help her, *anything*. Even this.

Chapter Six

"His name is Jake Holt. And I *know* he's still working for the agency," she said to her grandfather. "I need to ask him only one question. And I promise I won't make you contact the director again."

It had taken her two days to reach this point. Two endless days during which nothing had happened. She had talked to Minger, of course. Several times. And to the FBI. During those interviews, however, her mind had been only half-engaged, because she had known that it didn't matter what they asked or what she told them.

The police weren't going to find Gardner. Nor was the FBI. No one was going to contact her and demand ransom. That demand had already been made. Not to her, but to the person at whom this kidnapping had been directed.

And whoever had known enough about Griff and his team to pull this off was not going to be discovered by the local police. So whatever they were doing was pointless, and she knew it. This playing field was not on their level. Even the bureau was probably not capable of influencing events in this arena.

She couldn't tell the authorities that. She hadn't even told her parents or Mandy and Charles what was going on. Only her grandfather knew what had happened the night she had driven to Griff's house in Maryland. And the morning he had come here.

She had slept last night on the floor of Gardner's room, an exercise in trying to recapture the serenity their life had once held. To reconnect with her daughter. But Gardner was both too near and too far away in that room.

And Claire had acknowledged that Gardner might never be there in reality again if Griff didn't do what they'd asked him to do. And given the unforgivable things she had said to him, she could no longer be certain of anything he was doing.

So she had driven out to the Maryland house again today, searching for him, and had found it empty. There had been no sign that anyone had been there in months. No sign of her meeting with Griff. As if she had dreamed the entire episode.

I'll stay in touch, Griff had promised. But that had been before she'd lashed out at him, accusing him of being responsible for what had happened to Gardner. She had heard nothing from him during these two endless days. And she knew she couldn't live through another one without knowing what was going on.

"Cabot told you to let him handle it," her grandfather said. "That sounds like excellent advice, Claire."

"Actually," she said, finding a smile for him, because she understood he was trying to comfort her, "it sounds like blatant male chauvinism, but we'll ignore that for the moment."

"I don't know what you believe this Holt can tell you."

"Where they are," she said simply.

"They?" Her grandfather's voice reflected both his frustration with her and his puzzlement.

"Griff. Jordan Cross. A man called Hawk. And maybe Jake Holt as well. But...I think he would stay at headquarters. I think he's their contact there. And he would probably need the agency's computers.''

She was thinking out loud, of course. Articulating all the things she believed she had figured out in the last two days about what Griff might do.

"You think they're really going to do this," the old man said. "You think Cabot intends to do what the kidnappers demanded. And you want to try to stop them."

"No," she said. "I don't want to stop them. God forgive me, I want to help."

"I HAVE NO RIGHT to ask you," Griff Cabot said, his eyes touching on the face of each man in turn, "but I would like to have you with me," he said softly.

"I've got vacation coming," Jake Holt said, his voice laced with amusement, a contrast to the quiet solemnity of Griff's. "After all, *I'm* the only one who's still working for a living. Since you're paying all the expenses for this little excursion and since I think Florida's a really nice area to visit this time of year, you can count me in."

Griff nodded, not really surprised by Jake's acceptance, or by the cheerful nonchalance with which he'd made it. Jake wasn't a field agent, of course, but he had grown up around the area where they were going, so his knowledge of it would be invaluable. And Jake was a bachelor.

The other two men he had called had new lives, an existence outside the agency. And they had families. The fact that they had answered his summons spoke of the depth of their friendship, but Griff knew he had no right to ask them to lay their lives on the line for a mission that was purely personal.

"Quid pro quo," Jordan Cross said. "I owe Claire Heywood a couple of favors. And more than a few to you," he said, smiling at Griff. "I'm in."

Griff nodded, his gaze lingering unconsciously on Jordan's altered face. It was disconcerting, although he had known what to expect. And it was a little eerie when Jordan spoke to find his deep voice totally unchanged.

"Are you waiting for me to agree?" Hawk asked, and Griff's eyes swung to his face, its harsh contours reassuringly the same.

"I need to hear you say it," he said.

Just as he had needed to hear Claire tell him Gardner was his child, needed to hear her say the words, although there had really been no doubt after he'd received that ransom note. And he needed to know that each of these men knew going in exactly what they would be up against.

"Then I'm in," Hawk said.

Three words, but Hawk's ice-blue eyes, locked on his face, said all the other things Griff knew he would never hear from Lucas Hawkins. No words about bonds of friendship. Or old debts. Those would remain unspoken, because, between the two of them, they didn't need to be expressed. They never had.

"Then I'll let Jake tell you what he's found out," Griff said, fighting unwanted emotions, especially gratitude for a brotherhood that had been forged on missions just like this one would be. Dangerous. Precisely planned. And dependent on each other for its success.

"We'd never get him at home," Jake said, "not without losses. Security's too tight. Location's too isolated. Griff doesn't want to take that chance, and there's no need."

"So where?" Hawk asked.

"He has a meeting set up with his major distributors in three days," Jake said. "In the States. We need to do it here. But he'll fly out of Miami on the fifth or the sixth, so that's our window of opportunity."

"Not a lot of time," Griff interjected, "but doable. We've planned missions in less. Jake will fly down in the morning and make arrangements for the equipment we'll need. The three of us follow on different flights.''

"I don't understand how they could have known you're alive," Jordan said. "Or how they could know about the baby when you didn't.''

The fact that he hadn't been aware of Gardner's existence was something Griff had rather not go into. They had the right to ask questions, however, considering what they had just agreed to do, motivated by nothing more than friendship.

"People in the agency knew I was alive," he said. "They probably knew about the baby as well.''

"You think they could be behind this? Steiner and that crowd?" Hawk asked.

There was no love lost between Hawk and the man who had taken Griff's place, but as much as he had thought about the possibility that this was someone within the agency, Griff couldn't fathom a motive. Not for the assassination or for wanting him involved in something like this. The agency had more to lose with the possibility of his involvement becoming public than anyone else.

"Someone was in the system during the last couple of months," Jake said softly. "I could feel them. Someone who had to be operating from inside.''

"*I* was in the system," Griff said, remembering Steiner's frustration over how he had known what was going on with his team. "I kept expecting you to backtrack to me.''

Jake laughed, sounding a little relieved. "Guess I taught you pretty good.''

"You really didn't know?" Griff asked.

"Not that it was you," Jake said. "But that still doesn't explain how these people could know what they seem to know.''

"If I could get in, Jake, so could someone else," Griff said. "Someone from the outside.''

"When pigs fly," Jake said softly, but obviously challenging that conclusion.

"Then figuring out *how* they knew is your job," Griff suggested. "*While you're at it,* figure out how they sabotaged Claire's alarms."

"What about the exchange?" Jordan asked when Jake nodded.

Griff looked up and found Jordan's gray eyes on his face. At least they were still familiar.

"Down there," he said. "I've already arranged that with them. They're demanding proof. And that's going to be the tricky part, given how security conscious the subject is."

"But you've already figured out how we're going to do it," Hawk said, amusement threading the quiet comment.

Griff's mouth moved slightly in response before his eyes again found Lucas Hawkins's face. "I've figured out how *you're* going to do it," he said. "All I'm going to do is take a plane ride and work on my tan."

"Sounds like business as usual," Jordan said. "We take the chances, and you and Jake get a vacation."

Hawk laughed. For the first time in months, Griff heard the sound of his own laughter, joining that of the others. And despite the grim purpose that had brought these few members of his team together, he knew that Carl Steiner had been right. He had missed this. And he had missed them.

DESPITE HER GRANDFATHER'S efforts within the agency, Claire hadn't been able to get in touch with Jake Holt. Maybe she had been wrong in thinking he would remain at headquarters. Maybe he didn't need their computers to do whatever it was he did.

And that thought had led her to undertake tonight's journey—a drive to the old summer home on the coast of Virginia that the Cabots had owned for generations and that

Griff had utilized before for the activities of his team. A place where both Jordan and Hawk had sought refuge. A place where there was a lot of computer equipment that Griff had used for agency business.

And a place that now seemed as dark and devoid of human life as a tomb, she acknowledged, looking up to where the towers of the Victorian house loomed above her on the top of the seaside cliff. If Griff and his team were working here, they were being damned low-key about it.

Wild-goose chase, she thought, beginning the climb up the flights of wooden steps that snaked along the side of the cliff. She had managed more than half of them when she remembered Griff's cane and realized again how foolish this visit was.

Pausing to catch her breath, she looked up at the structure, so dark and forbidding and obviously unoccupied. She almost turned around and left, but since she was already here, she decided that she might as well make sure.

WILD-GOOSE CHASE, she thought again, as she directed the beam of her flashlight about the dark, empty rooms. She had been a little surprised that the codes for the security locks hadn't been changed. It seemed, however, that nothing had changed, she acknowledged, letting the light probe the perimeters of Griff's study.

She had already turned away, heading back to the hall and the front door, when a small flash attracted her attention. It had come from something on the desk, so she allowed the flashlight to play again over its surface. What she had caught out of the corner of her eye, she realized, was a reflection of her light off the glass of a photograph.

She stepped back into the room and walked over to the desk to pick it up. A snaggle-toothed, towheaded tomboy laughed out at her from the silver frame. A moment from her own childhood. A single moment that had been captured in time, almost as Griff's face had been that night in the garden. Frozen. Unchanging.

Griff's study. And her photograph. The only one he had ever asked her for. A picture no one could associate with the woman she was now. And that caution had been for security reasons, to prevent the very thing that had happened to Gardner.

Claire put the picture down where she had found it, but she didn't go back to the door. She stood there instead, remembering the times they had spent in this house. They hadn't been able to get away often, given their conflicting and equally crowded schedules, but the weekends they had stolen had been very special to them both. And rare. Far too rare in their relationship.

A relationship she had destroyed, she acknowledged, just as Griff had said. Destroyed deliberately and after careful thought. Over principle.

Her lips tightened, but resolutely she turned away from the desk and retraced her steps across the room. She had almost reached the door when she heard a noise. She stopped, quickly pressing the off button on the flashlight with her thumb. Then, holding her breath, she listened.

It had taken only a second to place the first sound. And then those she was hearing now. Someone had closed a door and was coming down the hallway, his steps echoing slightly in the long empty space.

Griff? she wondered, but instinctively she shrank against the wall beside the door. Not Griff. She had realized that by the even rhythm of the footsteps. She closed her eyes, putting her head back against the wall. Maybe there was a caretaker living nearby. Maybe he had seen her light and had come to investigate.

Whoever this was, she realized, he was apparently doing exactly what she had done, stopping in each doorway and examining each of the rooms that led off of it. But he was working from the back of the house.

She opened her eyes and turned her head toward the door. She could see the light he carried moving sporadically. Sometimes it seemed brighter—directed down the hall toward the room where she was hiding—and then it would fade as it was turned in another direction.

It was clear, however, that whoever held the flashlight was coming this way. She began edging to her right, toward the door that led from the study and out onto the gallery that ran around the back of the house. The footsteps were getting louder, and moving on tiptoe, she hurriedly closed the distance between herself and that outside door. She had her hand on its knob before she remembered the alarms.

She looked for the security pad, but couldn't find it in the darkness. And then, suddenly, it wasn't dark anymore. She whirled, and the beam of a flashlight focused on her face. Just as Griff had done that night, she put her hand up to block the intensity of the light, and it went out at once.

"Sorry, Ms. Heywood. I wasn't sure who was up here."

She lowered her hand, but her eyes were momentarily blinded. Gradually they adjusted to the return of darkness, and the figure standing in the doorway swam into focus.

"Jake said you'd been looking for us," Lucas Hawkins said.

She had met the man called Hawk only once, during the abortive meeting she had arranged for him with his superiors at the CIA. A meeting where he had traded his freedom for Tyler Stewart's life.

She had seen Hawk, however, before that meeting. At the time, she hadn't known who he was. She had realized when she'd met him later that he, too, had been visiting Griff's grave. And she wondered how *he* felt about the lie Griff had told them. Or had he had known all along Griff wasn't dead?

"And how did Jake know that?" she asked.

Since all her efforts to find Holt had ended in the same denials her previous inquiries about Hawk and Jordan had provoked, she was really curious.

"Jake knows everything," Hawk said easily. "Or didn't Griff tell you that?"

"You know he's alive," she said.

"I didn't. Not until this."

Not until this. Not until Griff had gotten the demand from the people who had taken Gardner and had called on his friends for help. She had been right about that, at least.

"And it doesn't bother you that they lied to us?"

Hawk had killed the man who'd ordered that terrorist attack at Langley. He had killed him because Griff Cabot had been one of the victims of that massacre. And since they now knew that he was not, she was curious as to how Hawk felt about the deception.

"I'm just glad he's alive."

"You *killed* a man because they told you Griff was dead."

Even to her, it sounded like an accusation. She didn't think she had meant to accuse him. Perhaps she just wanted to be reassured that Hawk felt as betrayed as she did by what Griff had let the CIA do. Or as angry, perhaps.

After all, Hawk's life had been as disrupted as hers by that lie. Perhaps more so. Only her intervention, and Jordan Cross's, had saved Hawk's life. And he had lost his profession as a result of the revenge he had taken for Griff's death.

"The man I killed had a lot of blood on his hands. A lot of murders through the years had been laid at his door. The five who *did* die at Langley were only his latest victims. And I'll save you the trouble of asking again. It doesn't bother me."

"And this?" she said, her voice very low. "Does…this bother you?"

"The assassination the kidnappers have demanded?" Hawk asked, putting the reality she had skirted into concrete terms.

She nodded and then was unsure he could see her clearly enough to detect the motion. "Yes," she whispered.

"I don't make those decisions, Ms. Heywood. I take orders. But I take them from a man I trust. And I always will. As long as he wants to give them to me."

The simplicity of Hawk's answer left her with nothing to say. *A man I trust.* That was the kind of loyalty Griff evoked in those who worked with him. Only she, apparently, had not been able to give him that unquestioning trust.

"If you want to talk to Griff," Hawk offered, "I'll take you to him."

She hesitated only a second before she stepped out of the shadows beside the gallery door and moved across the room to where the man called Hawk was waiting.

"WHAT ARE YOU DOING HERE, Claire?" Griff asked.

He glanced up when Hawk opened the door, but only long enough to see who was with him. Then he redirected his attention to the display on the monitor he had been studying, leaning over the shoulder of the man who was seated in front of the computer.

Jake Holt? she wondered. If so, apparently she had been wrong about what he needed. There didn't seem to be any more computer equipment in front of him than she had at home.

Finally, when she didn't answer his question, Griff straightened away from whatever he had been concentrating on and really looked at her. His eyes were shadowed, but even across the room, she could feel their impact. A physical impact.

Unexpectedly, a slow, roiling wave of heat moved through her body. The same hunger, the same need, that had driven her to come to him that night more than a year ago. The night Gardner had been conceived.

"I need to talk to you," she said.

He didn't say anything for a moment, but his mouth tightened, the grooves she had noticed beside it deepening with the pressure he was exerting.

"I think you know everyone here except Jake," he said.

"Hello, Claire."

Jordan Cross's deep voice, touched with that unmistakable Southern accent, came from across the room. Across the basement, she amended, her eyes lifting to find a man leaning against the original bricks of the cellar wall.

Jordan, she realized, although he looked very different from the man she had met at the Lincoln Memorial that day. The new face, courtesy of the CIA's surgeons, was almost as attractive as the old.

"It's good to see you again," Jordan added.

At least his tone seemed friendly, Claire thought. Uncondemning. But of course, Hawk's had been, too, even when he had made that pronouncement about trust. She had time to wonder what Griff had told them before the man at the computer turned, looking directly at her for the first time.

She was too far away to be able to tell anything about the color of his eyes. In the light from the computer, his hair appeared to be lighter than Griff's. A dark chestnut, perhaps.

Then he stood up and crossed the room toward her, putting out his hand. Automatically Claire took it, and found that his handshake was as warm and friendly as his smile.

And his eyes were amber, she realized. Far too golden to be called brown.

"So you're the head hotshot's woman," Jake said. "Nice of you to drop by. I wondered what you'd be like. We all did. Nobody but me will ever tell you that, by the way."

The head hotshot, she thought. She couldn't imagine anyone using that phrase to describe Griff. Especially not in front of him. Her lips tilted, despite the seriousness of the task that had brought her here.

"Don't mind Jake," Jordan said from across the room. "He likes to rattle cages. Sometimes he forgets what's inside."

"Hotshot number two," Jake said, almost under his breath.

"You're not...a hotshot?" she asked, smiling openly at him, a little of the stress of the last three days easing with his friendliness.

"I'm the geek. No field trips for me. I just tell them where to go and keep them safe."

She nodded, not quite sure how to respond to that. "You do that with the computers," she said finally.

"I see someone's been taking my name in vain," Jake said.

"Griff said that's what you do."

"I find things," he said.

"Have you found my daughter?" she asked softly.

The teasing light faded from his eyes. "No, ma'am," he replied, all amusement gone from the pleasant voice as well. "I wish I had, Ms. Heywood, but I haven't found out much that tells us anything useful about where your baby is right now."

"Then what is that?" she asked, gesturing with her head toward the screen they had been so focused on when she entered.

Jake held her eyes a moment before he turned to face Griff. "You want to tell her or do you want me to?" he asked.

"I think that depends on why she's here," Griff said.

Her eyes moved to Griff's. In their dark depths was a challenge. And clearly, there was bitterness as well. And she couldn't really blame him, not after what she'd said.

"I'm here because I want to know what you're going to do."

"Whatever it takes to get her back," he said simply.

His tone was as cold as his eyes. Cold because she had unfairly blamed him for what had happened to Gardner. And Griff was, she knew, the only hope for getting her daughter back.

Because of that, they would have to find some way to deal with their past. With their conflicts. Some way to put them into perspective and concentrate on what was important. She knew it was up to her to make the first move.

"I'd like to talk to you about that," she said. "Alone," she added softly, her eyes still locked on his.

"Upstairs," he said finally, and when he led the way, again she followed.

"HIS NAME IS RAMON DIAZ. He's one of the most powerful of the new below-the-border drug lords."

"Drugs?" she asked, feeling some small portion of her guilt over being here ease.

Griff had told her that a lot of people would want this man dead, but she hadn't known exactly what the implications of that might be. And frankly, understanding now what he had meant by that, she was relieved.

"A couple of years ago he was a middleman for the Colombians," Griff said. "Now he's a major supplier to the States. Mostly heroin."

"So...who would want to assassinate him?"

She was thinking that this might be someone official. Some government agency. Perhaps even the CIA themselves. Or the DEA. But surely the government wouldn't have used Gardner as a means to accomplish that.

"Someone who wants control of the network he's built. Someone who wants to run his show," Griff suggested. "Or maybe someone out for revenge. Who knows?"

"And their reasons don't really matter to you?" she asked.

Suddenly, she wished she hadn't. That sounded too much like the things she had said to him before. The arguments she had made. Too much like an accusation.

"Not in this situation," he said, his voice almost as cold as it had been upstairs.

"Why would they want *you?*" she asked. "How would they even know about you? About the team?"

"They want us because we can do it. Given the security Diaz surrounds himself with, there aren't many people who could. Apparently they were smart enough to realize that. And as to how they know about the team..." He shrugged. "We're in the process right now of trying to figure that out. But we're still trying to figure out a lot of things. And we don't have much time to do it in."

Claire didn't like the sound of that. Not when she thought about Gardner.

"What does that mean? The not-much-time part?" she asked.

"Diaz is coming to the States for a meeting with his major buyers. As soon as it's over, he goes back to his stronghold in the mountains of central Mexico. Once he's there, it becomes much harder to get to him."

"But...you could?" she asked, fighting the fear that even they might not be able to pull this off.

"Maybe," Griff said. "But it would be more dangerous.

Dangerous for those involved, so we'd rather hit him here. *Before* he leaves."

"When will that be?"

"Two or three days," Griff said.

Gardner had already been gone for three, and they had seemed endless. And endlessly painful. The thought that Griff might be able to bring this off and get her back in two or three more seemed overwhelming.

"And then...when you've done that, they'll give Gardner back?" she asked, hoping this was what they had promised him.

"As soon as they have verification of the hit."

Those words were like a foreign language in her safe, narrow world. A language she had never wanted to learn. Things she had never been able to think about without feeling sick. At least not in conjunction with her own life. Not in conjunction with the man she loved.

Now her daughter's life depended on the skills Griff Cabot and those hard men in the room downstairs had honed by doing the very acts for which she had once rejected him. The same things for which she had told him she never wanted to see him again. His past, on which she had blamed Gardner's kidnapping.

"I want to be with you," she said. "While you do this."

"Why?" Griff asked.

It was, she supposed, a simple enough question, but there wasn't a simple answer. Not that she had been able to come up with. Not one that would make sense to anyone else.

"Because if I go along with this... If I allow you to do this for Gardner," she amended, "then I should be part of it. Otherwise..." She hesitated again, but he kept his eyes steady on her face, waiting to hear whatever conclusion she had come to. And after two days of thinking about it, this was the decision she had made. "Otherwise, I'm a moral coward."

She wondered if he would even remember what he had said. He had accused her of moral arrogance. She certainly had none now. She wanted her baby back, and if the price was the death of a drug lord, then she would be able to face that. If Griff, who didn't even know his daughter, could deal with that guilt, then surely she could. *If* it was the price of her daughter's life.

"You don't have to prove anything, Claire," he said. "Not to me. Not even to the others. This isn't about morality. There's nothing moral about what they're demanding. Nothing honorable. You don't have to be involved."

"You'll ask Jordan or Hawk or Jake to help you. But not me."

"They all had a choice. You didn't. The people who took Gardner didn't give you any."

"And she's not their child," she said softly. "She doesn't belong to Hawk. Jordan didn't struggle to give her birth. None of them, including you, have held her when she cried all night. Or saw her first smile. None of you. So I don't need to hear about choices. Or about right and wrong. In case you've forgotten, I'm the one who made all those arguments before."

She hesitated again, and then she went on with what she had come here to tell him. "But right or wrong, I can't make them now. Not when Gardner's life is at stake. And if I'm not willing to tell you no, don't do this, then..." She hesitated, still holding his eyes, before she made her demand. "I have a right to be here, Griff. To be involved in this. I have more of a right to that than any of the rest of you."

She waited for him to deny her reasoning. She waited for him to turn the old arguments against her. Or to remind her of what she had once said. And of what she had done. Of what she'd accused him of. But of course, being Griff, he didn't do any of those things.

"Jake will show you what you can do to help," he said.

Without another word, he turned and limped back toward the hallway. She stood in the darkness watching until he disappeared. Then, after she had heard the door to the basement stairs close behind him and she was again alone in the dark, upstairs emptiness of the house, she walked over to the desk and picked up the photograph in the silver frame. Her photograph.

Given the coldness in Griff's voice when she'd arrived, she needed the hope this provided. Maybe the fact that he still had her picture on his desk didn't mean a thing. Maybe it had simply been forgotten in the turmoil of what had happened to him. After all, this house had been closed for more than a year, the same year during which she had thought Griff was dead.

But despite the fact that, several months before the attack at Langley, she had told him she never wanted to see him again, her picture was still on Griff Cabot's desk. And despite the terrible accusation she had made that morning in her kitchen, he hadn't made her leave.

Chapter Seven

Beyond the blue-green expanse of Biscayne Bay and in front of a backdrop of violet sky, the lights of Miami shimmered into life through the deepening twilight. The cruiser swayed gently on the swells, and except for the soft slap of water against the hull, it was surprisingly quiet. Surprisingly peaceful.

The unmoving figure at the rail added to the serenity. Claire had stood behind Griff for several minutes now, studying the broad shoulders and muscled back, both clearly delineated by the black cotton knit shirt. It was obvious, too, that under the tightly stretched material of the faded jeans he wore, his waist and hips were as narrow as before he'd been hurt.

It had been hard for her during the last two days to remember what had happened to Griff, especially when he was standing, unmoving, as he was now. At moments like this, he seemed unchanged. He hadn't used the cane at all during the two days they'd been on the boat. Claire assumed that was because they had traded the cold, wet climate of the D.C. area for the heat of the tropics.

In the two days she had been with the team, she hadn't sought Griff out. They had been together, of course, but always in the company of the others. Never alone. And they hadn't talked. Not about anything.

She wondered why he was up here, looking at the city. Was he thinking about what would happen tomorrow? Worrying about it, just as she had been all day?

"Do you really believe this will work?" she asked.

As she spoke, she moved up to stand beside him at the rail, her soft-soled shoes making no sound on the gleaming mahogany of the deck. Seeming to become aware of her presence for the first time, Griff turned his head, looking down into her eyes.

The bridge of his nose was sunburned from the long days they had spent on the boat. Even the high cheekbones were touched with color, despite the darkness of his skin. His blue-black hair, its natural curl enhanced by the humidity, moved slightly in the breeze.

In this forgiving light, the changes the past year had wrought in his face were less obvious. Right now, he looked exactly like the Griff she remembered. So much like that Griff.

Her breathing faltered with that realization, and she felt her pulse rate increase. A whisper of need brushed through her lower body, triggered by the memories of his lovemaking. Memories she couldn't afford to indulge in right now.

"If I *didn't* believe it would work," Griff said simply, "we wouldn't be out here." He turned his eyes back to the lights across the water, to the city where Hawk and Jordan had already begun to carry out the plan he had devised.

His hands were resting on the rail, and her eyes examined them now instead of his face. And found that contemplation no better for her peace of mind. Almost worse, in fact, because she could remember exactly how they had felt moving over her skin. Tantalizing and then satisfying.

Griff had almost been able to anticipate her needs. And certainly to read her responses. He had known everything about her. Things no one else had ever guessed. And, of course, there had never before been anyone who could evoke the feelings he had.

Before she met Griff Cabot, Claire had never considered herself to be sensual. Or sensuous. When she was with him, however, she was both. And she relished that. It was an incredible freedom, which he had first created within her mind and body and had then invited her to explore.

She pulled her eyes away from the temptation of remembering those long, dark fingers against her skin and looked out instead, as he was doing, across the panorama of sky and water. The lights of the city, glittering in the darkness like diamonds, rimmed the edge where the two met. She lifted her chin, closing her eyes and letting the breeze bathe her face. Enjoying its touch. Savoring the smell of the sea it brought with it.

"Don't worry," Griff said.

Surprised by the quiet command, she opened her eyes and turned to face him. He was looking at her again. Looking at her, and not through her, almost for the first time since she'd come to the summer house to find him.

"Nothing's going to go wrong," he said, his deep voice softer than it had been before. More intimate.

"Is that a promise?" she asked, smiling at him.

The question had been almost idly asked. Something to say besides "Do you remember…?"

"At least, nothing we can control will go wrong," he amended. "Nothing the team is responsible for will be left undone. Or left to chance. I *can* promise you that, Claire."

He had never broken a promise to her. He hadn't been the one who had broken the vow she had forced him to make. She had done that. Her arrival at his door that night had certainly been something out of his control. And just as much out of hers.

She nodded, turning back to the darkening sky. She knew the bare bones of the plan, although she hadn't really been in on its conception. Jordan and Hawk had left early today to carry out their part of it. And by this time tomorrow, it would all be over. *Nothing we can control will go wrong.* But there were, of course, so many things that couldn't be controlled.

She drew another breath, deep and slow. She supposed she was only borrowing trouble, and she had more than enough of that already, but today, as she had watched Hawk and Jordan's departure, she had felt a prickle of apprehension.

A premonition, perhaps, that there were elements about all this that none of them understood. Things that moved beneath the surface of what was happening, as unseen and unknown as whatever swam below them in the depths of the tranquil waters on which the yacht bobbed and dipped.

She looked down at the waves lapping against the hull. There was nothing there but the gentle rise and swell of the ocean. Nothing was visible under the surface of the water, which she knew teemed with life. Despite the humid warmth of the surrounding night, so thick it was almost palpable, she shivered.

"I told you not to worry," Griff said again.

She looked up, away from the hypnotizing rise and fall of the ocean, and straight into his eyes. They were as dark as the shadows behind the lights of Miami, and yet tonight they seemed to have lost the bitterness she had put there.

She wondered if he had forgiven her for the accusation she'd made. And she wondered if she had completely forgiven him for involving her daughter in the violence of his world.

But if there was any lesson she had learned from losing Griff, it was that there was never a guarantee of tomorrow. There might not *be* a second chance to make things right. And regret was something she had lived with a long time.

Despite the fact that Griff wouldn't be physically involved in what would happen tomorrow, and shouldn't be in the kind of danger that Hawk and Jordan seemed so willing to face, there were still things she needed to say to him.

"Griff," she said softly.

Suddenly, she shivered again, feeling the same chill of foreboding that had touched her before glide again along her spine. When she spoke his name, he turned to face her, propping his elbow on the railing and leaning against it.

"I should have told you," she whispered. "As soon as I knew about the baby, I should have called you."

She waited for some response, but his face was unchanging. No longer cold, but…something. Some emotion was reflected there that made her afraid again.

"You should have told me," he said finally.

Simple agreement. But in his tone was much more, a regret that almost matched that which had crushed her spirit during those months when she had guarded his child beneath her broken heart. Hearing it, she grieved anew that he had never known his daughter. Had not even known of her existence. And that loss had been Claire's choice. Something that had been within her control.

It had taken her these last two days to realize that if she had told him about Gardner at the beginning, everything might have been different. Griff would never have let her believe he was dead if he had known she was carrying his child. He would never have left her alone with that responsibility.

And he would never have left his daughter unprotected— *if* he had only known about her existence. And he hadn't, because Claire had chosen not to tell him. So if anyone was to blame for what had happened to Gardner…

"I'm so sorry," she whispered. "Sorry for not telling you I was pregnant. And…sorry for what I said. It's not your fault these people exist. I shouldn't have blamed you for what happened to Gardner.''

I'm sorry. The words seemed pitifully inadequate, but they were all she had. All anyone ever had.

His left hand lifted, and he touched her bare shoulder, exposed by the sleeveless tank top she was wearing. Offering comfort? she wondered. Or forgiveness.

He ran his thumb slowly down and back up, caressing the sensitive skin on the inside of her arm. And the unhurried movement was seductive.

What was in his eyes was just as evocative, reminding her of all they had once been to each other. Almost unconsciously, reacting to the touch of his hand and to what was in his eyes, she moved closer, drawn to him as she had been in the dream. Suddenly, his fingers closed hard around the soft flesh of her upper arms, pulling her to him. Her left hand found his cheek, cupping the pleasantly rough texture of his skin with her palm. And that, too, was a sensation she remembered.

His mouth lowered, opening slightly, aligning itself to fit over hers. She watched his eyes close, the thick fan of lashes dropping to hide their darkness. Then her own fell, surrendering to her need as a relieved and exhausted child finally gives in to the sleep it has mindlessly fought.

This was part of why she had demanded he let her come. Not only because she knew he was the only one who could rescue Gardner, but for this. For Griff. For his touch. His kiss. For all they had once shared. And could share again.

His mouth fastened over hers, moving with the same unquestioning surety. The same possession. And briefly, before her consciousness was overwhelmed by sensation, she remembered the hesitant movement of John Amerson's lips. This was why that kiss had been meaningless. Why anything else was unimportant. Anyone else. And why anyone else always would be.

Her hand found the back of Griff's head, and her fingers slipped into his hair, longer than it had been before, but warm and alive, as fine as silk. She pulled his head down, straining on tiptoe, pressing her breasts against the hard wall of his chest.

Trying to deepen the kiss. To prolong. To tell him again, this time without words, that she had been wrong. And that she knew and regretted her mistake. It had been such a long, aching emptiness of regret.

His hands found her shoulders instead. Gripping them, he pushed her away from him. The contact of the kiss was broken, of course, but his fingers still held her prisoner, and he was looking down again into her eyes.

Slowly, too lost in the sensations he had created to react immediately, she closed her mouth, still hungry for his. His eyes followed the movement and came back to hers.

"Whatever happens..." he began, and hesitated. His lips tightened, denying whatever he had intended to tell her. Thinking better of it, perhaps?

"Whatever happens?" she questioned. "Tomorrow?"

Had Griff, too, felt that cold undercurrent of fear that had run through her veins all day? A dread of the unknown? Terror of something they couldn't control?

"We'll get her back," he said.

"I know," she whispered. "I know you will."

For some reason their roles had reversed. She was comforting him. And she had never known Griff Cabot to be afraid before. Or in need of comfort. In need of anything.

His hands released her shoulders as suddenly as he had broken the kiss. Then he turned and, without looking back, limped across the deck to the stairwell and disappeared through it into the darkness below.

She listened a moment to the sound the waves made, and then she looked across the bay toward the lights. Griff's words echoed in her head. And in her heart. *"Whatever happens..."*

Warning? Premonition? Or was it possible that Griff had reacted as strongly to their kiss as she? Had he been as shaken as she had been by the reality that nothing had really changed between them? Nothing except Gardner's existence?

Somewhere in the darkness beyond those distant lights, two men were working to get a baby back. And somewhere below, the man who had devised the plan and had told them how to carry it out seemed as worried about what was about to happen as she was.

Worried about a daughter he had never known. And at this point, Claire wasn't certain if that genuine though unspoken concern was something she should be glad about.

IT WAS MUCH LATER that she heard the sound of the inflatable returning. Its motor woke her, and then she listened to its cushioned side bumping against the hull of the yacht as the two vessels rocked together in the current. It seemed that either Hawk or Jordan had returned. To report? Or for further instructions?

Either way, the meeting was one where she knew she wouldn't be welcome. So she lay in her bed and listened until she heard the inflatable's engine kick into life again and then roar away, gradually fading into the deep, night-time silence of the sea.

She lay awake even after it was gone, thinking about the kaleidoscope of events of the last four days. The images were fragmented, wheeling in her head exactly like those bits of colored glass, but refusing to make a pattern she could read. And underlying them all was the cold sense of dread that she had felt since she'd watched Hawk and Jordan leave the boat that morning.

She was asleep, however, when the cruiser itself began

to move, its powerful engines making little noise as it cut a path of foaming whiteness through the obsidian waters. Heading for a rendezvous that Claire had been told nothing about.

AT LEAST HE HAD TOLD HER the truth about one thing, Griff thought. Nothing they could control would go wrong. That had been a palliative, of course, intended to relieve some of her anxiety. He had been in this business too long to think there was much that could really be controlled. Meticulously planned for, yes. Anticipated. But never really controlled.

So far, however, the sequence had played out exactly the way it had been planned. As always, Jordan's and Hawk's execution had been flawless. By the time Diaz and his bodyguards had arrived at Opa-Locka Airport, the private jet that awaited them had been secured. The cameras, which would faithfully record Diaz boarding the doomed plane, had been set up. And the explosives that would destroy it were in place.

"Nothing we can control will go wrong," he had promised Claire, and nothing had. Everything about this had gone according to plan. It had almost been too easy, Griff thought. Too pat. But he was too much a professional to argue with success. He knew he should be celebrating instead of worrying.

Still, he acknowledged, the uneasiness that had been in the pit of his stomach for the last two days wouldn't go away, despite the fact that the operation, the dicey part of it at any rate, was almost over. Almost done.

Only his job remained, he acknowledged, as he put his hand on the throttle lever and eased it forward. The jet responded like a well-trained thoroughbred feeling the whip. It rocketed down the runway through the heavy tropical darkness.

He watched the needle on the air speed indicator climb, and when it reached the takeoff point, he gently pulled back on the yoke. The nose of the Citation came up, and the jet lifted away from the ground. Then he rotated it toward the ocean, which stretched dark and wide under the star-sprinkled sky.

Now it was all up to him. Up to him to keep the promise he had made. Another promise to Claire. And to a daughter he had never known.

WHEN SHE WAS JERKED out of sleep, there was no doubt in Claire's mind what had awakened her. The only question was whether the explosion had been real or a dream. The noise had been distant, but the echoing boom had been strong enough to bring her out of the restless, nightmare-filled sleep she had finally fallen into.

An explosion, just like the one that was supposed to destroy Diaz's plane. Tomorrow, she thought. That was tomorrow, and not…

Her gaze found the porthole and verified that it was almost light. Almost light. Almost tomorrow. *"Whatever happens…"* Griff had said. *"Whatever happens…"*

She threw the sheet off her body, the foreboding that had haunted her now so strong it was thick and vile, clogging her throat like a sickness. She opened the door to her cabin and hurried through the dark, silent salon, across the narrow galley and up the steps that led to the bridge. She could hear the soft, mindless noises of the instruments.

When she reached the top of the stairwell, she realized that Jake was at the helm, totally focused on the equipment in front of him, exactly as he had been during most of the last twenty-four hours. She wondered if he had even slept.

In the darkness the faint glow of the dials and screens that stretched before him was eerie. It gave the tense figure hunched forward in the command chair an otherworldliness—strange, supernatural, almost demonic.

"Jake," she said softly.

He jumped visibly, startled by the sound of a human voice in his familiar world of machines.

"God, Claire, you scared the bejesus out of me," he said, turning to look at her over his shoulder.

"Sorry," she said. She walked across to stand behind him as she had seen Griff do a hundred times in the last two days. Depending on him. "I heard a noise."

Before she reached him, Jake leaned forward and moved a couple of dials or switches. The pattern on the screen he had been studying changed. A radar screen, she realized, the sweep of the line around its circumference and its beeps making its function obvious.

"What are you doing up?" she asked, her eyes moving across the expensive array of gadgets.

Then, almost without her conscious volition, her gaze lifted above them to the dark gray world that stretched beyond the windows. An expanse of black sea meeting a slowly lightening sky, a void unbroken except for a distant glow.

Fire, she realized. Something was burning on the surface of the ocean. It was far enough away that it was only a smudge of light, flickering over the dark water, but near enough that there was no mistaking it for anything else.

"What's that?" she asked, raising her hand and pointing. "Could that be what I heard?"

She turned to look down at Jake, and found that rather than following the direction of her gesture, his eyes had remained locked on her face. And suddenly she knew why.

"That's the plane." She barely breathed the words, soft and shocked. "That's Diaz's plane."

This had been part of the plan, of course. They were planning to put explosives on Diaz's plane. A device that would be triggered by a certain altitude, one that wouldn't be reached until the jet was out over the ocean, well away from the city and the pleasure boats that dotted the bay. No danger to anyone on the ground and leaving no possible doubt in the minds of the kidnappers that the ransom they were demanding had been paid.

Paid in full, she thought, looking back at the fire. Now that she knew what it was, it was as ghostly as the other had been, as eerie as the light that had been bathing Jake's figure when she entered the bridge.

Out of the corner of her eye, she caught the movement of Jake's head. His attention had gone back to the screen he'd been watching when she came up. The long sweep of the needle and the soft automatic beep was monotonous. Unchanging. Finding nothing in the vast emptiness of the ocean that surrounded them.

Finding nothing. Her eyes tracked another slow circle. Still finding nothing. "Where's Griff?" she asked.

She knew Griff Cabot too well to believe he wouldn't be up here watching his plan unfold. Studying what was going on with the same intensity Jake had been when she'd interrupted him. Griff should have been standing at Jake's shoulder, just as he had during most of the last forty-eight hours.

The silence between her question and Jake's answer was too long. Long enough for her pulse to quicken and for the cold sense of dread that had been in her stomach all day to increase sickeningly. Long enough to know something was wrong.

"I don't know," Jake said finally. His voice was flat, emotionless. "I wish to hell I did."

"You don't *know?*" Claire repeated. "What does that mean?"

There was another pause, again prolonged and full of something she couldn't read. Reluctance to answer, certainly, but something else as well. Jake was keeping things from her, and if that were true... If that were true, then it meant Griff had been keeping them from her as well.

Son of a bitch, she thought, feeling anger surge through her body, almost strong enough to replace the ice of her fear. They had been keeping things from her. Griff's precious team. And apparently everyone had been in on the conspiracy.

"Where is he, Jake?" she asked again, her voice tight. "What the hell is going on? I have a stake in this, remember. A bigger stake than the rest of you. I deserve to know what's happening, damn it."

He didn't answer, but deliberately his eyes lifted from the screen, away from its meaningless, monotonous sweep to the vast ocean that lay beyond the window. Maybe even as far as the fading glow of the fire that was burning on top of the water.

THE WATER HAD BEEN much colder than Griff expected. Despite the fact that it was January, this was the tropics, and the water temperature should have been in the seventies. It certainly hadn't felt that warm when he had plunged into it.

Now he couldn't seem to feel his legs, dangling beneath the black-ink surface of the ocean. They seemed detached from the rest of his body, especially the right one, the leg that a burst of bullets from the terrorist's Uzi had shattered. But considering its usual protest of any kind of physical demand he might make on it, he supposed he should be grateful for the numbing cold.

"Like taking a bath," Hawk had said when they were planning this. Neither he nor Jordan had tried to talk Griff out of the role he had assigned himself. And neither had questioned that he would be able to carry it off. For that unspoken confidence, he had been infinitely grateful.

Griff was the only one of them who had flown a small jet before. They could have hired a pilot, but he had known he could do this. All he had to do was take the plane out over the ocean, set the automatic pilot to continue its climb, trip the time-delay on the explosives Hawk had rigged, and jump. His leg shouldn't be a hindrance in any of that, not even the drop into the ocean.

It hadn't been. Everything had gone as smoothly as he had anticipated. He had landed and gotten free of the chute in time to watch the plane's disintegration. It had blown apart in a firestorm of debris that rained down, far ahead of him, for seemingly endless minutes after the echo of the boom had faded away.

Now all he had to do was wait for Jake's equipment to pick up the radio signal from the ELT that was attached to his life vest. So in the darkness Griff floated on the surface of the water, waiting for the deep throb of the yacht's engine and thinking about Claire.

Chapter Eight

"You're telling me the transmitter Griff's wearing isn't working, and the chances of our picking him up on radar are somewhere between nil and zero."

Jake hadn't put it that bluntly, of course. Claire had had to pry every piece of information out of him. Like the fact that Griff had decided to take the plane up himself and trigger the explosives manually, to make sure it was far enough out when it blew. When he had, he'd bailed out, depending on an emergency transmitter to pinpoint his location.

"It's a damn big ocean," Jake said, his eyes on the unchanging sweep of the needle. "And the chances of the radar picking up a body—"

Obviously realizing the frightening connotations of that phrase, he broke off abruptly, and in the light from the screen, she watched his mouth tighten.

"Why isn't the thing transmitting?" Claire asked, her eyes drawn back to the dying smear of the distant fire.

"I don't know," Jake said. "It just…isn't. I checked it. Griff checked it. Hawk checked it right before he left. It was working then. It damn well should be working now."

She could hear the frustration in Jake's voice. And perhaps a thread of anger as well. In reaction to something in her tone? She wasn't accusing Jake of incompetence, even if her question had sounded that way. But he was the equipment man. It was his job to prevent something like this from happening. Suddenly, Griff's words echoed in her head. *Nothing we can control...*

How could a man's life depend on something this insignificant? Of course, if that radio signal was the only way Griff could be tracked in the vastness of the ocean that lay beyond the windows of the yacht, then the emergency transmitter really hadn't been an insignificant part of the plan at all.

And she still didn't understand why it was Griff out there. Someone else should have been flying that plane. Anyone else. Just not Griff. Not now.

"Why isn't there some kind of backup?" she asked.

"Because..." Jake hesitated, and then he turned in his chair to face her. "Look," he said, "we've used these things a hundred times. They're practically fail-safe. And we checked this one out, damn it. All of us did."

The anger she thought she had heard before was certainly there now. It was obvious Jake was blaming himself, and there was no use belaboring the point that there should have been some provision made in case this happened. But no one, not even Griff, as meticulous as he was, could control everything. He had told her that himself.

"What do we do?" she asked instead.

"We start at the debris field, while we can still find it, and we move out from it in widening circles."

He had probably already been thinking about that. And Jake was in charge, of course. She couldn't see any flaw in his plan, especially since she didn't have another one to offer.

"Okay," she said.

"Your job will be lookout."

It would have to be, given the necessity of Jake's keeping a watch on the instruments and directing the search. Her job would be to spot the small, living speck that was Griff Cabot in the vast blackness of the ocean that surrounded them.

THE DAY WAS WARMER than yesterday had been, Claire thought, wiping the sweat off her forehead with the back of her arm. And she wasn't sure whether that was good or bad. The water temperature wouldn't rise that much, and even the winter sun here was strong enough to burn. More than strong enough to lead to dehydration, which was the real danger.

Her eyes ached from the hours she had spent focusing them beyond the gray-green roil of water that foamed at the prow. She had swept the binoculars across the surface of the ocean, moving them slowly from horizon to horizon, too many times to count.

The cruiser was far enough out that they hadn't encountered much traffic. A Coast Guard cutter had passed them early this morning, undoubtedly heading out to check on the plane that had disappeared off Opa-Locka's screens. They had paid the yacht no attention, obviously in a hurry to reach the scene of the crash before there was nothing left to mark the spot. Claire suspected Jake had been relieved not to have to answer their questions.

She closed her burning eyes, wondering even as she did if she could afford that small luxury. At first, her heart had thudded wildly with each piece of flotsam that drifted in front of the boat. She had followed its movement with the binoculars, eyes wide and straining, until it was close enough to identify. And none of them had been Griff.

"You need to come in and get something to drink," Jake shouted from inside the bridge, gesturing broadly at her through the glass to make sure she understood.

Reluctantly she obeyed, wondering again if they should go back to Miami and report Griff missing. But Jake claimed that was the last thing Griff would want. His being in the water in this area would be highly suspicious. Griff wouldn't want any of them connected with that exploding plane, Jake had argued. And besides, in her naïveté, Claire had been sure they would find Griff before now.

As she entered the bridge, she glanced at her watch. No wonder her eyes hurt, she thought. She had been at this now for almost eight hours. Jake had been, as well, and at least she had gotten some sleep the first part of last night.

"You okay?" she asked, taking the bottled water he held out.

"Am *I* okay?" he responded, his voice quizzical.

"How long has it been since you've slept?"

"I'll sleep when this is over."

She didn't ask when he thought that might be. Or if he still believed they could find Griff. By now, even she had realized the odds of that. Claire wasn't willing to give up, of course, and she suspected that Jake, like Hawk and Jordan, would endure whatever was necessary until they had located Griff—alive or dead.

"I don't understand why we haven't found him," she said. "You said his chute would have come down somewhere between the wreckage and where we were anchored last night. We've already covered most of that."

She took another long drink from the bottle as she waited for his answer. She hadn't realized how thirsty she was until the first sweet, cold draught bathed the dryness of her mouth and throat. She poured a little of the water over her face and then her neck, letting its coolness trickle into the scooped neckline of the cotton shell she was wearing.

"You see that?" Jake asked.

He pointed at an object bobbing gently in the water. It was a large, rectangular piece of metal that she had watched through the binoculars until it had become something more than a distant blur. Until she knew it wasn't the man they were looking for.

"Maybe part of the plane," she suggested, her eyes automatically following its motion away from the yacht.

"Maybe," Jake said. "That's not really what I meant, though. Whatever it is, it's moving."

"On the current," she agreed, pulling her gaze away from the object and back to his. He wasn't looking at her, so she raised the water again to her lips.

"We're running out of time, Claire," Jake said softly.

She lowered the bottle slowly, eyes widened. "What does that mean? The water's warm. The sun's…bearable," she said, glancing up toward the afternoon dazzle of clear, blue sky and then, eyes narrowed, quickly away.

"That's the Gulf Stream. Probably the most powerful current in the world. If Griff is caught in that…"

Her eyes lifted again to the floating object. Even in the short time they had been talking, it secmed to have grown noticeably smaller. Of course, that was probably the power of suggestion, but it frightened her, just the same.

"Then we'll follow the current," she said, feeling a tinge of excitement at that thought. A resurgence of the hope that had begun to falter. "We can plot it. You know where we were last night. Where the plane went down. We ought to be able to figure out how far out the current would have carried him. Surely there are charts with the information we'd need to do that on board."

"Except we're supposed to be making contact with the kidnappers in a few hours," Jake stated, interrupting that more hopeful line of thought.

"Do it from here," she suggested. "We know Diaz is dead. Tell them that."

"Griff's the one they're expecting. He's the one who's talked to them. And the arrangements were very specific. And pretty sophisticated," Jake admitted. "They seem as security conscious as we would be in this situation. Calls from shipboard are too easily monitored, so the call Griff is supposed to make has to be placed to a particular Miami number from a specific pay phone there. They don't want any mistake about who they're dealing with.''

''What happens if he doesn't make that call?'' she asked, watching Jake's eyes, trying to read the truth of what he would tell her. And when he spoke, she thought she could.

''The crash will have been mentioned on the news. Word that it was Diaz's plane will probably get out to those involved. I'm not sure, however, if it will be enough to satisfy them that we've done our part. Or to satisfy them that, despite the delay, we'll be in touch. And they were pretty adamant about proof.''

''What kind of proof?'' Claire asked, trying not to think about Gardner. Trying not to picture her daughter in the hands of people growing increasingly angry about not receiving the message they were waiting for.

''Video of Diaz boarding the plane. The takeoff. Hawk and Jordan have that. We're supposed to rendezvous with them on one of the smaller keys and pick them and the video up. Then Griff makes the phone call in Miami and offers the package to the kidnappers. They tell us where to go from there. At least that's the way it was supposed to work.''

''Surely they'll wait,'' she said. ''If they know that Diaz's plane went down.''

''*If* Diaz was what these people are really after,'' Jake said.

''I don't understand,'' Claire said, shaking her head. What else was this all about, if not that? ''Griff thought this might be a rival who wanted to take over Diaz's operation.''

''Maybe,'' Jake said.

''*You* don't think that's what it is?'' she asked carefully.

"Drug cartels don't have access to information about the internal operations of the CIA," he suggested. "At least not about something as sensitive as what this team does. Or about how it operates. And how did they even know about Gardner? Or know that Griff was the only one who could set this up?"

"Maybe they got the information through the computers," she said, remembering what Griff had told her, about how much information was stored within them. And remembering what he had said Jake could do with them. But she also remembered that Griff had told her that these questions, the same ones Jake was asking, were things the team had already been trying to figure out.

Jake's mouth tightened again, as if he were thinking about what she'd suggested. "Maybe," he conceded. "I don't think so, but... I mean, I guess it's possible, but in my opinion someone like that breaching our system would be highly unlikely."

"So...who else would have that kind of information?" she asked. "Outside the agency, I mean."

Jake's lips pursed a little, and then he looked past her to the sea. An empty sea. And he didn't answer her question.

GRIFF CAME AWAKE with a start. He had no idea how long he had been asleep, but at least the sun was setting. It had beaten down mercilessly throughout the day. Despite the natural darkness of his skin, he knew his face and scalp were burned.

Of course, he thought, lifting his eyes to the shifting horizon that composed his limited view of the world, that was the least of his problems. His cracked lips lifted a little at the corners, despite the seriousness of his situation.

After all, he'd been in worse spots through the years. And the best thing he had going for him was the fact that they would be looking for him. The team. At least Jake. And Claire.

Obviously, the damn transmitter he was wearing wasn't working. Which meant, he supposed… He closed his sun-and-salt-burned eyes, trying not to think about all the things it might mean. And of course, those were the very things that continued to circle in his brain.

That maybe he wouldn't ever have a chance to say to Claire what he should have told her on deck last night. She had wanted him to kiss her. Had invited it. He knew Claire too well to have had any doubt about that.

Instead, he had pushed her away. And right now he couldn't quite remember why. Guilt, maybe? There had been a lot of that circling in his head as well throughout this endless day.

Guilt because he knew Claire had been right. The kidnapping had been his fault. Guilt because he hadn't told her the truth about what was going to happen. And because for a year he had let her believe the agency's lie. And Griff was honest enough to admit the things she had said to him when she had ended their relationship had played a role in that decision.

But he hadn't known about the baby. His daughter. His child, whom he had never even seen. And with everything else that had been going on, he realized he hadn't even asked Claire what she was like.

He had always considered himself to be a rational man. Logical. That had been the guiding principle in most of his relationships. Except with Claire Heywood, he acknowledged, his cracked lips moving again into a painful parody of a smile.

Except with Claire.

He turned his head to the left, resting his chin on the cushion of the life vest, and watched the sun begin to sink beneath the slow rolls and swells of water that lay between his line of sight and the bands of gold and red disappearing slowly into the sea. His eyelids began to drift downward, the urge to sleep almost too powerful to resist.

He pulled them up by sheer force of will. He scooped up a handful of water and splashed it on his face. The salt in it burned the sun-damaged skin, but its chill was refreshing. Stimulating. Helping him to think more clearly.

He dipped his cupped hand in the water again and raised it, a small silver stream overflowing each side of his palm. Almost unconsciously he began to carry it to his lips, painfully dry with heat and dehydration. He even knew how the water's soothing coolness would feel on them. And on his tongue.

He opened his mouth, burned skin cracking further with the movement. He couldn't gather enough saliva to swallow. All this water, all around him, and his mouth was too damn dry to spit.

His hand journeyed closer to his lips until it bumped against the forgotten bulge of the vest, spilling most of the water it held. Only with that bump did his brain kick in. Seawater. Saltwater. No matter how thirsty he was, that would only make things worse. He turned his hand, releasing the small, remaining puddle of water from his palm and letting his arm fall.

Claire and Jake would find him. Somebody would find him, he told himself. All he had to do was endure. Just hold on. Stay awake so he could wave if he spotted them. Or another boat. All he had to do was just stay awake. And not do anything stupid.

THE SEARCHLIGHT PLAYED slowly over the dark water. Claire wasn't sure anymore that even if her eyes found anything bobbing on the surface, the discovery would register on her tired brain. Too tired. Too many hours. Too many empty miles of ocean. And she felt as if she had examined them all.

She turned and looked over her shoulder toward the dim light coming from the bridge. She couldn't see Jake, but she knew he was there. The last time she'd gone inside, he had looked almost worse than she felt. If the two of them, who had access to water and shade during the course of the day, were like this…

She turned her head to look back over the sweep of ocean. It was dark enough that the point where the sky met the sea had been lost, but at least the moon was rising. Her eyes lifted to find it, floating silently, low in the sky.

Except she wasn't supposed to be looking at the sky. She followed the path the moonlight threw across the swells. Like a road. Yellow brick road. No, not brick. Water. A silver moon path lying across the black water, and in the middle of it…

She didn't dare breathe, watching the object rising and gently falling with the movement of the waves. Slowly, almost with a sense of dread that she might be mistaken, she raised the binoculars. It took a moment to find through them the path of moonlight. A moment to follow it.

And then to focus on the patch of color it illuminated. Yellow. Not the pale gilt of the moon path, but the bright yellow of a life jacket.

And then the glasses moved minutely upward to focus on the dark head that lolled lifelessly between the inflated sides of that yellow vest. She watched it, still not breathing. Without lowering the glasses, she closed her eyes, squeezing them together to make sure that they were moist. And when she opened them again, the object was still there. Still the same. A man.

Her hands began to shake because, she realized, she had really given up hope. Whatever had kept her out here looking for Griff hadn't been belief that they would find him.

Stubbornness instead. Endurance. And not having sense enough to know when to give up.

"Jake," she screamed. "I see him! Oh, my God, Jake, we've found him!"

GRIFF WAS CONSCIOUS when she reached him, but he seemed to drift in and out as they worked to get him on board. Claire had been the one who had gone down into the water because she couldn't wait to make sure Griff was all right. Now she had managed to maneuver him near the ladder. Jake was waiting at the top, ready to pull Griff over the rail, something which Claire, with less upper body strength, wouldn't have been able to do.

Jake was directing the small, portable spotlight down on them. From the surface of the sea, the side of the yacht stretched a seemingly impossible distance above them.

"Griff," she shouted, taking his chin in her hand and turning his head to face her.

His eyelids opened, moving in slow motion. In the glare of the light, she could see that his skin was burned. Beneath the surface red, however, it had a gray tinge, especially around the sunken eyes. His long, dark lashes were beaded with water, and the eyes they framed were rimmed with red, the whites bloodshot. His lips were cracked and almost blue. And yet, in the depths of his eyes, fastened now on her face, was the same intelligence and force of will that had always been there.

"You have to help me," she said, making each word a command, clear and distinct, her voice raised to reach him above the noise of the water and the idling engine. "You have to climb that ladder, Griff. Far enough up so that Jake can pull you over."

She gripped the rung that was just above the swell of the waves. The fingers of her other hand were fastened in the straps of Griff's life vest, and as a result his body floated nearer.

"Put your hand on the ladder," she ordered.

She was almost afraid to try to help him do that. Afraid that they'd move away from the yacht if she released the ladder and afraid that if she let go of Griff, he would somehow drift away and disappear again into the darkness. And she wasn't sure, if either of those things happened, whether she would have the strength to do this all again.

Sluggishly, Griff lifted his right hand, bringing a string of phosphorescent drops up with it. They shimmered in the glare of the spotlight. Although he reached out, his hand didn't connect with the rung of the ladder, but fell into the sea by his side. She could even hear the small splash it made when it struck the surface, distinct from the slap of the waves against the side of the boat.

"You have to hold on," she said.

In desperation, she released the ladder and fished under the water for his hand. By the time she found it, gripping his wrist and bringing it up to the surface, they were too far away from the boat for her to put his fingers over the flat, wooden rung. She took a few awkward strokes with her free arm, again bringing them against the hull.

"Put your hand on the ladder and hold on," she shouted.

"I'll get a rope," Jake yelled down, his voice seeming to come from a great distance above them. She glanced up, but couldn't see anything except the spotlight. She closed her eyes immediately, but was still almost blind when she opened them again.

Slowly Griff's face swam out of the darkness. If anything, he looked worse than he had a few minutes ago. Grayer. Less focused. Less capable of doing what she was asking him to do.

Which was probably, for a man in his condition, little short of impossible, she realized. Of course, finding him in this black wilderness of water had been little short of impossible. And she and Jake had done that.

Surely they could do this. They had to. They had come too close to give up. And, as Jake had reminded her more times than she wanted to think about, time was running out. Time to contact the kidnappers. Time to get to Gardner.

"We have to get back to Miami," she said to Griff. "We've already missed the deadline."

She was no longer shouting at him. She was so close her mouth was against his face. Close enough that she could occasionally feel the brush of his whiskers against her cheek as a wave lifted and then released them. Her lips were right beside his ear, and her tone had changed. She had stayed out here, looking for him, while those bastards had Gardner, and now...

"If we don't get back, they may kill her," she warned.

She didn't know that. But it was the thought she had fought since Jake had told her about the deadline, and finally giving utterance to it made it more real. Infinitely terrifying.

It had been five days since they had taken her baby, and Claire couldn't even remember how it felt to hold her. And if Griff didn't help her, didn't make this effort, then she might never hold her again.

"She's your daughter, Griff," she said. "Your daughter, damn it, and you promised me you'd get her back. And if you don't help me get you up that ladder right now, then we won't reach her in time."

A wave, stronger than the others, pushed them apart, the water slapping against the plastic of his life jacket. She ducked her head to keep the resulting spray out of her eyes.

When she looked up, she realized that Griff was looking at her, the dark eyes more focused. More coherent than they had been since her trembling fingers had first touched his cold cheek. She had been afraid that he was dead, and then,

with a rush of gratitude so overpowering it made her weak,
she had watched his eyes open and fasten on her face.

Almost the way they were fastened there now. Holding
on her eyes. Full of recognition. And understanding.

His hand lifted again, and the parched, cracked lips
closed into a taut line. This was a look she had seen on
Griff Cabot's face a hundred times, and seeing it there now,
her heart lifted.

His hand reached out and gripped the wooden rung of
the yacht's ladder. This time the long, dark fingers held.
And then he carefully fitted his foot into one of the rungs
that hung beneath the surface. And then his body began to
lift away from her. Moving upward.

Chapter Nine

"Just a little more," Claire said, fitting the rim of the bottle against Griff's lips again.

She was sitting on the bed in the largest stateroom, the one where she'd been sleeping. Her back was against the headboard and she was sitting behind Griff, her arms around his bare chest. Despite her concern for him, she was finding this physical proximity as evocative as watching his hands had been last night.

Griff was still shivering occasionally, but once she had gotten the wet clothing off and covered him with a blanket from the compartment above the bed, those involuntary tremors had gradually lessened. His lips were also regaining their color.

Just as he had obeyed all the other demands she had made, he obeyed this one, drinking from the bottle she offered. Jake had suggested she get the ginger ale from the galley while he helped Griff down the stairs. Because of its sugar content, he claimed the ginger ale would be better than plain water to fight shock.

Claire had no idea if that were true, but it made sense. And Griff certainly wasn't protesting. She suspected he would have just as readily drunk anything she gave him. Trustingly. Obediently.

After all, since his hand had first locked around the rung

of the ladder, he had done everything she'd told him to do. Even to putting his arm across their shoulders once she and Jake had finally managed to get him on board.

Getting Griff down the steps to the living quarters had been the worst. That had been the only time in that nightmare journey Griff had made a sound. Because the passage was so narrow, she'd had to step back and let Jake support his weight alone.

Until then, Griff hadn't revealed how painful his leg was. His groan of agony had obviously been torn from him against his will. And she knew something about the nature of Griff Cabot's will.

But he was safe, she told herself. At least he was safe, and the yacht, under Jake's tired but steady hand, was racing belatedly to the rendezvous with Hawk and Jordan that they had missed while they searched. And as for their being late for the other, for the call Griff was supposed to make from Miami…

Claire had refused to think about that. About the kidnappers' reactions. There was nothing she could do about those things. And there was a lot she could do for Griff.

It had been surprising—and a little frightening, knowing Griff—how much he had let her do. Supporting him across the deck. Undressing him. And now this.

Never before had she taken care of Griff Cabot. Not as long as she had known him. Of course, he had never before been in a position to need her care. She suspected that Griff had never really *needed* anyone. Right now, however, no matter how much he might hate this dependence, he did.

"Enough," he whispered, turning his head.

A drop of the liquid fell on her arm, still wrapped around his chest. She took the ginger ale away, leaning forward enough that she could see the side of his face. With her thumb, she wiped off the small trickle that had escaped the corner of his parched lips. Beneath her fingers, she could feel the growth of a two-day beard, rough and somehow very pleasant. Thankfully, the skin under it was beginning to warm.

"Better?" she asked softly.

She waited for his answer, but his eyes were closed, as was his mouth—a little too tightly closed. After a moment, she set the bottle on the table beside the bunk and leaned back against the pillows she'd stacked behind her. He didn't have to talk. She was content to hold him, to feel again the strong, steady rhythm of his heartbeat, lying just above hers.

"Why didn't you go back?" he asked. "Jake should have tried to make the call. Tried to do something."

"Go back without finding you?" she questioned.

"Of course," he said.

"It didn't seem like a good idea at the time," she answered, allowing a hint of gentle mockery to color her denial.

She didn't confess that she hadn't known it would be as hard as it had been to locate him. Then, once they had stayed long enough to know they would miss the deadline for the call, it didn't seem to make much sense to head back without finding him.

And they *had* found him. Eventually. Now Griff was safe. And maybe, while they had been looking, Hawk and Jordan had done what he was suggesting she and Jake should have tried. To make the call. To try to exchange the video for Gardner.

It had not been a conscious decision on her part to choose to look for Griff rather than make that call on time. They had been in the midst of the search when Jake first told her about it. And Jake had thought the kidnappers would deal only with Griff. He surely knew more about those things than she could.

But she had known that to leave Griff out there would

have been a desertion. And a decision that would almost certainly have condemned him to death. She hadn't been capable of making such a decision, and she was glad Jake hadn't suggested it.

She resisted the urge to put her lips against Griff's still-damp, darkly gleaming hair. She would only need to lower her face an inch or two to press a kiss against its softness.

Griff might not even be aware that she had. He might not feel the tenderness of the gesture she longed to make. And after the kiss she had invited, the one which he had deliberately broken off, she had no idea how Griff would react to her touch. No idea how he felt about her. About the unforgivable things she had said to him. All of them.

"What about Hawk and Jordan?" he asked into the silence.

"Jake's trying to reach them by radio."

"Trying?"

"The last I heard, he hadn't gotten an answer."

There was another silence, this one even longer.

"Why was it you in that plane?" she asked, remembering the fire flickering over the surface of the dark water. And the frightening hours she had spent scanning the empty expanse of ocean that stretched in front of the prow of the boat. "Why the hell did it have to be *you* who took that plane up?"

She waited through the silence, listening to the soft thrum of the cruiser's engine.

"Griff?" she said, finally leaning forward again to see his face. Trying to determine if he had fallen asleep.

But his eyes were open, focused on the opposite wall, or on the black, featureless porthole that looked out on the sea and the night.

"Why you?" she asked again, and watched a muscle at the corner of his mouth tighten and then slowly release.

"A macho bull-crap exercise in self-aggrandizement," he said softly.

She wondered for a second if he could be drifting into incoherence. Dehydration could do that. As could shock. And then, although she didn't really understand what the phrase meant, she laughed at the sheer absurdity of it.

Her breasts moved against the hard muscles in his back, and a wave of desire seared her lower body. She was breathless with the force of the memories it brought. Griff's hands. Her body moving against his. Under his. Things she couldn't afford to think about. Especially not here. Not now.

"What does that mean?" she asked instead.

"I wanted to prove I could still do it," he said.

"Still fly?"

"Still do this. Plan an operation. See it carried out."

She thought about why that might be so important to him. Important enough to risk his life for. And then she realized she had never once considered what his disassociation from the CIA might mean to Griff. His disassociation from the team, she amended.

That was a much more important disruption. A break in the bond of brotherhood these hard men had formed through the years. A bond that had, for most of them, taken the place of family. The place of love.

Once that bond had been broken by Griff's death, it seemed that for the first time some of them had become aware of the lack of those other things. Hawk had uncharacteristically rescued Tyler Stewart and then married her. Jordan had taken care of Rob Sorrel's small, vulnerable family and eventually made it his own. And Griff...

For the first time, she wondered what Griff had done during the long months she had existed without him. Apparently, none of his friends had known he was alive. His parents were both dead, and he had been their only child.

She had had Gardner to love and to care for during those months. But Griff, she realized, had had no one. In that terrorist attack he had lost his profession—a job he valued and was very good at. He had lost his friends. And even before that, he had lost what he and Claire had once had together. *She* had taken that from him. Her choice. Something within her control.

And Claire thought about what that particular loss might have meant to him. Wondered how he had handled it. Wondered, for the first time, if someone had taken her place in those long months of their separation.

Although Griff had not been her first lover, he had taught her more about her own sexuality than anyone else. And she had known, of course, that his sure, unthinking expertise came from experience. She had never wanted to think about that. About the time *before* she had known him. Before he had known her.

And she didn't really want to think about the possibility that there was someone in his life now. Was that why his initial approach to her had simply been an offer to help? Why he had made no attempt, other than the aborted kiss, which she had blatantly invited, to rekindle any of the physical connections that had existed between them. Was it because there was someone else in his life?

There had been for her an endless deprivation between the last time he'd made love to her and now. But maybe…maybe that had not been the case for Griff.

"I guess now I know the answer to that," he said softly.

Her concentration had gone so far afield that she had to think about what he had said before. Dredge it up out of a mind that had been totally focused on something much more important. Griff had been wondering if he could still plan and carry out an operation. And this one…

"It's going to work," she reassured him softly, no matter her own doubts. "That may be why Jake can't reach Jordan and Hawk. They may have gone ahead and made contact with the kidnappers. They may have already made the exchange.''

She couldn't know that, not given what Jake had told her about the arrangements, but there didn't seem to be any point in letting Griff punish himself for what had gone wrong. The things that had happened had been out of his control. And that was all he had promised her.

He didn't respond to her attempt at reassurance. She knew he didn't need to deal with this right now. He needed to build back the strength those long hours he had spent in the ocean, deprived of fluid, had stolen. He needed to sleep rather than to talk about what had gone wrong in this operation. Things he couldn't change now.

And she needed to check on poor Jake. He had had as little sleep as she in the last twenty-four hours. Maybe they could keep one another awake until they reached the rendezvous point where they were supposed to meet the others.

Griff didn't protest as she slipped out from behind him, carefully easing his upper body down onto the pillows she'd pushed against the headboard. When she was standing beside the bed, she realized that his eyes were closed again, the black lashes lying unmoving against the smudges of fatigue under them.

His eyes were a little less sunken than when she'd found him. At least they seemed to be, so the liquids she had given him must have had some positive effect.

"I need to check on Jake," she explained, not certain if Griff was asleep.

There was no response. She bent and pulled the blanket up over his chest. Her fingers made unintentional contact with his bare skin, but there was no reaction. She had already begun to turn away when he spoke.

"What's she like?" he asked. His voice was low, and

he still hadn't opened his eyes. He wasn't looking at her. Maybe deliberately.

Gardner, she realized. He was asking about Gardner. And that had been another regret, one she had thought a lot about as she and Jake searched. She had thought of all the things she wished she'd told Griff when she'd had the chance.

"Like you," she said, her throat tightening with the realization of how true that was. Being with Griff again had reinforced what she had already known. "She's really...a lot like you."

His eyes opened. In the dimness they were so dark they were black. Without color. Deep and fathomless.

"Like me?" he asked, his gaze touching briefly on her hair, which she knew had been lightened even more by its brief exposure to the tropical sun. Then his eyes settled on hers, which were nothing like Gardner's either, of course.

"Black hair. Your eyes. She's even got your chin," Claire said, remembering, in spite of how much it hurt, that small, determined tilt. Fighting the pull of emotion, she said, "You'd have a hard time denying she's your flesh and blood."

Until the words were spoken, echoing painfully in the quietness, she didn't realize how inappropriate they were. How out of place between the two of them. Griff had never attempted to deny Gardner. He couldn't have, because he had never known anything about her. And that was a result of something Claire had done. Her choice. Something within her control.

He held her eyes a long time, but he didn't say any of the hurtful things he might have said. None of the accusations she probably deserved.

Claire didn't move, waiting to hear whatever he wanted to say to her. Knowing that eventually it would all have to be said. She had denied him his daughter. And twice she had come very close to never having a chance to make that right.

Finally Griff turned his face toward the wall, closing his eyes. A signal that the conversation was over, she supposed, but she waited a few seconds longer. Then she turned again and went out of the cabin, leaving him alone.

"DAMN IT TO HELL," Jake said under his breath.

Startled, Claire looked up. She had almost been asleep, she realized. And she was supposed to be keeping Jake company. Keeping him awake. Except it seemed she was the one who was more in danger of succumbing to exhaustion.

"What is it?" she asked, her eyes moving around the small cove the boat was entering.

"They're not here," Jake said, expertly easing the cruiser into the shallow waters.

Claire glanced at her watch, but since it was dawn, she really didn't need to. They were hours late, and apparently Hawk and Jordan had given up waiting.

"Maybe they've taken the film and arranged the exchange on their own."

Jake didn't bother to answer. His eyes searched the tangled undergrowth that lined the narrow beach against which the aquamarine water became slow-breaking, cream-white rollers.

"The inflatable's not here," he said.

It wasn't until he said it that she understood what he'd been looking for. If the boat wasn't here, then neither were Hawk and Jordan. They wouldn't attempt walking out through that nearly impenetrable tangle.

"What do we do now?" Claire asked, glancing at Jake's set face. It was a question she had had to ask too often in the last few days. Now she was simply looking for something positive to hang on to. Some comfort. Reassurance.

"We contact the kidnappers," Griff said, his voice coming from behind her.

He had come up the steps while their attention had been focused on the cove. Neither she nor Jake had heard him. That might be explained by the fact that Griff was barefoot. He was wearing nothing but the same faded pair of Levi's he'd worn the night they'd stood together by the rail and watched the distant lights of Miami.

"Without the film?" Jake asked. "What do we tell them if they ask for proof?"

"We bluff," Griff said, moving carefully onto the bridge, his hand against the wall, using its support. "We pretend we have proof. And we set up a meeting to make the exchange."

Jake held his eyes a long heartbeat, and then, obeying Griff Cabot, just as he always had, he put the engine in reverse and began to back slowly out of the cove.

"YOU NEED TO REST," Claire said.

Griff looked over his shoulder and found her behind him. He had thought she and Jake were both still asleep, but it was obvious she'd been up long enough to take a shower. She had changed into fresh clothing, a pair of white shorts and a navy tank top, but she was barefoot.

Her hair was damp, and he could smell the soap or the shampoo she had used, its fragrance stronger than the hint of brine the morning breeze carried. He fought the images it evoked. They had showered together a few times. Washing one another's bodies. Slowly. Erotically. An act of love.

Without speaking, he turned back toward the front of the boat, the remembrance of Claire's naked body too strong in his head. He looked out through the bridge windows instead, fighting memory. He had thought about Claire Heywood almost every day of the last eighteen months.

Every day since she'd told him she never wanted to see him again.

And he had thought about her, and his daughter, almost constantly throughout these last few days. Days when he and Claire had finally been together again. And during those long, lonely hours he'd spent in the ocean, he'd had far too much time to think. About everything that had happened between them.

One conclusion he'd come to, sometime during the course of that ordeal, was that despite the argument he'd made about their agreement being no different than letting Claire believe he was dead, he knew better.

He had known she would have been devastated by his "death." He had known it, and yet he still hadn't contacted her to tell her it was a lie. Not until he'd sent her that single bloodred rose. A message that obviously hadn't meant to her what he had thought it would.

And as he had floated in that dark, cold water, finally forced to face what he had done, Griff had also come to the realization that there was only one explanation for why he hadn't. Somewhere inside, in a cold, bitter place in his soul, he had wanted to hurt Claire as much as she had hurt him.

When she had broken off their relationship, she had rejected who and what he was. And she had made some pretty damning accusations. Eventually he had retaliated, in the cruelest way imaginable. But he hadn't known about the baby, which would, of course, have changed everything.

"Where's Jake?" she asked.

"Still sleeping."

"He needs it," she said.

She was standing beside him, but Griff resisted the urge to look at her. Now wasn't the time or the place to try to make amends. He had a job to do first. A job that had been badly botched. And he could only hope that in spite of all that had gone wrong, he could somehow manage to get her daughter back. *Their* daughter.

When they had docked again this morning in Miami, he had gone ashore to contact the kidnappers, leaving Jake to see to getting the yacht ready to go out again, and leaving Claire asleep. Surprisingly, despite the missed call, whoever had answered at the number he'd been given agreed to a new rendezvous, giving him precise navigational directions. Which was where they were headed now.

He had bluffed his way through their questions about the delay by fabricating a mechanical problem. And he had lied about having the proof he'd promised them, just as he'd suggested to Jake they should do.

It had all been easier than he could have hoped for, probably because Diaz's name had already been released to the media. And that should also tip the odds of success a little more in their favor, despite the fact they didn't have the film he'd promised.

He was increasingly worried about Hawk and Jordan, however. According to Jake, they hadn't been heard from since the Citation left the airport two nights ago. They hadn't been at the prearranged rendezvous. And it seemed obvious from his phone conversation that they hadn't tried to contact the kidnappers on their own.

"When we get there..." Claire began, and then hesitated.

"We play it by ear," Griff said.

"Will they accept that Diaz is dead?"

"Would you?" he asked. It wasn't a trick. It was the same question he had been asking himself.

"I don't know. I guess it would depend on how trusting I was," she said finally.

He laughed, the sound low. Unamused. "I don't think these people are very trusting. But the plane crash has been widely reported, and they've released Diaz's name."

"What about Jordan and Hawk? What do you think's happened?"

Griff didn't like the images those words conveyed. He hoped to hell nothing had "happened" to them. They hadn't hesitated when he had asked for their help, but everything was different now than when they had been members of his team. This wasn't their job. And they had responsibilities they hadn't had then. People to protect. And to care for.

"I don't know," he said truthfully, wondering how he would tell those who were waiting for their return if Hawk and Jordan didn't make it back. What would he say to their wives, and in Jordan's case to Kathleen Sorrel's children, if something had gone wrong?

Keeping his men safe was something he had always managed to do before, no matter how dangerous the situation. No matter the odds against their survival.

"They seem capable of looking after themselves," Claire said softly, probably reading his anxiety.

And they were, of course. No one knew that better than Griff, but he was worried. There seemed no reason to respond to her comment, however, and again the silence stretched, tense and uncomfortable. Which he found sad, because, although they had been many things when they were together, they had never before been uncomfortable. Not even the first night.

"Well," she said hesitantly. "I just came up to check on you and Jake. I guess...I guess you'd rather be alone."

She turned, moving silently across the deck.

"No," he said. His voice was so low he wasn't sure she would hear. And he didn't understand why he had made that admission. Other than the fact it was the truth. He didn't want to be alone.

He was pushing the cruiser through the coastal waters as fast as he dared. Probably faster than was safe, but that wasn't why he wanted company. After all, he hadn't wanted Jake up here.

But Griff didn't want Claire to leave. He wanted her with him. Of course, he acknowledged, again remembering, he had always wanted that.

"Thank you," she said softly.

He looked up. She was standing at his side once more. He reached out and took her hand. The bones were fine and delicate, and they felt as fragile as porcelain under his fingers. He pulled her forward a little, directing her without speaking to the pilot's chair beside the one he was occupying.

She obeyed, but when she was seated, he didn't release her hand. Her eyes, focused on his, were questioning, and the smooth oval of her face was as beautiful to him as the first time he'd seen her.

She had borne his child, and he hadn't even been there. And she had mourned his death. Hawk, his controlled voice more emotional than Griff could ever remember it, had told him about Claire's visit to his grave. About the solitary rose she had left there. As much a message as Griff had intended the one he had sent her to be. A symbol of what had once been between them. And, in a way, what still was between them. Embodied in their child.

"I'd like to hear about her," he said.

He ran his thumb slowly over the fine-textured skin on the back of her hand, the gesture unthinking, provoked by the familiarity of her fingers resting, relaxed and unmoving, in his. Again. In spite of everything.

"I'd like to tell you," she said.

And so, her voice low and unhurried, and very intimate, she talked to him about Gardner until they reached their destination.

Chapter Ten

The path that disappeared into the low-growing vegetation on the tiny key had been visible even from the cruiser. And from there it had looked a lot less rugged than it was proving to be, Griff acknowledged, as they fought their way through the dense undergrowth of saw palmetto and saltwort.

He and Claire had waded through the shallows and climbed around the exposed mangrove roots. Then they had hit this. His damaged leg probably made progress over the terrain even more difficult for him than for Claire, which was particularly frustrating.

According to the instructions Griff had been given during the phone call he'd made in Miami, their meeting with the kidnappers was supposed to take place in the small gray house he could see beyond the overgrown palmetto and scrub palm.

Jake had stayed on board by the radio, hoping to hear something from Jordan and Hawk. Griff had intended for that to be Claire's job, but she had been adamant about going with him. She was going to be there when they gave Gardner back, she had said, her eyes challenging, just as they used to.

Jake had shrugged his agreement. His expression warned that he thought Claire had probably reached the breaking point. So Griff had given in, which, he acknowledged, was turning out to have been a smart move. This undergrowth would have made it difficult for him to carry a six-month-old. And neither he nor Jake, he had to admit, knew a whole hell of a lot about babies.

"Almost there," Claire said, as she turned to wait for him. He had let her lead the way after they'd gotten over the mangroves, preferring that to having her walking behind him, watching his progress.

Right now, her gaze was focused on his face—rather obviously focused there, he decided bitterly. And then, looking at her more closely, he realized that the thick vegetation and tangled roots had probably demanded an equally strenuous physical exertion on her part.

Her face was covered with a film of perspiration. A strand of hair clung to the moisture there after escaping the confinement of the long single braid, which lay over her left shoulder. As he watched, she pushed the tendril off her temple with the back of her fingers.

The gesture was so familiar, almost exactly like the one he had seen her make on television. Obviously feminine, it was enormously provocative as well. Griff lowered his eyes, fighting memory, fighting need, forcing himself to concentrate again on the uneven ground.

When he reached the place where Claire was waiting, he didn't look at her, but focused instead on the house that stood behind her. It was located in a ragged clearing, surrounded by more of the same vegetation they had just fought their way through.

It was apparent that the cleared area around the house had at one time been much larger. Given the climate, however, the creeping undergrowth had reclaimed almost everything that had originally been hacked away.

Weathered, squat and close to the ground, the house had

probably withstood its share of tropical storms. It certainly looked as if it had been designed for that purpose.

Griff wondered briefly why anyone would want to live in this place. Maybe someone's idea of paradise, but its isolation, the unremitting heat and humidity, and the prospect of what might be hiding in the surrounding scrub meant it wasn't his.

"Do we just knock on the front door?" Claire asked.

Her question had a thin edge of sarcasm, probably injected to hide her anxiety. She was now facing the house as well, standing at his left shoulder.

"If they're in there, they know we're here."

"If?" Claire repeated.

"There was no boat in the cove. No sign of activity there or around the house."

"But Jake *is* sure that this is—"

"This is where they told him," Griff confirmed before she could finish the question. "Jake knows these keys like the back of his hand. Come on," he ordered.

Without waiting for her to obey, he started across the clearing. In the heavy stillness, there wasn't a bird cry. Not even a whisper of wind rustling through the dry spikes of the palmettos. The silence around them might simply be the result of their presence in a place that didn't get many visitors, but it was strange that there seemed to be no sound here at all, other than their own labored breathing.

When he reached the front door, Claire trailing closely behind him, Griff hesitated, again listening. The quietness of the clearing was unbroken, and despite it, Griff could hear no sound from inside the house. No conversation. No radio. Nothing. It felt as if he and Claire might be the only two people on the planet. Certainly the only two on this island.

As he thought that, Claire reached past him and fastened her hand around the knob of the door. She didn't turn it immediately, hesitating long enough to give him time to protest. But despite his misgivings, and a growing sense that something was very wrong here, he knew they had to go in.

When Claire's hand began to move, the knob turning slowly beneath the same fingers that had rested in his while she had told him about his daughter, he didn't stop her. She pushed the door open, revealing a sheltered dimness that seemed almost inviting after the outside glare.

There was still no sound. Nothing emanated from the dark interior but a miasma of late afternoon heat, mildew and rot, all ubiquitous in the tropics.

Griff moved past her and into the entrance hall, pausing just across the threshold to give his eyes time to adjust. He heard Claire follow, the soles of her running shoes making a faint noise on the old-fashioned terrazzo floor.

He fought the urge to call out to the people who were supposed to meet them. Whoever had set this up had to know they were here. They should have been watching ever since he and Claire climbed down the ladder of the yacht and waded into the shallows.

Claire, who was now beside him again, touched his arm, questioning his hesitation with arched brows. He tilted his head down the hall and then stepped forward, making no effort to mask the sound of his steps.

The hallway, when they reached the end of it, opened into a spacious room, obviously the main living area of the house. The ceiling seemed very high, especially compared to the low entryway they'd just left. On one side was a wall of glass, fogged by years of buffeting by the sea wind.

At one time the vegetation, which could still be discerned through the salt-hazed windows, must have been kept cut back, revealing a view of the ocean. All that could be seen of the water now was a blear of turquoise beyond the palmetto spikes and moss-draped dwarf cypresses.

Part of the musty odor that pervaded the house came from the furniture. Sun-faded cushions covered a matching set of chairs and couch that hadn't been in style for more than forty years. Now, especially along the seams of the pillows, black mold almost obscured the once-bright colors of the fabric.

There was no one waiting to meet them. And still no sound except an indistinct buzzing. Insects, Griff decided, dismissing the low, distant hum from his evaluation of the situation.

His gaze slowly circled the long room. There was a kitchen on one end, separated from the living area by panels of white latticework. On the other end was an opening that led into another hall, this one even darker than the entryway had been.

"Stay here," he ordered, starting across the expanse of terrazzo to explore it.

His uneven footsteps echoed off the stone floor. But he had already decided it didn't matter how much noise they made. The house was empty. It *felt* empty, devoid of life, and obviously it had been for a long time.

He didn't know what game the people who had taken Gardner were playing, but the frustration he had fought throughout the last year was again boiling up inside. A sick disappointment about failing at something this important. And almost as powerful as those, his dread of having to justify his failure. To Claire, and perhaps even more importantly, to himself.

When he entered the hallway, he discovered there was a windowless bathroom on his right. A few steps farther down on the left was the open door of what he assumed would be the bedroom. The hum he had vaguely been aware of since they'd entered was louder back here.

A broken window? he wondered, walking toward the doorway. It seemed strange he hadn't heard the insects outside. He'd been aware of that hum only after they had come inside. Only after they'd reached—

The sick sweetness of the smell should have warned him, but he didn't put it all together until he stepped into the room. Then he didn't need any of the clues he had missed.

Whoever had done this had opened all the windows in the bedroom before they'd left, very probably to ensure that what was going on would happen. The open windows had made the smell less obvious in the rest of the house. And of course, the body had to have been here less than forty-eight hours.

Griff closed his eyes, blocking out the image of what was on the bed. He fought a surge of nausea so strong he literally swallowed against it, trying desperately to push the bile out of his throat. And he forced himself to stand in the fetid dimness, trying to make his mind work. Trying to make this an intellectual exercise. Trying to figure out exactly what message he was supposed to receive from this obscenity.

Because there was no doubt in his mind this *was* a message. And that it was what they had been sent here to find.

"Dear God," Claire said, her anguished whisper coming from behind him.

Griff opened his eyes. They felt as burned as they had yesterday, unprotected from the blaze of the sun reflecting off the water. Listening to the sounds of Claire's retching behind him, he made himself take another look at the thing on the bed.

His lips flattened with disgust, but he realized he hadn't been mistaken. The second look left no doubt. Despite the condition of the body, he hadn't been wrong about his identification.

He turned around, moving a few steps out into the hallway before he took a breath. He hadn't even realized that he had been avoiding breathing while he was in the bedroom, an action automatic and unthinking.

Claire was standing at the end of the hall, her head bent forward, her right hand resting high on the wall beside her, as if for support, her left clamped over her mouth. The diffuse light from the salt-glazed wall of windows limned the back of her body and touched the long blond braid with silver.

He walked up behind her and put his hand on her shoulder. Immediately she turned, leaning into him, laying her head against his chest. His left arm enfolded her. He could feel her trembling, her slim body vibrating as strongly as his had when they'd pulled him out of the water last night.

"It's all right," he whispered. "We're all right. Whoever did that is gone, Claire. Long gone."

Without thinking, he lowered his head, setting his chin on the top of her head, feeling the sun-warmed softness of her hair under it. He closed his eyes, remembering other times he'd held her. The good times.

The fragrance of the shampoo he had noticed before had been released by the heat and exertion of their trek. He took a deep breath, welcoming the sweet normality of its scent. It cut through the sickness that was thick in his throat. Purifying it. And him.

"Who *is* that?" Claire whispered, her face still buried against the front of his shirt.

He thought about lying to her, but he had done enough of that. There had been more than enough tricks. On both sides. More than enough cleverness to go around. Griff's mouth tightened briefly before he opened it, but he told her the truth.

"Ramon Diaz," he said.

It took a few seconds for the name to register, as he had guessed it might, and he waited through them. It might take a few more for all the implications of what he had just said to sink in, but Claire Heywood was very bright.

Her head lifted suddenly, and she took a step back, moving away from him. Breaking whatever bond had been between them.

Her eyes seemed very blue now, as blue as the water in the lagoon they had crossed to get here. And despite yesterday's ordeal, the whites were clear. The dark pupils had widened, however, as they focused on his face. Trying to read it despite the dimness. Trying, he knew, to understand.

"Diaz?" she whispered.

Her voice sounded puzzled, but the knowledge of what this meant was already in her eyes. Her intellect was fighting against accepting it, he supposed. Just as his had done when he'd identified the body.

"He's...he's supposed to be dead," she said finally.

"He is," Griff said bitterly. "Spectacularly dead."

They had cut his throat, the wound deep and running from ear to ear. There was a lot of blood, but most of it seemed to be on his clothing rather than on the bed, which argued that Diaz hadn't been killed here. This was strictly for show. A message intended for Griff.

Claire shook her head, the movement contained, and her eyes didn't release his, still questioning. "Dead and in the ocean," she clarified. "That plane *exploded*."

She said the last word as if there was no doubt. As if that phrase answered everything. Diaz's plane had exploded over the ocean. She had seen it or heard it, and had seen burned and broken evidence of the crash in the water. Therefore, Diaz shouldn't be on the bed in this house with his throat cut.

"But he wasn't *on* the plane," Claire said softly, coming to the obvious conclusion. "He was *never* on that plane."

The last was accusatory. And Griff deserved it. Whatever

she wanted to say, he knew he deserved to have to listen to it. And to have to explain.

"Briefly," he admitted.

"Just so the cameras you'd set up could film him boarding."

When he nodded, she went on, piecing together what they had done. What they had done and not told her about. That was the one part of this, he suspected, she would find unforgivable.

"Then you got them off the plane somehow...." She paused, thinking about it. "Hawk and Jordan got them off, out of camera range—Diaz and his bodyguards—and you took the plane up alone. You exploded an empty plane over the ocean, so..." Again she faltered. "So the kidnappers would *think* Diaz was dead."

Maybe this was better, letting her work it all out in her head. Without him having to tell her all the reasons he had chosen to do it that way.

"But you never intended to kill him," she whispered, her voice shocked and then accusing. "Not from the first. But you didn't tell *me* that."

"What we do... What the team did," Griff amended, "was never like what they wanted. We never killed for personal reasons. I would never ask my people to do that, Claire. Not even in this situation."

As far as he was concerned, killing Diaz had never been an option. What the team had done instead was to arrange a performance. A trick to make the kidnappers think they had done what they been asked to do. And he hadn't told Claire what was going on.

"You wanted me to think I had agreed to Diaz's death," she said accusingly.

"I thought if you didn't know we were planning to do it that way, you wouldn't worry as much about something going wrong. About the kidnappers finding out. We've always operated on a need-to-know basis. If you don't have a role in the operation, then you aren't briefed about it.''

"Oh, I'm sure that's true,'' she said softly, her voice bitter. "But that isn't why you didn't tell me, Griff. You didn't tell me because you wanted me to agree. You wanted to *hear* me give permission for Diaz to die.''

Griff hadn't demanded that. He could have, and to his shame he had even thought about it. What he *had* done, however, had been almost as despicable. *"Unless you tell me no,''* he had told her. And she hadn't. Because her baby's life was at stake.

"You wanted me to understand that the decisions you had to make were always hard,'' she said. "Maybe as hard as that one.''

Perhaps he had, he admitted, remembering their arguments. Remembering how many times he had explained the difficult choices involved in what the team did. Remembering how many times he had tried to make her see that sometimes a madman has to be destroyed to protect the innocent. But he had never succeeded in convincing her that taking someone's life was ever justified. Not under any circumstances.

"You wanted me to *know* what making that decision feels like,'' she said, her eyes cold.

He had been right before. Claire Heywood was very smart. Because that *was* what he had done, of course. He had destroyed the validity of those old arguments by showing her that she, too, would come to that same decision. No matter what they felt about the sanctity of human life, about the sin of destroying it, almost everyone would make such a decision in order to safeguard those they loved.

"You never intended to kill Diaz,'' she said. "You never intended to keep your part of the bargain with the kidnappers, did you, Griff? And Diaz wasn't dead when you left him with Hawk and Jordan.''

He hadn't been. They had all been alive—Diaz and his bodyguards. But like everything else... Just like everything else, this had gone wrong. And it shouldn't have, Griff thought, going over all the meticulous details of the plan in his mind.

Hawk and Jordan had gotten everyone off the plane, using the refueling truck as cover. All they'd had to do then was to take Diaz and his men to the rendezvous and hold them there. After Griff blew up the plane, he and Jake would pick up the video of Diaz boarding the plane and exchange it for the baby. Then they would turn Diaz over to the DEA, and hope he'd cut a deal with them, talk his head off in exchange for protection.

That's what was supposed to happen. But they hadn't made that initial rendezvous because the emergency transmitter had failed. And when they'd finally arrived, Hawk and Jordan hadn't been there. Now Diaz was dead, his body miles from where it was supposed to be. And Griff had no idea who had killed him and brought him here. No idea where Jordan and Hawk were.

"What do we do about Gardner?" Claire asked softly, her voice full of fear as she realized the rest of it. As she came to the conclusion he'd already reached. "If the kidnappers *know* this was a double cross, and they must, since they put Diaz's body here, then..." Her voice faded, her eyes almost pleading. "Then how are we going to get Gardner back?"

And that was the question, of course, Griff had already asked himself. A question for which he had no answer.

"SOMEHOW THEY KNEW you hadn't killed Diaz," Jake said, "that you didn't plan on killing him, so they did it for you."

They were headed back to Miami, the cruiser cutting through the water like a knife, leaving behind them the island where Ramon Diaz's body rested in a dark bedroom. Exactly where they had been sent to find it.

Claire waited for Griff's response to Jake's comment. His features were hard, as if set in stone, his eyes as bleak as she had ever seen them. Bleaker even than they had been the night she had made him promise he would never try to see her again.

"How could they know?" Griff asked quietly. "How the hell could the kidnappers have known we didn't intend to kill him?"

That wasn't the primary question Claire wanted an explanation for, but it was a good one. She had assumed it was rhetorical, but surprisingly, Jake answered it. Whether what he said was *the* answer, she had no way of knowing, but when Griff heard it, the grooves around his mouth deepened, his lips compressing into a thinner line.

"They knew because somebody told them," Jake said.

He looked braced for a scathing denunciation, but Griff said nothing for a long time, his silence indicating that he was at least considering the idea.

"Only four of us knew," he said finally. "Are you suggesting that someone on this team—"

"I'm *suggesting* there have been a hell of a lot of things going on in the last six months I didn't understand. Like the situation with Jordan..."

Jake hesitated, glancing at Claire, as if reluctant to discuss business in front of an outsider. And to them that's exactly what she was, she realized. She had been forced to acknowledge just how much an outsider when she learned that not only had Griff double-crossed the kidnappers by faking Diaz's death, he had double-crossed her as well.

"Go on," Griff ordered, without following Jake's gaze to its focus on Claire's face. "What *about* the situation with Jordan?"

"There were too many things about what happened to

Cross that never made sense to me. Things nobody should have known about then, either. But they did.''

''Like what?''

''How did Helms know where to find Jordan and Kathleen Sorrel? How did he get past the security system in your summer house?''

''Jordan says they tracked him through the e-mail he sent you,'' Griff said.

''An encrypted e-mail, Griff. And nobody's gotten into one of those. Not yet. And while Jordan was on the run, somebody got into the agency's system. I told you that. I couldn't backtrack them, but I knew they'd been there. They could have been reading files. Reading everything I was doing to help Jordan. Tracking his movements, just as I was.''

''I told you *I* was in the system, Jake.''

''Did *you* betray Jordan?'' Jake asked softly.

The logic was irrefutable. Griff Cabot would be the last person who might be suspected of doing that.

''And if you didn't,'' Jake continued, ''then who did? And how the hell did they do it if *not* like I said?''

Griff remained silent for a moment, his eyes considering Jake's face. ''There's not a system built that can keep a talented hacker out,'' he said finally.

''Not even mine?'' Jake asked mockingly.

His was an arrogance that, given what everyone said about him, was probably deserved, Claire thought.

''The agency's got the best security system in the world,'' Jake added. ''We both know that.''

''Helms was FBI. He used the bureau to get information about Jordan's movements.''

''And the kidnappers? Who you think are some rival drug cartel? Are they using the bureau, too?'' Jake asked.

Griff's eyes didn't leave Jake's, but he didn't answer.

''How else can you explain how they could have

known—'' Claire began, only to have her question over-ridden by Griff's.

''You really think this is someone operating from inside the agency, Jake?'' Griff interrupted. ''Is that what you're suggesting?''

Jake's mouth pursed, and then he nodded. ''Realistically, who else could know about this team and what it does?''

''How would they find out what we intended for Diaz?''

''I don't know. But...Jordan was at the summer house when Helms found him.''

''You said the house was clean. No listening devices.''

''Maybe I was wrong,'' Jake said.

''Why would the agency set this up?'' Griff asked softly. ''What would they have to gain?''

The silence grew and expanded. Finally Jake broke it, his voice low, expressing the fatigue and disappointment they all felt at what they hadn't found on that island.

''I don't know. Just like I don't know what's happened to Hawk and Jordan. Or why we were sent to find Diaz's body. Or who killed him. But if *you've* got some other logical solution for all that's happened on this operation, believe me, Griff, I'd be more than happy to listen to it.'' He stopped, his eyes holding Griff's, seeming to ask for a denial.

Griff said nothing. Finally, he turned and limped across the control room toward the stairs that led to the cabins below. Claire listened as the sounds of his footsteps faded, and then she turned back to Jake.

''What do we do now?'' she asked, the words producing a sick sense of déjà vu.

''Damned if I know,'' Jake said softly, his gaze on the dark stairwell where Griff had disappeared. ''Damned if I have any idea at all of where we go from here.''

Chapter Eleven

"Jake's just trying to make sense of what happened," Claire said, the tone of her voice comforting. "I think I need help doing that as well."

She was standing in the door of his stateroom. Griff wished he'd remembered to close it, but he wondered if even that would have kept her out. He had hoped for more time to come to grips with what had happened, but this confrontation was inevitable.

He wished to hell, however, that Claire didn't feel the need to comfort him, he thought savagely. What he heard in her voice now was almost as difficult for him to accept as her help had been last night.

He had expected to have to deal with her anger over his deception about Diaz. He had been prepared for that. Hearing concern in her voice instead was pretty damned disheartening. Too much had changed between them. Their roles had shifted, somehow. Moved out of the familiar and comfortable dimensions they had once assumed. Or maybe, he acknowledged, those had only been comfortable for him.

Claire had the right to know the truth, no matter how unpalatable that might be. And figuring out that truth was exactly what he had been trying to do since he'd left the bridge.

"Jake's probably right about some of what he said,"

Griff admitted, looking up at her, eyes lifting from their pretended contemplation of his joined fingers.

When Claire appeared in the doorway, she had caught him with his elbows on his knees, forehead resting in his hands. Which went a long way toward explaining what he had heard in her voice. As soon as he realized she was there, he had lifted his head, obviously too late to prevent her from reading the despair his posture implied. A despair he was actually feeling.

"Right about which parts?" she asked.

As if taking his response for permission to enter, she stepped into the room and walked over to sit down on the other end of the bed. Griff's eyes didn't follow her movement; he was looking down again at his hands instead. Which was safer, of course. And he didn't look up even as he answered.

"Whatever's going on here—and probably most of the problems the members of the team have experienced during the last few months—haven't been coincidental. Nor have they originated with someone from outside the agency. There are too many things that indicate events are being…manipulated," he said carefully. "Too many things that point to insider knowledge."

"Events are being manipulated by someone on the team?" she asked. "Is that what you're saying?"

"From someone within the agency," he clarified.

"Why?" Claire asked.

That was the pertinent question, of course—one he thought he had answered a couple of weeks ago. An answer that had prompted his message to the director. And the timing of that and Gardner's kidnapping seemed obvious now. He wondered why it hadn't before. Because he had allowed himself to be thrown off track by Steiner's visit, he acknowledged. And by Carl's dismissal of his suspicions.

"Are you drumming up a conspiracy because you miss it?" Steiner had asked. *Because you miss the team? The excitement? The thrill of the chase?"* And Griff had thought that maybe, just maybe, Carl was right. But now...

"They're trying to destroy the team," he said softly.

He had suspected all along that was what the agency was up to. He had known it in his gut, and he had let Carl's ridicule push those well-honed instincts aside. Because he liked Carl. And because he trusted him.

"I thought..." Claire hesitated. "I thought they had already done that."

"I don't mean disband it," Griff said, thinking about the reality of the phrase he had used. "They're out to destroy *us*. To get rid of *us*. I think that's what has been going on from the beginning."

To Claire that would probably sound like a lunatic-fringe theory, Griff supposed. Paranoia, maybe. Or maybe it would simply sound like an excuse to explain his own ineptitude. A cop-out for his responsibility in the fiasco this had become.

Carl had said they'd retired him because, given the extent of his injuries, they were afraid he could no longer do the job. Maybe they had been right.

"Destroy you because the existence of the team is potentially an embarrassment to this government?" Claire asked.

He looked at her then, turning his head and focusing on her face. He could still remember the things she had said in that last brutal argument. About him. About what the team did. And suddenly he remembered Steiner's remark. *"There are a lot of people who think that about all of us in the agency."*

Griff Cabot had heard all the variations on that theme through the years. All the accusations and insinuations about what the CIA did. He had learned to ignore most of the comments, even those about the immorality of the so-called black operations in which he had played such a major role.

He had been able to play that role because he truly believed what the team did was essential to the survival of democracy. And because he saw their missions as necessary to defeat the evil that too often threatened the world. Claire, however, had seen the team as something as reprehensible as what they were fighting against. Which meant Carl Steiner was probably right about public opinion. In any case, the new leadership was determined to distance themselves from the kinds of activities the External Security Team had once been involved in.

And apparently to distance themselves from the men who had once carried out those sanctioned missions. *Permanently* distance themselves, he thought. And who would be left then to defeat the next madman with a hunger for world domination and a few nuclear weapons at his disposal?

To preserve and protect. To stand guard over this country. And those they loved. *Standing guard.* He had repeated that phrase to his team like a litany. Because that had been what he truly believed they were doing. But now the worldwide arena where he had once operated was no longer where that war was being waged. His fight was here. His battle. And at stake this time was the life of a little girl. A baby.

His baby, he amended, for the first time allowing himself to view this not as an assignment, about which he could be coldly detached and intellectual, but as a personal crusade to find and rescue his daughter. A daughter whom he had never even seen.

"If what we did ever becomes public knowledge," he said, "there will be a hue and cry from certain aspects of our society. And a demand for heads to roll," he added.

Claire laughed. Surprised, he looked up. Although he

hadn't intended that comment to be a joke, he supposed in a way it was. Ironic, at least. They were the ones being targeted for destruction because they had once done the exact same thing.

The current government didn't have the stomach to admit what they knew and had even condoned in the past. That violence is sometimes necessary to preserve democracy. Necessary to insure peace—the fragile, uneasy peace that was all the world had at the moment. A peace that would end in an instant with the detonation of just one of those nuclear weapons so readily available on the terrorist black market.

"Why do they think it might?" Claire asked. "Become public, I mean? Why, all of a sudden, are they so afraid of that?"

"They made the decision to dissolve the team and then belatedly realized that the connections between the members were far stronger than they had believed. Our loyalties had become more...personal than professional."

Carl had even told him that, but Griff hadn't realized then how much they feared it. The CIA valued loyalty to the agency above almost anything else, because it insured that the code of silence would be maintained. Once they began to suspect that another loyalty might supersede that one, then they would suspect disloyalty where none had existed. Their own brand of paranoia.

"That's why they were afraid of Hawk," Claire said. "Because he threatened to go public with what he knew. Because he disobeyed *their* orders in order to get the man who had killed *you*. The man he thought had killed you," she corrected.

"Maybe," Griff acknowledged.

"So they tried to insure that even if he went public, he would never be able to make anyone believe him. They destroyed all record of Hawk's existence so he could never tell what he knew,'' she said.

And suddenly, as Claire remembered the cold hatred that had been in Hawk's eyes that day, a hatred of Steiner and everything he represented, the explanation for everything that had gone wrong with what they were trying to do shifted into place like a piece of a puzzle slipping smoothly between two others. Completing the pattern.

''Hawk,'' she said softly.

Griff's eyes, which were once more focused on his hands, lifted to her face. She could only imagine what it must reveal.

Griff believed that the CIA was out to destroy the team. And maybe he was right. They had been furious because Hawk had disobeyed their orders. Maybe they had targeted Jordan because he had helped Hawk rescue Tyler Stewart at the airport that day and had then protected Hawk by taking the blame. Claire could go along with all that, but maybe...

The more she thought about it, the more it made sense. There was something else going on here as well. Something that would explain how the supposed kidnappers could have learned that it had never been part of Griff's plan to kill Ramon Diaz. Something that would explain how Diaz's body had shown up miles from where it was supposed to be. And would explain why Hawk and Jordan had disappeared.

''Hawk?'' Griff questioned, his voice puzzled.

''Hawk's behind this,'' Claire said, all at once absolutely certain of the validity of her reasoning.

She understood, even as she said the words, how difficult that would be for Griff to accept. It was, however, the only thing that could explain why everything from the beginning of this operation had gone wrong. Griff had said it himself—insider information.

"*Whatever* is going on," Griff said, "I can promise you Hawk has nothing to do with it."

Claire's eyes remained on his, but she didn't answer the denial she had been expecting. Not for several long heart-beats. Instead she reviewed everything she knew, her mind searching for flaws in her logic. And she could find none. Because it all made sense.

"The CIA destroyed Hawk," she said. "They did it deliberately. Mockingly. I was there, Griff. I saw how Steiner treated him. And then, after Hawk had done everything they demanded of him, Steiner almost let Tyler Stewart get killed."

"So Hawk betrays the rest of us?" Griff said, his voice almost amused—or pretending to be.

"He doesn't see this as a betrayal," she said. "None of you have been hurt. Not that we can verify, anyway," she amended, wondering about Jordan. What would Hawk have done with Jordan?

Or… The thought was as sudden as the first had been, but it, too, made sense. Was it possible Jordan could be in on all this as well?

If he believed, as Griff and Jake now seemed to, that what had happened to him had been set up by the agency, if Hawk had convinced him of that, then maybe Jordan would be more than willing to go along with whatever Hawk had planned.

"Hawk would never—" Griff began.

She interrupted, her tone uncompromising. She didn't understand it all, but some of this just made too much sense not to be true.

"The CIA cut him off, destroyed him, without even the pension he was entitled to. Hawk's smart enough to know there are a lot of ways to make money. Especially with the skills he's acquired. Maybe he saw the contract some rival put out on Diaz as a way of bankrolling the retirement they'd forced on him. Or maybe he just figured somebody owes him something.''

''You think Hawk is bitter enough about what Steiner did to pull something like this? Something that would put friends in danger? Something that would endanger a *baby?* And do all it for money?''

Hearing the anger underlying the mockery in the deep voice she knew so well, Claire said nothing, but again she held Griff's eyes, letting his questions hang unanswered between them. Giving him time to work out the answers for himself.

''I asked you a question, Claire,'' Griff demanded. ''Are you suggesting Hawk set this up? That *Hawk* took Gardner?''

Was she? she wondered. Could the man they called Hawk be angry enough to design this kind of elaborate hoax? It would almost be comforting to believe that. To believe that someone she knew had taken her baby.

''I...I don't know,'' she admitted.

''Look,'' Griff said, moderating the fury that had been in his voice, maybe because of that faltering admission. ''If Hawk *had* arranged all this, what would be the purpose? Even if he wanted money, even if someone was offering money for killing Diaz, Hawk could have done that by himself. That's exactly the kind of job he did for the team. So what purpose could it serve to take Gardner?''

''Because it involved you,'' Claire said.

Again Griff held her eyes a long time before he answered her. ''Hawk's the one who went to Baghdad,'' he said.

For Griff. To avenge his death. That was probably the strongest argument Griff could make against what she had just suggested. Out of all the members of his team, Hawk had been the one who had sought vengeance for his death.

But maybe he didn't realize that particular act didn't argue against what she had suggested. If anything, it seemed to prove her case. Hawk *was* the kind of man who would never let something go. He would always be the one who would seek revenge.

"You're right," she said. "He *is* the one. He put his life on the line for yours. And doing that cost him his career."

"So he's angry at the agency for retiring him. Angry at Steiner for destroying his identity. For putting Tyler in danger. I agree, but I don't see how any of that would lead you to the conclusion that he took Gardner to involve *me* in this."

"Think about how all of that started," she said softly.

It had started with Griff's death. Which had not, of course, been a death at all. Only another forced retirement. The destruction of a member of a black ops team the CIA had decided no longer had a role in today's world.

"You think Hawk's angry at *me* for letting the agency put out the story that I had been killed?" Griff asked incredulously. "You think he blames *me* for setting him off on that hunt?"

"A hunt that eventually led to everything else that happened," Claire said. "To his situation. Tyler's danger. Even Jordan's. If Hawk *hadn't* gone to Baghdad to get revenge for your death, then the agency wouldn't have made him a target. And none of those other things would ever have happened."

"So in revenge he kidnaps a baby?" Griff suggested, his voice sardonic, ridiculing the whole idea.

"*Your* baby," Claire corrected, and saw the impact of that in his eyes.

She could imagine how difficult this would be for Griff to believe. But it had a twisted kind of logic if he would only think about it. A man like Hawk wouldn't like being manipulated or lied to. It was obvious he felt the agency had done both. And that they had betrayed him after his years of service. Those feelings had been very clear during the meeting with Steiner—clear to her, at least.

"How could Hawk know Gardner is mine?" Griff asked.

"I can accept Hawk knowing Gardner is your child more easily than I can accept that some Mexican drug dealer knew it," she said. "Besides, Hawk also knows exactly how this team works. They couldn't. He could *do* this, Griff. Nobody else could."

There was another long silence. Which meant he was thinking about it, she supposed. He was at least considering what she had said. And the longer she'd talked, the more convinced she was that she was on the right track.

"Why?" Griff asked again.

"I don't know. Not...exactly. Maybe to prove to Steiner that he was smarter than they gave him credit for? Or because you let their lie stand? You were his friend. Hawk was more than willing to put his neck in a noose for you in Baghdad. Willing to take the official flak for that hit. But then he found out somehow it was all a lie. One you'd gone along with."

She remembered how that felt—to realize Griff had let her believe he was dead. Hawk had denied that finding out the truth of that had affected him, but she hadn't believed him. She *couldn't,* because she knew how she had felt.

Griff's eyes, still fastened on her face, were very dark, almost empty. After all, she was asking him to believe the worst of a man he considered a friend. And she could be wrong, of course. At least wrong about Hawk trying to get revenge on Griff. But she knew she wasn't wrong about the other. It made too much sense.

"Maybe he did it to get back at the CIA. At Steiner," she said, trying not to go too far. No further than she could really defend. "And at the same time he sets himself up very nicely financially."

"How does this get back at Steiner?" Griff asked. "Or at the agency?"

"Because Hawk created a situation where he believed you'd be forced to kill someone. He thought you'd have no compunction about targeting Diaz because of what he was. Hawk wouldn't have. He also knew you'd call for help from the team. And he knew he'd be included in this mission."

That bond between the two of them had been obvious, even in the short time she'd been around them. And as Griff had reminded her, Hawk had been the one who had gone to Baghdad.

"Then, when it's done, when Diaz is dead, Hawk goes public. He takes this assassination, along with the history of the External Security Team, to the media. And *this* time, Griff, they'll believe him. After all," she added softly, "this time he has the film to prove what you did."

She could see it happening in his eyes. She watched the anger fade as his intellect began to push aside the emotional barriers that had prevented him from accepting how much sense this made. How much it explained. And despite the fact that he hadn't told her about Diaz, she ached for his betrayal.

"Griff," she said softly, sorry that she had had to be the one to do this, but she wondered, given how he felt about Hawk, if Griff would ever have figured it out on his own. She had always imagined him to be so rational. Almost unemotional. But looking into his eyes now, she knew how wrong she had been.

She put her hand on his arm. The feel of it must have broken the spell of horror her words—or rather his acceptance of them—had created. He turned his head away, no longer willing to look at her.

She could see only his profile. She watched the muscle in his jaw slowly tighten, his gaze focused on the dark, empty doorway. After a moment, his lips compressed. Then, as if willing himself to move, he turned back to face her.

"He wouldn't hurt her," he said.

In the midst of dealing with this treachery, she realized, he was trying to reassure her about Gardner. She nodded, her throat tight. She had once believed Hawk and Jordan would be more than willing to help her find her daughter because she had helped them. And now, it seemed...

The threat of tears bleared her vision. Fighting them, she focused on her fingers resting against Griff's forearm. She didn't really believe Hawk would hurt Gardner. Or allow her to be hurt. For all his hardness, Hawk had never struck her as cruel, and Griff knew him much better than she. But of course, this entire episode had been the ultimate cruelty. To take someone's baby. No matter what your motives.

Griff shifted his body, turning toward her. He lifted his hand to her cheek. His thumb moved under her chin, applying an upward pressure, and she obeyed it, raising her eyes to his.

"I told you I'll get her back," he said.

"I know," she whispered.

"I will. I promise you, Claire. No matter what else is going on here, I *will* get Gardner back."

She nodded. Seeing the moisture in her eyes, Griff smiled at her. The smile was intended for reassurance, she supposed, but without thinking, she returned it. He ran his thumb across her lips, a small, intimate caress.

She had invited his kiss on deck that night. Less than forty-eight hours ago, she realized. It seemed longer, because so much had happened in the meantime. She had wondered then if there were someone else in Griff's life. And if so...

His head began to lower. His dark eyes held hers a long moment, and then they closed. Even as she watched, his head tilted so that his mouth would fit over hers, a natural and familiar alignment. And she wanted his mouth there. No matter what else was going on, she wanted Griff to touch her again. To kiss her. To keep the senseless terrors of the world they inhabited at bay. Only Griff had ever been strong enough to do that. For her. And for Gardner.

Claire had always known that, but for some reason, she had fought against it, using intellectual arguments rather than acknowledging the truth of what he believed. That the world was evil. A terrifyingly dangerous place. And that there must be someone willing to stand against its depravity. She had just never wanted that someone to have to be Griff. She didn't now.

She closed her eyes, lifting her chin until she felt the warmth of his breath on her lips. Her mouth opened, welcoming the heat and movement of his tongue, which immediately pushed inside. Seeking. Demanding a response. And finding it.

Whatever anger she had felt or whatever foolish arguments she had once made against the possibility of their being together disappeared. Any remaining trace of doubt about the rightness of this melted away in the promise of his kiss.

She put her hands lightly on either side of his face, the rough, masculine texture of his skin familiar, branded on her senses and never forgotten. *Never* forgotten.

With only the force of the kiss, mouth against mouth, he pushed her down onto the bunk. Once she was on her back, he placed his hands flat on the mattress, one on either side of her shoulders. She put her feet up on the bed, and he moved his right knee to the other side of hers.

Then, bending his elbows, he lowered himself until he was lying on top of her. Her breasts crushed by the weight of his chest. His hips aligned on top of hers, the strength of his hard erection blatant. Exciting.

She had tried to maintain contact with his lips, but their movements down onto the mattress had resulted instead in a series of touches and releases between their open mouths. When she felt his arousal pressing into her hips, she caught his bottom lip in her teeth, biting it teasingly.

She heard his gasp of reaction, and then his tongue invaded, once more hard and demanding, almost punishing. Controlling. The same control that had once taught her so much about making love. Enough that when he was gone, she had dreamed of this. Of him. And she had awakened trembling with need and regret.

He pushed his hips into hers again, rocking them against her pelvis. The movement was small, very deliberate. And so tantalizing, especially with the barrier of their clothing between them. The soft gasp of breath this time was hers.

His right hand moved, sliding under her top. His palm was rough against her bare skin, more calloused than she remembered. Its feel was incredibly masculine. As it slid over her stomach, the abrasiveness was also exciting, provoking a rush of desire, heat and moisture spreading like smoke, thick and rich, through her lower body.

She wanted the roughness of his palms against her breasts. Imagined the sensation. Envisioned it. The softness of her breast enclosed in the masculine strength of his dark fingers.

It had been too long since Griff had touched her. An endless loneliness. That had been at first through her own choice. And then because of the cold despair of his death. And finally, again, they had come to this.

She eased her own hand under her shell, placing it over the back of his and urging it upward. He obeyed, cupping his fingers under the fullness of her breast.

She had only recently stopped nursing Gardner. Neither of them had been ready for it, but because of the demands of resuming her profession, because of its long, uncertain hours, the process had become increasingly frustrating for them both.

Her breasts were, therefore, much fuller than they had ever been before. Much more sensitive. A thousand nerve endings were demanding Griff's attention. Aching with need.

His lips had drifted away from her mouth to find her throat. They slid, opened, hot and wet, over the small pulse that had begun to race under the thin, delicate skin beneath her ear. Her fingers slipped into his hair, holding his head against her body as his mouth moved downward, trailing moisture against her neck. And then lower.

The anticipation with which her aching, milk-filled breasts had once welcomed the touch of Gardner's mouth surged through her belly. Perhaps there was something strange, Claire acknowledged, in the juxtaposition of those two images—Griff's mouth and her daughter's fastened over the nipple of her breast. Something she should push from her head. But she didn't. She wanted to feel Griff's lips there as much as she had wanted Gardner's. Both were natural. And right. Her right.

Desire for the fulfillment of that right was so powerful she tried to tell him, but the sound she made was inarticulate. Husky with need, it originated too low in her throat to be verbal communication.

It must have delivered its message, however, for Griff moved his hand, slipping it out from under her top. It lifted, his thumb hooking around the straps of her shell and her bra to pull both off her shoulder. Then he reached into the scooped neckline of the garment and cupped the globe of her breast, lifting it free.

She waited for the descent of his lips, her breathing ragged. Griff had gone very still. The hands that had been caressing her body were now unmoving.

Slowly, she opened her eyes. His face was just above

hers. His eyes were dark and hooded, screened by his lashes. She could see enough to know, however, that they were focused on her exposed breast. It was only with the intensity of his gaze that she realized why the seductive movement of his hand had stopped. He had known her body so well, and he was now becoming aware of all the changes that had occurred during the last fifteen months.

Changes in her breasts. Not just in size, but in shape as well. In the subtly increased darkness of their nipples. And in the tracery of small, silvered lines. All the telltale evidence left by her pregnancy and by nursing his daughter.

Griff had never seen any of those before. Because the last time they had made love, of course... The last time they had made love... Thought suspended, she waited, almost frightened by his stillness.

His eyes lifted to hers. They seemed unfocused. Then they traveled over her face as if they had never really looked at her features before. Examined them one by one. And still she waited, wondering what he was thinking. What he was feeling.

She knew there were other subtle differences in her body. Things he had not yet seen. Or felt. And now, suddenly, she was unsure of what she was doing. Of what they were doing together. Unsure for the first time that the sheer physical passion that had always, instantly, arced between them would be the same.

His eyes moved down to her breast, and then, so slowly her throat went dry and her bones melted, he lowered his lips to the dark, slightly distended nipple. She watched his tongue touch it. Circle. Lave with such incredible deliberation that she held her breath. Waiting. Waiting. The heat and wetness between her legs building in anticipation.

And then his mouth began to lower again, descending a fraction of a millimeter at a time. Her eyes closed, an involuntary response because she truly wanted to watch what he was doing, and she couldn't. She could do nothing but anticipate what he would do next. She was powerless to resist him. Without will. Without control.

His lips finally settled around the areola, exactly as Gardner's had often done, and then he, too, began to suckle. With the first pressure, her lower body exploded, arching upward again and again into the hardness of his.

She was mindless with want. With need. And when his teeth delicately touched on either side of the sensitive nipple, nibbling erotically, she lifted her legs, locking them around his hips.

An effort to increase their closeness. To become one with him. Again and again she arched into his arousal as waves of sensation roared through her body. The roughness of his jeans rubbing against the skin of her inside thighs was as erotic as his callused palm had been. As erotic as his mouth moving over her breast.

But she wanted more. She wanted the heat of his sweat-dampened skin sliding against hers. His moisture jetting to join the torrent of hers. His body moving inside hers, driving away the pain and loneliness and need of the months she had been forced to exist without him.

Despite everything that now lay between them, all the hurt and lies and betrayals, nothing about this had changed. And she could no more deny what she felt for Griff than she had been able to deny herself the night she had come out of the fog to place her trembling hand in his. The night Gardner had been conceived.

Her fingers found the fabric of his shirt, tearing at it, desperate to pull it free of his jeans. She wanted to spread her fingers against the dark, hair-roughened chest. To move them slowly over the flat, ridged stomach. To slip the tips of them inside the low waistband of his jeans. To unfasten the metal buttons one by one until flesh met flesh.

"Claire," Griff whispered.

His mouth was no longer against her breast. The moisture it had left there was caressed by the breath released with her name, and she shivered with the subtle eroticism of that sensation.

"I need you so much," Griff said, his voice hoarse, the soft Virginia accent she had loved more pronounced.

A need she understood. And echoed.

"Tell me yes," he begged softly.

The words were almost shocking. Interrupting what had been happening. They seemed...out of place. Certainly out of place between the two of them.

She had *never* told him no. Not even the first time. And Griff had never before verbally asked her permission. He hadn't needed to, of course, and she wondered why he would believe he should now.

It confused her. And then it made her wonder. In all the years she had known him, Griff Cabot had never begged her for anything. Why would he now?

The frantic movements of her hands had stopped, her once-desperate fingers locked unmoving in the material of his shirt. *"I need you so much,"* he had whispered. A need based on his love for her? Or on something else? Something that had never before had any place in their relationship.

She had seen his despair when she had stood hesitantly at the door watching him. And had seen his pain when she had tried to convince him of Hawk's betrayal. Had Griff turned to her for comfort? Using her body for solace for failure and betrayal?

But whatever happened here, whatever happened between them, shouldn't be about comfort or loneliness. Not even about her fears for Gardner. If she and Griff made love again, it should only be about them. About how much they loved one another. Just as it had always been. And maybe...maybe this wasn't what tonight was about.

With her continued stillness, Griff pushed himself up, lifting his upper body away from hers to look down into her eyes. His were again cold. Dark and unreadable.

"Tell me yes," he had said. And she hadn't.

And still she didn't. No matter how much she wanted to make love to Griff, she knew it wasn't the time for this. It wouldn't solve any of the unresolved issues that lay between them. It would simply be another complication. And there were already enough of those in what was happening. More than enough complications.

"Claire?" Griff said softly. A question.

"No," she whispered.

No explanation. She couldn't have made one. Even she didn't fully understand why she hadn't said yes. Why she hadn't agreed to what they both wanted.

Griff nodded, his lips thinned, cruelly compressed. The same lips that had drifted so knowingly over her breast. Then he pushed away from her, the movement abrupt. Removing his body from all contact with hers.

The positions involved in making love are always slightly awkward, but there was something inherently more embarrassing about assuming them and then having to retreat from their intimacy. When she looked up, Griff was standing beside the bed, looking down on her. She realized that she was lying exactly where he had placed her, unmoving, her breast exposed, still damp with the moisture of his mouth.

Slowly, she pulled the straps of her bra and shell up over her shoulder again, her own movements clumsy now. An awkwardness between two people for which intimacy had never before been awkward. Or uncomfortable.

"I'm sorry," she whispered.

She rolled to her side and put her feet on the floor, sitting up on the edge of the bed. She realized that she was shaking. She wanted to stay here a moment, maybe put her head in her hands, as Griff had done.

But this was his room. His retreat. So she put her palms against the edge of the mattress and pushed up. Tiredly. Moving like an old woman. She expected him to try to stop her, but he didn't. He didn't move. He didn't say another word to her.

"Tell me yes," he had begged.

She hadn't.

And right now, at least, she supposed there were no other questions between them that really mattered.

Chapter Twelve

The cruiser was no longer moving. Perhaps that was what had awakened her, Claire thought, lying in the stifling darkness of her stateroom, listening to the silence. There was no lulling vibration of the powerful engines. She had been far too aware of their sound as she tossed and turned in this lonely bed after leaving Griff's cabin last night. Now there was no engine noise thrumming like a heartbeat through the hull. Which meant, she supposed, they were back in Miami.

That's where Griff had ordered Jake to take them last night. Back to where this misadventure had all begun. And, after too few hours of restless, nightmare-interrupted sleep, she was back again to wondering what happened next. And to the realization that she had no control over any of it.

Claire Heywood wasn't accustomed to feeling helpless. She had always had control. Of her career. Of her life. Always. Until someone opened a second story window on New Year's Eve and took her daughter. She closed her eyes, trying not to think about the images that had seethed in her brain last night.

Images of Gardner. Wondering if someone would make sure she was warm and hold her when she fretted. Wondering how they would know to sing the same lullabies to her as Claire had. Wondering if her baby were alone and frightened instead, somewhere in a darkness that matched this one.

Images of Hawk. Remembering her impressions of him, formed in the few times she had met him. Wondering if she were right to suspect him. Right to tell Griff what she believed. Wondering if Lucas Hawkins could really be cruel enough, vindictive enough, to have been the guiding hand behind Gardner's kidnapping and everything that had happened since.

And images of Griff... Those had been the hardest to deny. It was so hard to push all thought of him from her consciousness. Almost impossible because he was here. And because she knew that all she had to do to change what had happened between them was to go back to his cabin.

To open the door to that dark room where he was sleeping and let him make her forget. Forget the pain of this. At least for an hour or two. To have that respite from thinking about things she could do nothing about, all she had to do, she thought again, as she had thought so many times last night, was to go to him.

Instead, she closed her eyes, squeezing them tight against the burn of tears. She pushed her legs out from under the weight of the sheet. It was too hot, heavy against her bare skin and damp with the ever-present south Florida humidity.

She opened her eyes, turning her head toward the porthole, wondering if it were too early to get up. There was the faintest hint of gray in the blackness of the sky. It was not yet dawn. Which meant Jake was probably still asleep in the narrow crew cabin that had been built into the side of the pilothouse. As Griff almost certainly would be in his stateroom next door.

Next door, she thought. Next door. But of course, considering what had happened last night, he might as well be as far away from her as he had been before this all started.

She sat up on the edge of the bed, wondering about the oppressive heat. Maybe the air-conditioning didn't work if the engines weren't running. Or maybe Jake, sleeping topside, hadn't realized how hot it would be down here without it.

There would be a breeze on deck. At least there would be a breath of fresh air that wasn't contaminated by regret and worry, which seemed to have permanently thickened the atmosphere of this room. And it would do her good to watch the sun come up.

The promise of another day that, please, dear God, *had* to be better than the one that had just passed. Claire had always found a sense of renewal in watching the streaks of gold edge upward from beneath the rim of the ocean and push into a dark sky. Despite everything, she knew she would feel better watching that eternal phenomenon.

She stood up, not bothering to look for the robe she had bought to go with the thin cotton nightgown. There would be no one else on deck, and besides, part of the purpose of going up was to escape the heat and humidity. Putting on more clothes wouldn't accomplish that.

On bare feet, she crossed the floor to the door. Once there, she hesitated, unconsciously listening. There was nothing. No sound. Only a silence that seemed as deep as the unnatural stillness on the island had yesterday.

Pushing away the image of what she and Griff had found there, she opened her door and walked down the short, deserted companionway to the stairs, resisting the urge to look toward the door of Griff's room. As she climbed, the air around her seemed to freshen as well as brighten. She took a deep breath, savoring it.

Daylight was a little nearer than she had thought. Near enough that objects were almost discernible. As she watched, eyes adjusting, shapes began to form out of the surrounding darkness. The ghostly white hulls of the other cruisers in their moorings nearby. The outlines of the marina.

She walked over to the rail, her bare feet making no sound on the varnished deck. Or if they did, it was soft enough to be hidden by the low splash of the waves. No one was stirring on the nearby boats.

They would be soon, she decided, leaning against the rail. Pleasure boats or working boats, for most of them the day started at dawn and ended when the sun set. The water lapped seductively against the side of the yacht, a larger wave occasionally hitting the bottom rung of the ladder with a sharper, distinctive slap.

The monotony of sound was relaxing. She lifted her face, trying to let the salt-tanged breeze blow away the miasma of disappointment and worry that had oppressed her since there had been no kidnappers to meet them on the key. Griff had promised, she told herself. Promised her that no matter what, he'd get Gardner back. And she still believed that if anyone could—

There was a sound behind her. It was dark enough that she reacted just as she would have in the city, looking over her shoulder, eyes searching for whoever or whatever had made the noise. She expected to see Jake walking across the deck to join her. Or Griff, appearing at the top of the stairs, unshaven, the stubble of yesterday's beard on his lean cheeks, his eyes as tired as they had been last night.

There was no one. She turned all the way around to be sure. Her eyes moved across the cruiser, sweeping slowly from stern to bow. Everything looked eerie in the strange half-light of dawn, but it seemed there was nothing—and no one else—on deck.

Maybe the noise, whatever she had heard, had come from the yacht on the far side. She took a step in that direction, craning her neck to see if someone had come out on deck. Her bare toes bumped against something.

The object was small and light enough to go skittering across the polished deck as if she had deliberately kicked it. Curious, she bent, eyes searching in the near dawn dimness to find it. The defective transmitter, she realized. She picked it up, holding it up to the light. It must have fallen off when she and Jake had been struggling to get Griff on board.

A reminder of all that had gone wrong, she thought. A reminder she didn't need. She turned, intending to toss it over the side. She had raised her arm, poised to throw, when she realized there was no reason to add this to the other garbage polluting the ocean. She had seen more than enough flotsam during the hours she'd searched for Griff to understand how much was already out there.

Instead, she closed her fingers around the transmitter. She'd dispose of it later. Or give it to Jake. Maybe it could be fixed, although she wouldn't want to trust anyone's life to it again. She glanced toward the helm in response to the thought of handing the transmitter over to Jake.

Hawk was standing by the rail on the opposite side of the yacht. He was watching her, blue eyes luminescent in the darkness, his strong features set, composed and unsmiling. He must have just come over the side, she realized. That had been the noise she heard.

He was wearing jeans and nothing else. And he was barefoot. As hers had been, his footsteps would be silent crossing the deck. By intent, she realized. Silent by intent. Her eyes lifted slowly from his feet. When they reached waist level, they stopped again, no longer focused on Hawk or on what he was wearing, but on what he held in his hand.

It was a knife, as broad and long as a bowie knife. The blade turned slightly as he adjusted the grip of his hand on the haft. The moving blade caught a shaft of light from the rising sun, reflecting it onto the varnished planks.

Her heart jumped, literally skipping beats in its normal rhythm. Other than that fluttering pulsation, nothing about her body seemed capable of movement. Her terror, invoked by that subtle flicker of light off the edge of his knife, was paralyzing.

She had always hated the thought of blades. The thought of being cut. Some people feared being trapped in a fire. Or drowning. Some were terrified of airplanes. But her own personal phobia had always been a fear of being attacked in some dark alley. Of feeling a razor-edge blade slice into her skin.

Still unbreathing, she watched Hawk take a step toward her. He turned his head, looking toward the helm. She couldn't make her eyes follow his. Not even to see if Jake were there. Then Hawk looked toward the stern, blue eyes searching the length of the yacht, just as hers had done only seconds before.

When his gaze came back to her, his brows lifted, their meaning obvious. A question. Despite her fear, she certainly recognized the expression. She wasn't sure, however, exactly what he was asking. Where the others were? Did he really expect her to tell him that?

Slowly, she shook her head. He was Griff's friend, she told herself. Even the scenario she had described to Griff to explain what Hawk had done didn't mean she believed he would be angry enough, or crazy enough, to want to hurt the people who were on this cruiser. Jake was his friend. She had helped Hawk set up the meeting he wanted with Steiner. And Hawk had once been willing to die for Griff—or to kill for him. Surely now…

As he took another step away from the railing, his eyes again scanning his surroundings, he reminded her of some sleek predator. Totally alert. Looking for danger.

Looking for danger. For some reason the phrase echoed in her head. That was exactly what Hawk appeared to be doing, she realized. But why would he expect danger here?

Because he thought Jake or Griff would by now have figured out what he had done? After all, she had, and she wasn't nearly as skilled at this game as the two of them.

Was Jake still asleep? she wondered. And why not? So far there had been no sound. The cruiser, the whole marina, was as quiet as the island had been yesterday. Suddenly the unwanted image of Diaz's body was in her head. His throat cut from ear to ear. With the knife Hawk was holding?

With that thought, she took an involuntary step backward, pressing again the rail. Hawk's fair head tilted again. Listening to something? Or questioning her movement? Using the knife, he pointed at the stairs that led belowdecks.

Where Griff was sleeping. Was he looking for Griff? My God, could he be insane enough to want to do to Griff what he had done to Ramon Diaz? What someone had done, she amended, trying to think rationally, despite her terror.

This time she made no response to his question, not even the small negative movement of her head she had made before. He pointed again with the knife, stabbing it toward the companionway. Demanding information?

It was almost daylight, she realized. The sun was creeping up over the horizon behind her, illuminating the marina with its thin, pale light. Surely someone on one of the other boats would come up on deck soon and realize what was going on.

Or maybe, disturbed by the rising sun, Jake would stir, come out of the crew cabin and see Hawk. See the knife he held and understand what was happening. Jake never seemed to sleep. Surely—

"That's far enough," Jake said.

His voice was low, but commanding. Maybe Jake wasn't

one of the hotshots, as he had called Jordan and the others, but still, right now he seemed an answer to prayer. It was almost as if she had conjured him up with the force of her fear.

Somehow Claire managed to pull her eyes away from their terrified fascination with the knife and look to her left. To where Jake's voice had come from. He had come around the bridge, and she wondered how long he had been hiding there. Since before the first sound she had heard, of course. The narrow cabin where he slept was on that side of the cruiser, so Jake would have had more warning of Hawk's arrival than she.

Jake was on the same side of the yacht as she was, looking across the expanse of its deck at Hawk. And he was holding a gun. A big gun, which he held as if he knew what he was doing.

"Jake?" Hawk said, his tone questioning.

Surprised? Or trying to sound as if he were? Or trying to sound...innocent? Claire wondered.

"Are you all right?" Hawk asked. "We were worried that—"

"Put the knife down," Jake ordered, his words louder and more forceful than that first quiet command had been. The muzzle of the gun lifted a little, pointing at the center of Hawk's chest. "Bend your knees, arms out to your side, and lay the knife down on the deck. *Then* we can talk."

The cold blue eyes of the man they called Hawk held on Jake's face. He seemed to be considering the demand, but he didn't obey. For endless seconds nobody moved.

"Do it now," Jake said. "Don't *make* me have to shoot you, old buddy. I sure don't want to have to do that."

Despite that seemingly reassuring avowal, Jake's voice had hardened. Sharpened with certainty. And suddenly there was no doubt in Claire's mind that he would do exactly what he had threatened.

Hotshot or not, Jake Holt was a CIA agent. No one got to that position without the kind of training it would take to pull that trigger. The kind of courage necessary to put a bullet into the heart of a man he had once considered to be his friend. A man that he had evidently decided, as she had last night, might be an enemy instead.

Apparently Lucas Hawkins heard in Jake's voice the same quality Claire had heard. His arms moved slowly upward, lifting carefully away from his body. His eyes remained on Holt's face as they did. His knees began to bend, however, the powerful muscles in his thighs stretching the faded material of his jeans.

When Hawk had stooped as low as he could, his right arm began to lower, that movement as smooth and unhurried as the other had been. He laid the knife on the deck.

"Push it toward me," Jake directed, while Hawk's fingers were still touching the hilt. "Hard enough for it to get here."

There was a half second of hesitation before Hawk sent the knife sliding along the slick surface. It came to rest about two feet from Jake's right foot. Jake's eyes had never left their contemplation of the man who was still squatting, balancing on his bare toes, across the cruiser from him.

"Good job," Jake said softly.

His lips tilted a little as he made the compliment. The smile didn't have a warming effect on Hawk, whose lips were thinned and set, his eyes even colder.

Moving slowly, he began to reverse the process that had brought the knife close enough to the deck for him to leave it there. Arms again lifted slightly away from his sides, he pushed up out of the low squat until he was standing once more.

"What's going on?" he asked.

"You tell me, man," Jake countered softly. "You tell me what the hell's going on."

Hawk's eyes held their focus on Jake's face for a few seconds more before he nodded and began to talk. "When we got to the rendezvous, we were ambushed. They took Diaz and his bodyguards and left us tied up."

"Must have been a hell of an ambush," Jake said, sounding amused. Sarcastic. "Your reputations obviously hadn't preceded you."

He didn't believe Hawk's story, Claire realized. Jake had worked with these men for years, and of course, considering all she had heard about them, it would be pretty difficult for her to believe that someone could catch Hawk and Jordan unaware.

She had just seen a demonstration of the kind of caution Hawk would bring to an operation. No wonder Jake had his doubts about the scenario Hawk had described.

"We were expecting to meet Griff," Hawk said. "We weren't expecting a trap."

"Neither were we," Jake said.

"You had trouble?"

"You could say that," Jake said.

"Where's Griff?" Hawk asked.

For the first time, his eyes left Jake and moved back to the stairs that led below. Then they rose, finding Claire's.

"Griff downstairs?" he asked.

There was no doubt the question was directed at her. She just wasn't sure what Jake would want her to say. It was an obvious attempt to get information, but she wasn't sure why Hawk needed that particular piece. Just to place everyone? More of that habitual caution? Or because he was really concerned about Griff, which was what his tone implied?

In any case, she opted for saying nothing, waiting for Jake to step into the breach and tell Hawk whatever he wanted him to know. And after a second or two, he did.

"Griff's asleep. He had a pretty rough couple of days."

Hawk's eyes had remained on Claire, even after Jake answered the question he'd posed. And then, moving with what appeared to be a deliberate redirection, they went back to Jake's face. He had never once looked at the gun, which was still pointed, steady and unmoving, at his heart.

"What does that mean?" Hawk asked softly. "A rough two days?"

"Spending more than twelve hours in the sea for one thing," Jake said. "The transmitter didn't work. You got any explanation for that, Hawk?" Again there was an edge in Jake's voice. Mockery. Or a challenge.

"It worked when I checked it," Hawk said. "There wasn't a damn thing wrong with the transmitter when we left."

"Well, it didn't work when it needed to. And that's a real big ocean out there. Too frigging big to be lost in. If it hadn't been for Claire..." Jake shrugged.

Hawk's eyes came back to her face, quickly this time.

"That's why you weren't at the rendezvous," Hawk suggested, his own voice without inflection.

"We had a choice. We leave Griff out there or we miss picking you up," Claire said, wondering how long Hawk was going to pretend that he hadn't known any of this.

"And the kidnappers?" Hawk asked.

You tell me, she thought. That's exactly what she wanted to demand of him. *Tell me where my baby is, you bastard. Tell me how to get her back.*

She opened her mouth, and Griff's voice interrupted.

"What's going on?" he asked.

From where she was standing, she couldn't see him. Obviously, he was in the stairwell that led down to the companionway. Hawk was far enough away from the other rail that he probably *could* see Griff.

"He climbed over the side," Jake said. "Carrying a knife."

"We thought something must have gone wrong," Hawk said. "That something had happened to you. You didn't make the rendezvous, and we got ambushed when we did."

"Ambushed?" Griff repeated.

"Somebody sneaked up on Jordan and Hawk and tied them up," Jake said.

His voice was no longer sarcastic. Or amused, but somehow he still made it obvious he didn't believe Hawk's story. And obvious he didn't expect Griff to, either.

"Where's Jordan?" Griff asked, instead of commenting on the ambush.

"Trying to contact the kidnappers," Hawk said. "Trying to find the baby."

"And you came here to rescue us?" Griff asked.

Unlike Jake's, his voice was totally devoid of inflection. Even Claire, who knew him so well, couldn't read the emotion behind those words.

Hawk shrugged. "We thought you'd run into trouble, too. We thought the same kind of thing might have happened to you that had happened to us. I've been waiting to see if the yacht showed up back here."

"How did you get back to Miami?" Griff asked.

There was a fraction of a second's hesitation. Hawk's eyes went back to Jake before he answered, and when he did, Claire knew why.

"They left the skiff behind," he said.

"Whoever tied you up left the inflatable?" Jake asked, his tone openly disbelieving now. "How very considerate of them," he said, smiling. "That was just real convenient, old buddy. Wouldn't you say?"

It *was* a little ingenuous, Claire thought, but maybe it was the best Hawk could come up with. Maybe he hadn't ever intended to have to answer questions.

"What *I'd* say is that's exactly the way they planned it," Hawk said quietly, his voice controlled, not responding to

Jake's obvious incredulity. "Just exactly what they intended."

"Why?" Griff asked.

Hawk looked at him again. Griff was standing now at the top of the stairs. That air of being in charge, of being the one who had the right to ask the questions, emanated from him. Despite the fact that he was, as she had envisioned earlier, unshaven, and his eyes were as tired as she'd remembered them being last night.

"Setup," Hawk suggested, blue eyes focused on Griff's face, his voice still unemotional. "And I think I know who's behind it. Jordan and I have figured out who's been behind everything that's happened to all of us. And more importantly, Griff, we think we know why," he added.

Chapter Thirteen

Whether or not he had been right yesterday about the agency's intentions, Griff thought, watching Jake hold the semiautomatic on Hawk, the result of what they had done had been exactly what he'd feared. The destruction of the External Security Team had become a reality.

And that it was happening in this way seemed far more painful than the other would have been. All the bonds they had formed during the last ten years were being irreparably broken by the distrust that spread like a virus between them.

"Unless you're not interested in who's behind this," Hawk said softly.

Griff realized that Hawk had been waiting through his silence. Waiting for a response. For some indication that Griff wanted to hear whatever theory he and Jordan had devised. But Griff kept thinking instead about the one Claire had suggested last night. And, despite his feelings about Hawk, despite their friendship, about how much sense it had made.

"I'm interested," he said aloud.

Hawk nodded, the acknowledgment small, totally controlled, as was every action Lucas Hawkins ever took.

"This has to be Steiner," Hawk said.

Griff realized that after he'd appeared, some of Hawk's tension had eased. Of course, one would have to know

Hawk very well—and few people did, certainly not as well as Griff—to even recognize that he had been tense. Or to recognize that he'd relaxed as a result of Griff's appearance.

Griff wasn't entirely sure why that had happened. Because Hawk believed he would never allow Jake to pull that trigger? Or because he and Hawk had always been so close, closer perhaps than anyone else on the team? Griff knew the reason for that, although he had always recognized the dangers inherent in that closeness. In the jealousies it might foster. Hawk, however, had never had anyone else. Nothing besides the team. The next mission. And Griff's friendship. At one time those had comprised the whole of Lucas Hawkins's world.

They didn't anymore, of course. Hawk had found a woman who loved him, without any questions about who he was or what he had done. Like the rest of them, however, Jake Holt excluded, Hawk no longer had a profession. Or the missions. The friendships.

"Why do you think it's Steiner?" Griff asked, watching Hawk's face, a face he would have said only a week ago he could read like an open book. Somehow, that no longer seemed so easy.

"If they could get us to do this," Hawk said, "if they could make it appear we'd done it—that's all the excuse they'd need."

"Excuse for what?" Jake asked. "What the hell makes you think the bureaucrats ever need an *excuse* for what they do?"

"Because there are people who understand the value of what we did," Hawk said. "People who know *you*, Griff. And who aren't going to be so easily convinced that doing away with the External Security Team is the best thing for this country."

Jake's snort of laughter expressed his ridicule. It was

loud enough to be distracting, and Hawk's eyes briefly left their concentration on Griff to track back to Jake's face. His thin lips tightened before he went on.

"The oversight committees have read the reports. I think Steiner will have a hard time convincing them that there won't be a need for our kind of missions in the future."

More words than he'd ever heard Hawk put together before, Griff thought, resisting the urge to smile. Because he recognized that most of them were words he'd learned from Griff. *Standing guard.*

"Why now?" Griff asked.

After all, the decision to disband the unit had probably been made not long after the terrorist attack in which he'd been injured. A year ago.

"Somebody in a position to do something about it finally got wind of what they were planning," Hawk suggested.

"How?" Jake asked, the sarcasm that had been in his voice no longer there. It had been replaced by interest.

"Because they haven't been particularly discreet about their intentions for standing down the team," Hawk suggested. "Ms. Heywood's grandfather may have figured out what they were doing. You asked for his help in setting up that meeting with Steiner," Hawk said.

His eyes had shifted again from Griff's face, this time to focus on Claire's. Griff found his own gaze following Hawk's, and then he wished it hadn't. Deliberately, he hadn't looked at her since he'd come up from below, but he had known exactly where she was standing. He had been totally and completely aware of her position. Just as he had always been when they were in the same room. Completely and totally aware of everything about her.

She was on the other side of the deck from Hawk, with the rising sun behind her. The thin white cotton of her nightgown was made transparent by its light, the outline of her slender body clearly revealed.

And despite the seriousness of what was happening here, Griff's thoughts went back to last night. When she had lain on his bed and allowed him to touch her. Allowed him to see the changes the last year and a half had made in her body. Changes that had come as a result of the birth of a child they had conceived together. A baby who was now a pawn in a game that seemed to grow more complicated as each layer of motivation and corruption was peeled away.

"I asked for his help," Claire agreed, "but…I never told him what that was all about. And he never asked me," she said.

"Maybe because he had his own sources," Hawk suggested. "He knew Griff. With his connections, your grandfather had to be aware of exactly what Griff did for the agency. He probably knew that Steiner had taken Griff's place. Your request could have been enough to make him start asking questions. And questions from a former DCI about what they were doing with External Security would make a lot of people nervous. Your grandfather has been a player in Washington politics for half a century."

"Nobody has better connections than an old spook," Claire said softly.

That was a truism often repeated in the capital, maybe because it *was* so damn true, Griff thought.

"But even if that's what happened," he said, "even if Claire's grandfather asked questions they didn't want to answer, how does kidnapping Gardner fit into that?"

"Taking your daughter—Ms. Heywood's daughter," Hawk amended, "was guaranteed to get you involved. Guaranteed to make you take the bait. To force you to kill Diaz. They know they have to discredit *you* in order to discredit the team."

Hawk's voice was softer than it had been before. But the conviction in it seemed just as sincere. His eyes had been on Griff as he made that argument. And then he glanced again at Claire before he went on.

"And it might also have been intended as...a reminder to your grandfather. A warning that no matter how much influence he has, he can't protect his own family. He can't protect anybody. Not if they really want to get to them." The silence that fell after those words was broken when Hawk added quietly, "And maybe it was even a warning to you."

"To me?" Claire said. "A warning to *me?*"

"You threatened Steiner with going public about what they were doing to me."

Griff hadn't known that, but he wasn't surprised. That was exactly the kind of courage Claire had always had. The same courage it had taken to constantly challenge him. To make him argue the right and the wrong of what he did. If she really had threatened Steiner—

"And then you helped Jordan gather the media when he needed them to turn over the money Sorrel took," Hawk added. "Maybe Steiner just figured he ought to remind you of the nature of the league you'd chosen to play in."

A tough, dirty league, Griff acknowledged. Tougher and dirtier than anything Claire Heywood had ever faced in her entire life. And the agency was certainly capable of issuing that kind of warning. In this case, however, Griff didn't believe anything they had done had been intended as a threat to Claire. Or to her grandfather, although he didn't doubt that the old man was capable of digging deeper than they would be comfortable with.

Griff believed this had all been arranged with him as the target. Because he had dared to question their intentions for his men. And because they were people who didn't like being questioned. Griff had known that all along. He just hadn't dreamed they would retaliate against his family. Even as the word formed in his mind, he recognized that he had no right to use it. He and Claire weren't a family, despite the fact that they had conceived a child. A child who, even now...

"Put it away, Jake," he ordered quietly, remembering the mission. But Jake's gaze didn't falter from the man he was targeting. And the muzzle of the Glock didn't lower.

"Griff," Claire protested.

"Hawk had nothing to do with this," Griff said to her. "He thinks he's the cause of it, but he isn't even right about that. And if you couldn't hear what was in his voice when he talked about your standing up to Steiner on his behalf, then you're not nearly as intuitive—or as intelligent—as you used to be."

He had allowed a thread of amusement into that explanation, intending it to reassure her, just as listening to Hawk had reassured him. Hawk had nothing to do with Gardner's kidnapping. Griff would stake his life on that. It was obvious the others thought he was.

"He had a knife," Jake said, the focus of his gun unchanged. And unchanging. "He came up over the side, Griff, barefoot and carrying a knife."

"He thought we'd been victims of the same people who attacked him and Jordan. This was a rescue, Jake, not an assassination."

Assassination seemed to reverberate through the suntouched air that shimmered between them. Griff wished he had been more careful in his choice of words. Because that was exactly what Hawk did, of course. Assassinations. That had been his job in the years he'd been with the team. He had assassinated a few madmen—including the one with the suitcase nukes.

It was what he had done in Baghdad. That time to revenge the death of those senselessly killed at Langley. To avenge Griff's death. Which had not, of course, been a death at all.

"Claire thinks I owe you an explanation for the CIA's version of my retirement," he said.

"You don't owe me anything, Griff," Hawk said softly. "You never have."

There was far more unspoken in that quiet statement. A lot of memories hidden in that soft, deep voice. Memories of a mission that had gone wrong. Of a long, unpleasant recuperation in Virginia, which Hawk had silently endured. As he had endured Griff's inept nursing. And maybe a long delayed acknowledgment of friendship that had been offered to a bitter loner long before there was any sign that it might be reciprocated. Acknowledgment of things they had never before seen any need to express because they both understood them so well.

"Put the gun down, Jake," Griff ordered again, his voice even lower than it had been before.

This time, however, his words had an effect. Slowly Jake lowered the weapon he held. Then he turned and walked over to the rail near where Claire stood, every motion an indication that was an order he had unwillingly obeyed.

"What if you're wrong?" Claire asked.

Griff looked at her, pulling his gaze from Hawk's face, more than satisfied by what he had seen there.

"I'm not," he said simply. And then he smiled at her. "But you're more than welcome to argue the point."

His sudden surety about Hawk was like a weight lifted from his spirits. Maybe things had gone wrong. Maybe he had made mistakes. But not about this. And the people he would have staked his life on when this started were, thank God, unchanged.

"You have to know that *someone*—"

"Not Hawk," he denied, breaking into her disclaimer, despite the invitation he had just issued. This wasn't the time or the place for the debate he'd invited.

"This is my daughter's *life*," Claire argued.

"My daughter as well," Griff said. "I haven't forgotten."

Perhaps because she knew him so well, well enough to recognize the implacable quality of his voice, she didn't try to plead the case she had made last night. Instead, she walked across the deck toward Hawk. She stopped just before she reached him, looking up into his harsh features.

Although Claire was tall for a woman, Hawk topped her by at least six inches. He met her eyes, unflinching before their assessment. She studied his face for a long, silent minute.

Finally, she shook her head, moving it from side to side only once or twice. Not so much, Griff believed, a denial of what he had said as an indication of her own uncertainty. She had turned away, starting toward the stairs that led belowdecks, when she hesitated, turning back to face Hawk again.

"Here," she said.

She held out her hand, fingers cupped downward over what it held. Automatically, Hawk held his out, palm up. Claire placed the transmitter on his outstretched hand.

"A souvenir," she said softly, her tone bitter.

Without waiting for a response, she turned again and walked across the deck to the stairwell. Griff moved out of her way, but she didn't even meet his eyes as she went by.

Hawk was still looking at the object that rested in his palm. Then he closed his fingers over it and raised his eyes to Griff's.

"Is Jordan where you can reach him?" Griff asked.

"I can try," Hawk said after a small delay, after seeming to think about it.

"Can you do it from here?"

Hawk nodded, walking toward the helm. Griff glanced to his left, where Jake was still standing at the rail, his back to them, shoulders stiff. With anger? he wondered. Or with resentment over having his judgment questioned?

When Hawk got to the helm, he reached toward the bank of instruments and turned a dial. Immediately there was a small steady beep, the sound soft, but very clear in the dawn stillness. Hawk's brows lifted slightly, blue eyes finding Griff's again. His mouth moved, one corner lifting.

"Your locator seems to be working," he said.

"Damn cold comfort," Griff said. "And just a little late."

"That's what I heard," Claire said, her voice coming from behind him. "That night," she said. "I came up here after the explosion, and as I was coming up the stairs I heard that sound."

The three of them listened to the small steady message the beacon was sending out. The same message it had apparently been sending the night Griff had exploded Diaz's private jet and parachuted out of it into the emptiness of that cold, dark sea.

"I heard it," she whispered. "And then Jake reached out and touched something and...the sound stopped."

He should have reacted sooner, Griff thought, when his eyes swung to find Jake. Because Jake certainly had. But then Jake had probably known exactly what was going to happen as soon as he heard the first beep of the beacon's transmission.

By the time he and Hawk had figured out what Claire's words implied, it was too late to do much about it. Nothing beyond staring at the dark eye of the weapon Jake was once again holding, competently directed this time at the two of them.

"Join them, Ms. Heywood," Jake ordered, "or I'll put a bullet in his kneecap. The good one," he added softly.

Considering all that had already happened, including Diaz's brutal murder, no one could afford to doubt Jake would do exactly what he had threatened. Griff didn't. And his stomach tightened, guts clenching in sick anticipation.

Apparently, Claire didn't doubt Jake's threat, either. She walked across the deck, putting herself in Jake's sight. And in the line of fire.

"Thank you," Jake said softly when she had joined them. "Now if we only had Jordan here…" he suggested, the thin edge of sarcasm back in his voice, touched now with triumph as well.

Because he had bested the hotshots? Griff wondered. Had that familiar raillery, which they had all dismissed as Jake's way of putting them in their place, played any part in this? *Jake's way,* Griff thought, fighting the same sense of failure Claire's accusations of Hawk had caused last night. It had been Jake all along. One of his team.

The problems associated with this particular mission had been Jake's doing. And perhaps he had been involved with what had happened to Jordan, as well. Maybe even with what they'd done to Hawk. Jake had certainly been in a position to affect the outcome of those events.

Suddenly, he remembered Carl Steiner telling him that it had been Jake who had confirmed that Sheik al-Ahmad's assassination was an extremist plot. Which was the reason Steiner had released Tyler Stewart from protection and almost gotten her killed.

"Why, Jake?" Griff asked. Why would he endanger people he had worked with for more than ten years?

"Because I got tired of the bureaucratic BS," Jake said, his voice seeming too calm to reflect enough anger or resentment to enable him to do what it was obvious now that he had done.

"We're not the bureaucrats," Griff said.

"This had nothing to do with you, Griff."

"Nothing to do with me?" Griff asked, his voice incredulous. "It's my *daughter* they took, Jake. Or are you saying you weren't in on that?"

He thought about that possibility, but if Jake had used the transmitter to keep them from making the rendezvous with Hawk and Jordan, obviously to give his fellow conspirators a chance to get to Diaz, then he had to have been in on this from the beginning.

"Nothing's happened to the baby," Jake said. "Harming her was never part of the plan."

"Then what exactly *was* the plan? What the hell has been going on here?"

"You don't have a clue, do you, Griff? But then I shouldn't be surprised. You never had a clue about what it's like for the rest of us. They screw you over, they destroy you, and you retire and live out your life in luxury. They screw us, and we stay screwed. I didn't like that."

"So you target the rest of *us?*"

"There's nothing personal about this," Jake said. "None of you were ever the targets of what I did."

"And now?" Griff asked quietly, allowing his eyes to fall to the Glock. "Aren't we the targets now?"

Jake didn't answer, and in the waiting silence, they could hear subtle sounds beginning to emanate from the boats moored around them. Their occupants were starting to stir. Maybe even to come out on deck. And soon, someone would notice what was going on here.

"It wasn't supposed to be this way," Jake said finally. His voice had lowered, perhaps in recognition of what was taking place on the boats around them.

"How *was* it supposed to be?"

"I had something coming to me. But I watched what those bastards were doing to the others, and I knew that unless I did something, it wasn't going to happen for me. Not unless I made it happen. But nobody on the team has been hurt by what I did. Not Jordan. Not you."

"And Tyler Stewart?" Griff asked. "You're the one who told Steiner to release her. You had to know what would happen to her when you did."

Beside him, he felt Hawk move. A start of reaction, small enough that it would have been indiscernible to the others.

"I thought if Steiner believed it was just regional politics, he'd see that he didn't have any legitimate reason to hold Hawk. As soon as I realized that idiot had released her, I called Jordan. What happened at the airport..." Jake shrugged. "You can't hold me responsible for Ahmad's insanity."

"And what happened to Jordan?" Griff asked. "Or can't you be held responsible for that, either?"

Jake's denial of his responsibility for Jordan's situation was several seconds longer in coming than it should have been.

"You son of a bitch," Hawk said softly as the silence stretched. "You set Jordan up. That whole deal was a setup."

Hawk didn't move, however, despite the fury in his quiet voice. Griff thanked Hawk's habitual control for that—a control that had been acquired the hard way.

"Nothing happened to Jordan," Jake said, seeming to be trying to make his case to Hawk now. "I saw to that."

"You *saw* to it?" Hawk repeated unbelievingly. "You were controlling things? You were up there playing God with people's lives?"

People's lives, Griff thought. Jordan's life. And the lives of the Sorrel family, which included a couple of small children. And apparently—

"Jordan rescued Sorrel's wife and kids," Jake asserted. "He got them out of a situation they'd been living in for three years. Nobody else could have done that. And nobody was hurt."

"Except an FBI agent named Helms," Griff said.

"Helms was willing to take his chances."

For a sixteen-million-dollar payoff. A lot of people would have been willing to take their chances. Including Jake Holt.

"You and Helms were in on that together," Hawk suggested.

They had to have been, Griff realized. And that's how Helms had found Jordan and the Sorrel family at the Virginia mansion. Not through an outside invasion of Jake's computers, as Jordan had thought, but through Jake.

"You did it all for the money, Jake?" Griff said unbelievingly.

For the Mafia's sixteen million dollars. Money that everyone else was looking for. Except Jake Holt had the inside track. Insider information. And he had had Jordan's friendship and trust, as well.

It had taken him too long to put this all together, Griff conceded. It had taken all of them too long. Distracted by what he had known were the agency's intentions for his people, he hadn't been aware of the traitor in their midst. A traitor who had tried to use the skills of the team Griff had built to provide for his own retirement, something Jake obviously believed was impending. Except, of course, his situation was different from the rest of them. Because Jake wasn't one of the hotshots.

"You could have written your own ticket, Jake," Griff said. "Whatever the agency did with the rest of us, they weren't going to let you go. You're too valuable to them."

Jake laughed, the sound short and bitter. "Like I said. It's okay for you to work all your life for the company rate and a miserable little pension when it's over. The rest of us weren't born with any silver spoons in our mouths. And I don't intend to analyze satellite data in a hole in the wall at Langley for the rest of my life."

For *money*, Griff thought again. He really had done it all

for money. But of course, Jake was right about a part of that. Griff had never needed the salary the agency paid him. Just as he hadn't needed the generous pension they had given him when they had put him out to pasture.

And as soon as they had, they had begun dissolving his team and retiring his men. The beginnings of this hadn't been Jake, of course, although the agency's own disloyalty seemed to have set him off.

"Where's my daughter?" Claire asked, breaking into his useless self-recrimination.

Jake's eyes focused briefly on her face before they came back to concentrate on the men, whom he wisely saw as the greater threat. "Somewhere safe," he said.

"Did you do what Hawk said?" Claire asked. "Did you try to use Gardner to discredit the team? To embarrass the agency?"

"His motives weren't quite that noble, Ms. Heywood," Hawk said. "How much was the contract on Diaz, Jake? How much did you stand to make on this?"

"What do you care?" Jake asked. "You didn't do the hit. Nobody owes you."

"And when you found out that Griff wasn't willing to kill Diaz, you told whoever had put out the contract where to find us. And you gave them Diaz, bound and gagged, so they could do it themselves."

"Actually, they kind of liked it that way," Jake said. "A little bad blood between the parties involved. And nobody got hurt," he added.

"Nobody but Diaz," Hawk reminded him softly.

"You know, old buddy, I find concern for Diaz pretty funny coming from you," Jake said. "Diaz deserved to die every bit as much as those bastards you lined up in your sights and blew away."

"That was never my decision," Hawk said.

"No, it was always Griff's decision. Based on information *I* supplied. Situations *I* analyzed. Based on *my* assessment of the threat they presented. And there was nothing different about this one. So let's don't pretend to be sentimental over some scumbag drug runner, Hawk. Morality doesn't become you, good buddy. It doesn't really become any of us. Not after the things we've been a part of through the years.''

"If you felt that way—" Griff began, only to be cut off.

"None of your sermons, Griff. I've had a bellyful of those, too. Sanctimonious defenses of just exactly what I did to Diaz. I made my choices. And you made yours. Who's to say one was better than the other? They're all still dead. There aren't going to be any resurrections.''

Griff said nothing, his eyes on a man he had known for ten years and had realized only now he hadn't known at all. Maybe he hadn't really known any of them.

Hawk's hands were clenched at his sides. But after his small, involuntary reaction to the knowledge that Jake had been responsible for what almost happened to Tyler, he hadn't moved.

"Now what?'' Claire asked softly.

Not the ideal question in this situation, Griff thought, but she couldn't know that. He just didn't want Jake pressured into making any sudden choices. They might not be the right ones.

"We get the hell out of here,'' Jake said. "Before somebody gets curious.''

"What about Jordan?'' Griff asked.

"I'll deal with Jordan later,'' Jake promised. "Take her out, Griff,'' he ordered. "We're going back out to sea. And once we're there…'' He hesitated, thinking about his narrowing options. "Once we're there, *I'll* decide what we do next.''

Chapter Fourteen

"I'm afraid it isn't going to be quite that easy, Jake."

Only Jake didn't react to the quiet voice they all recognized. The eyes of the other three lifted to find Jordan Cross standing on the flybridge of the cruiser in the next bay. He held a rifle, sighted carefully at the back of Jake Holt's head.

Griff supposed he should have been expecting Jordan to show up. If they suspected something had gone wrong on the cruiser, Hawk and Jordan wouldn't have split forces. They would have done exactly what it appeared they had. They would have come at the situation from two angles, prepared to back each other up.

Griff didn't know how long Jordan had been up there. Since the beginning? Since Hawk had come over the side? Or maybe the sounds he had heard seconds earlier had been Jordan climbing to his perch.

With Claire on deck, he had never allowed his concentration to waver from Jake and the gun he held, always prepared to put his body between hers and a bullet. Whenever Jordan had arrived, however, it was obvious that he had been up there long enough to figure out what was going on.

And Jordan, of course, had been as much affected by Jake's treachery as he and Claire had been. Maybe more so, Griff acknowledged, remembering what had happened at the summer house. Jordan had taken a bullet from Helms in order to protect the Sorrel children.

"Put the gun down, Jake," Jordan ordered softly. "This is over. Even you have to realize that. You can't kill us all."

"I can take one of them out before you can squeeze that trigger," Jake said, his voice still calm, seemingly unaffected by the threat Jordan represented. "I'd even be willing to let you choose which one it's going to be."

That offer was sheer bravado, designed to make Jordan think about the reality that one of them would be dead, no matter how fast he got off his shot. Jake would have already selected his primary target—long before Jordan's challenge.

And of course, Jordan should have killed Holt outright instead of talking to him. That's how it *should* have been done. How any professional would have handled this. Jordan, of course, realized the dangers inherent in trying to do it this way. In trying to make Jake see he couldn't win. And that there could be no going back to how it had once been.

Somehow, however, Griff found he couldn't fault Jordan for choosing not to shoot Jake in the back. He, too, would have had a hard time putting a bullet into the back of any one of them. And Jake and Jordan had been friends for a long time, a friendship that was maybe as close as his and Hawk's.

Which was why Jake had been able to get away with what he had done when he'd sent Jordan to find the Mafia's sixteen million dollars. Of them all, Jordan was the best equipped for that job. Jake had known that. He had used Jordan's skills then just as he'd intended to use the skills of the team to kill Diaz and collect on the contract. And his plans had worked in both cases because they had trusted him.

Holt's gun didn't waver as he waited for Jordan's response. From where Jordan stood, Griff knew it would have been hard to say which of the three Jake was targeting. It was even hard for him to be sure.

Not Claire, Griff thought, the unspoken words almost a prayer. It would be him or Hawk. There had been enough underlying bitterness in the things Jake had said to see either of them the focus of his resentment. And his target.

Griff, because he had been born with everything Jake had plotted and schemed and betrayed to acquire. And Hawk? Maybe because he was what Jake had never been. One of the hotshots. Jake had undertaken only one mission, which had come down, finally, to this moment.

"You can kill one of them," Jordan agreed. "I'm not Hawk, but I'm still good enough that I won't miss, Jake. Not from this distance. You said you never intended to hurt any member of the team. That you had tried to take care of us. If that's true, why kill one of us now?"

Jake didn't respond, but the muzzle of the gun he held didn't shift a millimeter. Neither did Jordan's.

"It's over, Jake," Jordan said. "Nothing you've done so far is a capital offense. Even in Diaz's death you're probably only an accessory. But if you do this—"

Jake laughed, the sound as harshly derisive as that he had made earlier. "Wrong threat, old buddy," he said. "Wrong argument."

And then the gun he held began to move.

It wasn't Jordan who reacted. It was Griff who started across the deck, but of course, he never had a chance of reaching Jake in time to prevent what was about to happen. Even though Jake's hand seemed to be moving in slow motion as Griff ran toward him, his uneven gait making the desperate sprint awkward, he knew he'd never get there in time. The muzzle continued to lift inexorably toward its target.

"Jake!" Griff shouted.

The protest was too late, of course, sounding almost on top of the gun's report. Even in the open air the noise of the shot was shocking.

Not as shocking as the sight of Jake, his mouth closed around the barrel of the Glock, slumping onto the mahogany deck. His fingers, instructed by some dying reflex of nerves and muscles sent from his shattered brain, seemed unable to release their hold on the weapon, not even in death.

At the shot, Griff had stopped so suddenly he skidded on the polished boards. He knew that this image would linger forever in his head. Etched on his memory by his sense of failure, which was as strong now as the acid of Jake's betrayal.

"Jake," he said softly, regretfully. The whispered name had no more effect than his shout had had. And then he closed his eyes, at least physically blocking the sight. Because, just as Jordan had said, it really was all over.

THEY HAD HAD TO DEAL with the authorities, of course. Jake's death had been too public an event to avoid that. The gunshot had shattered the peaceful south Florida morning as effectively as it had blown out the top of Jake's skull.

And it had been sheer, blind luck that they had been able to avoid a media circus as well. The only reason they had was that the cops arrived before the cameras. Although it was obvious Jake's death had been a suicide, after the gunshot enough people had seen Jordan on the flybridge of the next boat, rifle pointing downward, to cause the authorities to take them all in.

None of them was carrying any official identification. If it hadn't been for Carl Steiner's long-distance intervention with the locals, Claire thought, they would probably still be answering questions back in Miami.

"Tell them as much of the truth as you can," Griff had advised before the police arrived. And that's exactly what she had done. Told them the truth. That Jake had been involved in the kidnapping of her daughter. That they had been in south Florida to pay the ransom the kidnappers had demanded.

Exactly what that ransom demand had been was something she knew Griff and his men would never disclose. If they did, it might lead back to the team. And eventually to the agency. In their loyalty to the CIA, they would see that as a betrayal. And so, for some reason, Claire hadn't told the cops what they had been asked to do in order to get her daughter back, either.

Not because she had any loyalty to the CIA. But Ramon Diaz was dead. So was Jake, who wouldn't, of course, now benefit from Diaz's death. And she had never known who'd put the contract out on Diaz's life. Or where they had taken Gardner.

That was a secret Jake Holt would take to his grave. Just as Jordan had said, it was all over. And they still didn't have any idea where Gardner was.

Claire closed her eyes, turning her head toward the dark window of the plane, so that if she couldn't conquer the almost constant urge to cry, at least no one would see her. She wasn't sure why that mattered anymore.

She had acknowledged, to herself at least, that her courage was broken, her hope that they would find her baby almost too faint to allow her to go on. For some reason, however, she was determined that those hard men who were flying back to the capital with her wouldn't be allowed to see her cry.

Griff's fingers closed around hers, lifting her hand from where it had lain throughout the flight, cold and unmoving, in her lap. She didn't resist the gesture, but she didn't respond to it, either.

Illogically, she had again been blaming Griff. He should have known, she thought. Jake Holt was his man, a member of his precious team. And Griff should have known what was going on.

"We have more to work with than we did before," Griff said softly. "That house on the key, for one thing. We'll run the ownership records. It should give us somewhere to start. When we figure out who would benefit the most from Diaz's death, we'll have an idea about who put out the contract Jake accepted. The DEA is already working on that."

She turned her head to look at him. Maybe to tell him that it wasn't enough. Or that all this was his fault. His fault for knowing the Jake Holts of the world. For associating with them. For trusting them.

When she looked into Griff's eyes, she realized that whatever she was feeling, whatever pain and anger choked her heart, making her chest too tight to take the next breath, she couldn't say any of those things to Griff. Not now.

His eyes were as haunted as hers. She had caught a glimpse of herself in the mirror of the police station rest room, and startled by the stranger who appeared there, she had turned back to examine her reflection, too clearly illuminated by the garish fluorescent lighting.

Someone else's face stared back at her. Eyes that had seen too much horror and were imagining more. Skin that beneath its superficial tan was as gray with fatigue, as lined with worry, as Griff's was.

And so she nodded, clamping her lips over the bitter, accusing words she wanted to throw at him. Intellectually, she knew this wasn't Griff's fault. This was simply the world he had always warned her about. And she had denied what he said, never believing that its evil could touch her life. Or her daughter's.

"Claire," he said softly.

"Don't," she whispered, too angry and disillusioned to deal with this rationally. To deal with him. "Just...don't."

Don't make me any promises. Or tell me any more lies. Just get my baby back. And then... Maybe then...

She was unsure what the "then" that had formed in her head would be. Or even what it *could* be. So she turned her eyes back to the window and the night sky and tried very hard not to think. Not to think about anything. Especially not about Gardner.

"WE GO PUBLIC," Claire's grandfather suggested. "We flood the media with pictures of Jake Holt, together with pictures of Gardner. And we ask anybody who's seen either one of them, but especially anyone who has seen them together, to call."

They were sitting around the kitchen table of Claire's house in Georgetown three days after their return from Florida. Its familiarity should have been comforting, she thought, but nothing had felt familiar since she'd been home.

Her world no longer existed—the one she had once occupied. The one where babies slept safely in their cribs. Where the worst thing she had to worry about was whether the house was warm enough or whether she'd get home in time to spend an hour or two with Gardner before the nanny put her down for the night.

Now the image of Jake's body, the back of his skull blown away, was her world instead. The reality of a trusted friend's betrayal. The mutilated corpse of Ramon Diaz was there as well. Diaz, who might have been killed by the same people who had taken Gardner. And if that were true...

"I'm not sure that will do any good," Jordan said.

"Has anything else done any good?" Claire asked.

She regretted the bitterness in her voice. She knew Griff would believe she was still blaming him. She was past that now. Her sense of fair play, or her logic maybe, had reasserted itself. It wasn't Griff's fault that he had trusted Jake Holt.

After all, that was what she had railed at him for so often in the past. For *not* trusting. For believing people were capable of the things his team was supposed to guard against. But if one of his vaunted team could do these despicable things, then what hope was there for the rest of the world?

Of course, that was an old argument. One she had made to him during their last quarrel—that Griff and his team were no better than the people they were fighting against.

"What could it hurt?" Hawk asked, his deep voice considering. "Besides sending Steiner and the agency ballistic."

"For one thing, it will bring out the crackpots to muddy the waters with a lot of false information—all of which would have to be investigated," Griff said. "It might be better to concentrate on the legitimate leads we have."

"Which have led exactly nowhere," Claire said, her bitterness more open this time. She was sorry about that when Griff's eyes lifted quickly to her face.

The FBI had discovered that the house where they found Diaz's body had once belonged to Jake's family. Jake had lived there when he was a child. But as far as they'd been able to ascertain, he had never returned to the island where he'd grown up. Not until he'd put this plan into action.

And as for tracing the people who had put out the contract on Diaz, the DEA was still working on that. There were a dozen emerging potential rivals for Diaz, all of whom would probably like to get in on what he had put together. And all of whom had enough money to make them suspects. So it seemed to her that she and the others were right back where they'd started.

"Doing what your grandfather suggests would also mean a further loss of privacy for you and the baby," Griff said.

For you and the baby. No mention of his role in their future. Her eyes searched his face, but she could read nothing there. Nothing but professional detachment.

"You're afraid this would make them...more vulnerable," Hawk suggested. "Afraid someone else might try the same thing. Maybe not for the same reasons," he added.

"Up until this happened, Claire had kept the baby out of the spotlight," her grandfather said. "Virtually no one knew of her existence. No one but family and close friends. It didn't seem to make much difference."

No one knew of her existence. No one except Jake Holt, Claire thought. She remembered Jordan's words: *Jake knows everything.* He had known Griff was alive, maybe from backtracking Griff's invasion of the CIA's computer system, although he'd denied that. Or maybe from the message Griff had sent to the director just before this had all begun. And he had known about Gardner, the second piece of information he had needed to bring this off. Then he'd just used his computers to interrupt Claire's security system and he was on his way.

"With all due respect, sir," Griff said quietly, "I don't think anything Claire could have done would have made a difference in what happened."

"Because Holt was really targeting you?" Monty Gardner suggested, his eyes piercing, the intelligence behind them still obvious and demanding, despite his age.

"I'm not even sure that's true. At least not the whole truth. Jake Holt was brilliant, but...there were a lot of things going on under the surface that none of us suspected. But...maybe it wasn't about any of us. Maybe it was just what he said it was. Just about the money."

"But *you* don't believe that," Claire's grandfather suggested.

No one said anything for a long time, and then Griff said, "Ultimately...I'm not sure I do."

The old man nodded, and then he turned to look at Claire. "It seems to me we've got nothing else to lose, my dear," he said. "And everything to gain. Cabot's right, however, about the loss of privacy. About future threats. And especially about the crackpots. They'll come out of the woodwork. So...I think it must be your decision."

Nothing to lose. And everything to gain, she thought. First she had lost Griff. And then Gardner. Her grandfather was right. She really had nothing else to lose.

She knew that if they didn't succeed in getting Gardner back, then nothing could ever be the same between her and Griff. Not because she wouldn't want it to be, but because she understood Griff Cabot well enough to know that he would never be able to forgive himself for that failure.

Most marriages didn't survive the loss of a child. And she and Griff didn't even have a legal connection that would have to be dissolved. Griff would just disappear. He would go out of her world. Disappear from her life. Again.

She knew now that wasn't what she wanted. What she really wanted was to go back to how things had been before. Such a simple phrase for all it encompassed. Back to what she and Griff had once had. Back to being Gardner's mother. Back to the idealism about the world that had seemed so easy and so noble.

Maybe she could never go back to the last, but it still seemed that she had to pursue every avenue available to get Gardner back. And then Griff. *Nothing else to lose. And everything to gain.*

"Do it," she said softly. "Put Gardner's picture on the front of every newspaper and on every TV station that beams a signal out tonight," she said, looking around the table. "A description of what she was wearing. A description of anything about her that might make someone realize…"

Her throat closed suddenly over the rest of it. *That might make someone realize they have my baby.*

"And I want Jake Holt's picture right beside hers," she added, controlling that first surge of emotion with her anger over what Holt had done to them all.

Her grandfather nodded approval. Neither Jordan or Hawk said anything. She could imagine what the CIA would feel about making Jake's identity and his role in the kidnapping public. They would be afraid, of course, that somehow the media would trace Holt back to them. Maybe even back to the unit known as the External Security Team.

But she didn't care how Carl Steiner would feel. And by the time he had a chance to do anything about it, this could already be accomplished. That would be up to Griff.

"Can you do that?" she asked him. "Can you give them Jake's picture? And tell them his name?"

His eyes held hers, the concern in their dark depths obvious. He probably knew how fragile her control was. After all, he knew her so well. He knew, and understood, everything about her.

"I can do it," he said softly.

And he would. She was certain Griff would do what he'd promised. He'd do exactly what she'd asked, no matter what Steiner or anybody else in the CIA thought about it.

"THE CLOTHES ARE different," Detective Minger said, "but that doesn't mean anything. They probably bought everything they gave this woman new. Just in case."

"But you really think this is Gardner?" Claire said softly, her voice strained.

Griff understood her caution, of course. They had almost been afraid to hope. Although, with Claire's connections, the media outlets had given the news release a lot of play, the pictures of Jake Holt had been out there less than six hours when they got Minger's call.

"Let's just say we haven't discovered anything to make us think she might *not* be. She seems to be just what she claims. She even gave us references from people whose children she'd cared for in the past," he said, his voice touched with amusement. "There's nothing in the computers about her. She doesn't seem like a crazy, and believe me, I've got radar where those are concerned. We all do around here. We think she's the real thing, Ms. Heywood, although I should warn you we're still checking out her story. And of course, we can't be sure about any of the rest of it until you ID the baby," he added softly.

The crux of the matter, Griff realized. And why they had been sent for. Claire's identification would end this entire episode as far as the cops were concerned. Minger had already been told what had happened in Florida. Not all of it, but as much as the Miami police knew.

"Of course," Claire said.

Her eyes left Minger's and found Griff's. In them he read all that he was feeling. Hope, of course. And the fear that this wouldn't be what they were hoping for. That in spite of what Minger said, in spite of his reaction to the woman who had called, this might not be what they had been praying for.

"She's naturally concerned that she'll be in trouble," Minger said. "But as far as we can tell, she really is innocent. Totally unaware of what was going on. And we've had a doctor check out the baby, Ms. Heywood. If this *is* your daughter, she's none the worse for her experience. And if she is your baby, I think you'll have to thank this woman for that."

"If this is Gardner," Claire said quietly, "I assure you I intend to."

"Do you think we can see her now?" Griff asked.

Minger had explained enough. It was time to do this before Claire reached her breaking point, something he had been anticipating since Jake's death. Griff wasn't sure how much more she could take. With the question, Minger's eyes shifted to his face, probably wondering who the hell he was and why he was here.

"You want to see the woman?" he asked.

"We want to see the baby," Griff corrected.

There would be time enough for expressing gratitude. *If* Minger was right. But right now...

"Of course," Minger said. "I'll have them get her."

He picked up the phone on his desk and punched one of the buttons. "Bring the kid up," he said.

"Alone," Claire suggested softly. "May we see her alone?"

Minger looked up at her as he put the receiver into its cradle. His lips pursed, and then he shrugged. He took his suit coat off the back of his chair and held it, the loop at the neck hung over one beefy finger as they waited.

So far tonight they had managed to escape the media's attention. The news crews had been stationed in front of the precinct house, lights and cameras set up behind the barricades the cops had erected to keep them away from the front entrance.

They had come in one of the back doors, arriving in Claire's grandfather's car. Hawk had backed Claire's out of the garage of the Georgetown house ten minutes before they themselves had left, drawing most of the media who had been waiting in the cold darkness outside it away with him.

And Jordan, who had volunteered to drive them here, had somehow managed to lose most of the others. The small success had generated more satisfaction than it probably deserved, Griff thought. Something that had finally gone right. As he hoped releasing the pictures to the media had.

This was the moment of truth, he supposed. He wasn't sure Claire could stand it if this woman turned out to be one of the crackpots he had warned her about. But Jake had said that the baby hadn't been harmed. That hurting her had never been part of his plan. If this were on the up-and-up, then at least Jake hadn't lied about that.

The door opened, and a young, black female cop came in. She was holding a bundle wrapped in a pink blanket. The covering had been drawn around the baby's head, probably because of the damp January chill that pervaded the police station.

It had been long after dark when they'd gotten the call. Long after the evening news broadcasts where the story had run. But the wheels of the bureaucracy turned slowly. Even in situations like this.

The woman's eyes touched on Claire's face and then on Griff's before they settled questioningly on Minger's. The detective tilted his head toward Claire, and the cop walked over and held out the baby.

Claire hesitated a few seconds. Griff saw the ratcheting breath she took before she reached out and took the child from the officer's arms, the transfer as smooth as if they had done it a hundred times.

Then, after another quick, inquiring glance at Minger for direction, the officer stepped back, removing herself from whatever would happen next. Claire's hand was trembling enough for the movement to be visible as it slowly lifted.

She touched the edge of the blanket, and then, without looking at any of them, she turned it back, revealing the face of the sleeping child.

After that, she remained completely still, looking down at the baby's features a long time. Almost as long, Griff thought, as it had taken Jake Holt's gun to reach its destination. An eternity of waiting.

Finally, her eyes lifted. To meet his rather than Minger's, as he'd expected. Griff realized that their blue shimmered with tears, one of which had already escaped, making its slow way down her cheek, which was totally devoid of color.

He couldn't read what was in them, however. It was neither the triumph he had been hoping for nor the despair he had feared. It was almost as if she were looking through him. As if she didn't see him at all, and his thundering heartbeat faltered.

Then she broke the connection between them to look at Minger. She nodded, a small up-and-down motion of her head, quickly made, before her eyes returned once more to the face of the sleeping baby she held.

Chapter Fifteen

"Holy Mother of God, I said to myself when I seen the news. Not blasphemy, you understand," Rose Connor said earnestly, her eyes moving from Claire's face to Griff's. "But I was that surprised, I can tell you. He seemed such a *nice* man."

She paused, her eyes again searching each face. There could be no agreement for that assessment, of course. Neither he nor Claire would ever feel that Jake Holt was "such a nice man," Griff thought. Not now.

"And yet here was this darling he'd brought me. Which must be, I knew, the baby they was looking for."

Without asking permission, Rose Connor leaned closer to Claire, smoothing a proprietary hand over Gardner's head. The baby was awake now, disturbed by the noises of the squad room they'd passed through on the way to the office where Rose Connor was waiting to meet them. Claire held the little girl upright, securely against her shoulder, but the baby seemed enthralled by her surroundings, dark eyes trying to take in everything.

"I don't know how to thank you for looking after her," Claire said.

Griff was aware that she had to force herself not to turn her body and move the baby away from this woman, who was, despite everything, a stranger. That tendency to overprotectiveness would take awhile to disappear, he supposed. If it ever did. And he certainly couldn't blame Claire for feeling it.

"That's my job," Rose Connor said proudly. "And my joy. Looking after the little ones. I looked after my brothers and sisters when I was only a bit of a girl myself. So I've been doing it all my life, you might say. I don't suppose..." The pleasant lilt faltered, Rose Connor seeming shy for the first time. "I don't suppose you need someone," she said finally, raising her eyes hopefully from Gardner's face to Claire's. "To look after her, I mean."

The broad, winter-reddened fingers dipped under the baby's double chin for a tickle. Despite the strangeness of her surroundings and the lateness of the hour, Gardner grinned, new teeth prominently displayed, and then she ducked her head as if embarrassed to respond to such blatant cajolery.

"I have a nanny," Claire said softly, her eyes meeting Griff's above Rose's shoulder. "But...we want to do something to compensate you for your trouble, of course."

"Oh, no trouble," Rose said, smiling back at the little girl, whose eyes were again fastened on her face. "He paid me. Give me the money up front, he did. For two weeks. And it hasn't been quite that, now has it?"

Not quite two weeks, Griff thought, and yet everything about his life had changed. Both their lives—his and Claire's.

"Not quite," Claire said, her eyes still on his.

He nodded to let her know that he'd do something very generous for Rose Connor. "We'll stay in touch, Mrs. Connor," he said. "To let you know about Gardner. About how she's doing."

"I'd appreciate that. You get attached to them so fast. But it's just Rose," she corrected. "Never was a Mrs. Too old to hope for that now," she added, laughing.

Then she stepped back, moving away from the baby. She plucked her coat, a serviceable gray wool tweed, off the coat rack. And when, with Griff's help, her ample girth had been stuffed into it, she retrieved the knitting she'd been working on from the table and put it into a tapestry sewing bag. Finally, almost reluctantly, she removed the strap of a well-worn vinyl purse from where she had hung it over the back of her chair.

"You keep that darling good and warm on the way home," she said. "It's a bitter night for having a baby out."

"We will," Claire promised. "Detective Minger has your address?"

"All the particulars," Rose assured her with a smile. "I thought I was in trouble for sure. All them questions."

"You're not in trouble," Griff said. "And we *will* be in touch."

"Well, I'll be looking forward to hearing about the darling, no mistake about that. No matter how long or how little they're with me, they're mine, you know. For the moment. And I don't ever forget them."

Her eyes fell again to Gardner, who was chewing her fist. She had been following Rose's movements with big brown eyes.

"She looks like you," Rose said, her gaze moving consideringly from the baby's face to Griff's. "You'd think for a girl, she'll take some after her mother, but I'm guessing from the looks of her she's going to be all you when she grows up."

Griff studied his daughter's face. He was unable to see any reflection of himself, other than the obvious one of shared coloring, in the baby's delicate features. Claire had said the same thing, however, so there must be something of him in the softly rounded cheeks and doll-like mouth. His daughter, he thought again, almost in wonder. His daughter, and he realized this was the first time he had seen her face.

"You take care of her," Rose Connor ordered. The pleasant voice had softened. "You take good care of the both of them."

Griff's eyes lifted to Claire's, seeking permission perhaps to do just that. She had been watching him, but whatever emotion he had surprised in her eyes was hidden by the quick fall of her lashes. Then she lowered her face, cupping her hand on the side of Gardner's head and pulling it gently toward her. She pressed a kiss on the silken down of her daughter's hair before her eyes rose again to meet his.

And whatever he thought he had seen in them before was gone.

WHEN THEY GOT BACK to the house in Georgetown, there was no one there. Hawk had picked Jordan up at the police station. They had left the keys to Claire's grandfather's car with the desk sergeant. It seemed the old man had gone as well, maybe taking a taxi back to his daughter's house or to Maddy and Charles's.

However the arrangements for emptying the big, dark house had come about, they found themselves alone. Together and alone for the first time since that night on the cruiser when Claire had made it clear she wasn't willing to resume their relationship. At least not the same relationship they had once had.

And maybe, despite the daughter they had conceived together, she never would be, Griff acknowledged, looking out into the winter darkness. Claire had taken the baby upstairs to put her down in her crib. She hadn't invited him to accompany them.

He had retreated to the kitchen, where only this morning, sitting at the round oak table, they had finally planned the strategy that had been successful in securing Gardner's return. Unlike the one Jake had planned for them, he thought bitterly. Unlike the operation Jake had controlled from the beginning.

With the others around during the last four days, there had been less tension between him and Claire, just as there had been in the Keys. There had been too many distractions to be able to dwell on all the unresolved issues that lay between them. The CIA's lie about his death. The fact that he hadn't told Claire they didn't intend to kill Diaz. Her long-ago decision not to tell him she was pregnant. And of course, underlying those was still the central question that had driven them apart.

If he and Claire and Gardner were ever to become a family, all of those, he supposed, would have to be discussed. If Claire were willing to discuss them. And he wasn't sure at this point she would be. He knew, however, that she would come back downstairs tonight, to double-check the locks if nothing else. Claire Heywood had never run from anything in her life. Nothing except who and what he was, he reminded himself.

And it was always possible, of course, that she would choose to do that again. Maybe leaving him alone down here, purposely excluded from her joy in Gardner's home-coming, was her way of telling him that. He took a deep breath, wondering if she would ever forgive him for exposing their daughter to the world he had inhabited for so long. A world that, despite his retirement, Griff knew he could never completely escape.

It was his past. His life. His world. And its echoes and images had probably been too clearly demonstrated to Claire during the last few days for her to ever be able to forget that.

"I could make some coffee," she said.

He turned and found her standing in the kitchen door-way, watching him. She was still wearing the dark slacks and white sweater she had put on this morning. There were smudges of exhaustion under her eyes, and her mouth was tight again, almost as if it had forgotten how to relax.

"No," he said. "Thank you, Claire, but...no."

The silence drifted between them, as wide as the stretch of shining white kitchen floor that separated them. Wider even, because it was full of regret. Too many mistakes. And all the baggage of the past. Of their divergent views of the world. Of their roles in it.

"You must be tired," he said. "You probably want to get to bed."

Despite his offer, he didn't move away from the sink where he had been standing when she had come into the room. Looking out at the night through the windows above it. There was nothing out there, of course. Nothing threatening. Nothing dangerous. There was only the safe, pleasant quietness of the exclusive neighborhood where his daughter would grow up. Maybe without him.

Claire nodded, her eyes on his face. She seemed to be waiting, but there was nothing else he could say. Nothing that could erase the nightmare he had brought into their lives. Nothing that would change the possibility that no matter what precautions they took, his past might again touch them. Contaminate them with the violence he had lived with so long it hadn't seemed so terrible to him anymore. Not until it had threatened those he loved.

He didn't even have the right to do for them what he had once believed he was good at. The one thing in this insane world that had always made sense to him. The commitment his entire professional life had been built around. *Standing guard over those we love.*

Claire took a step forward and then another. The leather flats she wore echoed slightly on the ceramic tile. Just before she reached him, she stopped, her eyes again searching his face. Almost as if she had never seen it before. Or as if she were trying to imprint it on her memory. With that thought, his heart began to pound, just as it had at the station.

She had done this once before. Sent him away. Told him to get out of her life. And in his pride, he had refused to beg. Refused to change who he was because he knew he was not what she thought him to be. But this time...

This time, he admitted, he would beg if he had to. His mind briefly visited the nursery upstairs, a room he had never seen, but a room where someone had opened a window one cold dark night and stolen a baby. His baby.

Claire was crying, he realized suddenly. The slowly welling tears emphasized the blue of her eyes, their color as intense as that of the shallows around the island where Jake had taken them.

Slowly she raised her hand. And he forgot to breathe. Forgot to hope. He only knew that whatever she demanded this time, he couldn't agree to. He couldn't leave the two of them alone again.

Standing guard. It was all he had that was worth offering. His life, willingly given, for either of theirs.

Her hand flattened. Palm up, she held it out before him. Several long heartbeats passed before he accepted that this was an invitation. Exactly like one he had once made. The night she had shown up at his door.

He had demanded no explanation for why she had come, despite the bitter things she had said to him. He hadn't needed an explanation of why she was there. It was enough that she was. Enough that when he held out his hand, she had laid her cold, trembling fingers into it and let him draw her inside.

Unquestioning now, as he had not questioned that night, Griff put his hand into hers and felt her fingers close around it. Warm and strong, they didn't tremble tonight. Not even when they led him on the same journey they had taken together once before.

CLAIRE HAD LEFT the bedside lamp on when she came downstairs to find him, and its soft light was welcoming. And familiar. He had often spent the night here. More often than she had come to his house in Maryland.

And tonight, given all that lay between them, that familiarity was soothing. The door to the adjoining room was not completely closed. He assumed that what had once been Claire's upstairs office had been transformed into a nursery for Gardner.

Knowing their daughter was sleeping next door had been inhibiting, at least in the beginning. But of course, any anxiety either of them had felt when they entered this room quickly faded.

After all, for him there could be no doubt Claire wanted him here. No doubt about the message she had intended when she'd offered him her hand. That night, the last night they had spent together, was too clear in their memories for either of them to doubt the significance of her gesture.

And so, when he had finally pulled her to him, slipping his hands under the soft wool of her sweater and tracing, through the silk of her skin, the outline of each rib as his fingers moved upward, his mouth sought hers, certain of her response. He had not been disappointed.

That night on the yacht all the things that had come between them had seemed insurmountable. Here, tonight, they seemed unimportant. And that was because of Claire's generosity. In issuing her invitation, she had demanded nothing. Asked for no explanations. Either for who he was or for what he had done. Or for what he had allowed to happen to their daughter.

"Make love to me," she whispered, her lips moving

against his temple as his mouth caressed the delicate skin of her throat. "Make love to me, Griff."

It was permission that he hadn't needed. Not after the other, but hearing her whisper those words drove the hot blood through his body in a demanding wave of need and desire.

He had always desired Claire. And always loved her. But after what they had been through, it was more important than ever to show her. To prove to her again how he felt.

And through the course of the night, he had done that in every way he could conceive. With his hands, drifting against the well-known and beloved places he had slowly discovered, one by one, during their previous lovemaking. With his lips, brushing with tantalizing tenderness over the most erogenous areas of her sensitized body. With his teeth, teasing nerve endings that had never before seemed so responsive to his touch.

He had once known Claire's body better than he knew his own. Yet in the course of this night, he learned things he had never imagined about her ability to respond. And found places newly awakened to his touch and to his tongue's caress.

He had left nothing unexplored, delighting in inventing ways to make her gasp his name, in hearing it float away into the darkness, or in feeling the breath of its single syllable sighing against his own skin, as his lips trailed wet heat over hers.

There had been nothing one-sided about their lovemaking. One by one, Claire had examined each of the scars he had acquired since they had been together. And she had traced with her tongue and her fingertips the uneven ridges left by the surgeries.

He had been surprised to feel the hot fall of tears, but somehow they had served to burn away his guilt. Guilt that she hadn't been allowed to be with him. Guilt that they hadn't even told her he'd been hurt, as desperately as she would have wanted to know. As desperately as he would have wanted her beside him.

Maybe if he had been able to express that desire, they would have sent for her. Then the long, dark coldness that had come between them wouldn't have existed. But he hadn't, and by the time he had been capable of making his own decisions again, that tragic one had already been made for him.

He could have defied the agency, of course, but in his new bitterness over the changes the terrorist's bullets had made in his life and his body, he had included the old bitterness over Claire's rejection, as well. She had told him she never wanted to see him again, and for months he had savagely, angrily, complied with that demand, fighting other battles, physical ones, while he struggled to conquer his never-ending need for her.

He had been such a fool, he thought, his mouth lingering over the hardening nipple of her breast. So much time wasted. So many things missed. So many things. He raised his head, looking down on the smooth, milk-white skin around the dark areola of her breast, marked with a thin tracery of blue veins and faint, silvered lines.

"You breast-fed her?" he said, his eyes lifting to hers.

There was a moment's hesitation before she answered, and he wondered if that had sounded like a criticism. And then she smiled, the corners of her mouth, relaxed as they had not been throughout the ordeal of these long days, tilting in amusement.

At least she could still read him well enough to know that his question was simply the result of his fascination with a subject he knew nothing about. A process he had missed having any share in. Another regret. Another loss.

"I thought about that the night on the boat," she said.

"About your mouth—and Gardner's. Both of them on my breasts."

The image produced by those words, which had been so soft he had to strain to hear them, was surprisingly erotic. His hard erection suddenly strengthened. And Claire was certainly aware of that, given the intimacy of their positions.

"Very different sensations, I would think," he said, lowering his lips to fasten around the nipple again, the idle suggestion made just before his teeth nibbled at its peak.

"No," she whispered.

He raised his head so he could see her face.

"Not so different. Not the feel," she said. "Not the way it made *me* feel. Not at the beginning."

He nodded, watching the memories move in her eyes.

"A little like the first time with you," she said. "Making love the first time. Nervous. Unsure, I guess, but...anticipating so much what it would be like."

"You don't do that anymore?" he asked.

"Anticipate making love to you?" she teased.

"Feed her."

"You like talking about this," she said, a hint of surprise about that discovery in her voice.

And he realized that he did. He wished he had seen them, Gardner's small dark head against Claire's breast, a contrast to the almost alabaster skin of her body.

"You think that's strange?" he asked. "That I like to think about you feeding her? About seeing you like that?"

"I used to look down at her while she nursed. At her hair. The shape of her head. And I'd remember *your head* there. So, no...I don't think it's strange that you would like to think about that," she said. "She's a part of us. Both of us. A part we created. Just...like this."

"Is that a warning?" he asked, smiling at her.

"Maybe," she said softly. "If you want to be warned."

He thought about the possibility of another baby. He didn't even know the one they had. He had already missed so much. So much of watching her learn and grow and develop. Of being around to take an active role in that.

"I don't think I do," he said, lowering his mouth to reclaim her nipple. "Want to be warned, I mean," he whispered, just before his lips closed around it, beginning to mimic the image that had been in his head.

"Yes," she whispered. And then again, after a long time, as his hands moved against her body, "Oh, yes."

That was what he had asked her to say on the cruiser, he remembered. A word he had thought he needed to hear. And now, tonight, it hadn't seemed important anymore. Because between them it was just as it had always been. And would always be.

"I THINK SHE'S HUNGRY," Griff said.

Claire struggled to open her eyes, squinting against the sun that was pouring into the room through the windows whose draperies she had forgotten to pull. Griff was standing beside the bed, wearing nothing but his slacks, wrinkled because he had dropped them on the floor early on last night.

His belt was through the loops, but he hadn't taken time to buckle it. The waistband gaped a little at the closure, revealing the trail of fine, dark hair that ran down the center of his flat stomach and crossed his navel to disappear into the opening.

"Feed her," Claire suggested, closing her eyes against the temptation that sight offered. She pulled the pillow over her head, trying to block out the painful sunlight and the endless allure of Griff's body.

She must have had at least a couple of hours sleep last night, but she couldn't be sure. After all, she and Griff had

had a lot of lost time to make up for. A lot of cold, empty nights to forget. And forgive.

Despite the pillow, she could still hear the baby. Gardner was always talkative in the mornings. An incomprehensible string of syllables, gradually growing in volume, always accompanied the sound of her rattle being drawn back and forth against the bars of her crib, exactly like a prisoner's protest to the warden.

Claire must have missed the rattle signal this morning. *If* Griff had left Gardner in her crib long enough for that second stage of waking to begin. But the baby was certainly well into the talking phase.

Claire lay there, head under the pillow, listening to those familiar sounds and knowing that for the first time in a long while things really were right in her world. Gardner was safe, and Griff... Griff was back.

Unable to resist, she furtively inched the edge of the pillowcase aside with her fingers until she could see them. Griff's size dwarfed Gardner's. It was obvious that he was holding her very carefully—and a little awkwardly—ready for any unexpected move. Amused, Claire wondered if Griff Cabot had ever before held a baby in his entire life. If not, it seemed to her that the experience was long overdue.

A lot of things had been overdue, she acknowledged, but she refused to let regrets spoil today. Or spoil the sight of Gardner's small fingers now gingerly touching the dark mat of hair that covered Griff's broad bare chest. That would certainly be a new texture for her to explore, Claire thought in amusement.

Griff was looking down on those tiny fingers, so that she could see only the top of his head. There was more gray intermingled with the raven's wing blackness of his hair than she had realized before. The morning light highlighted the contrast, but it also emphasized how very much alike were those two dark heads, together for the first time.

"You want to give me some instructions here, Claire?" Griff said impatiently, raising his head and focusing his attention on the pillow under which she was hiding.

At the sound of his deep voice, Gardner leaned back in surprise, and then, quickly overcoming that reaction, she poked her fingers toward his mouth. Griff automatically avoided them by raising his head, ending up with a couple of chubby fingers grazing his chin. Gardner reached out to touch him again, apparently deciding that she liked the feel of whiskers almost as much as the texture of chest hair.

"Cereal," Claire said, her voice muffled. "There's some in pantry. It says cereal on the jar. She isn't picky."

"Just spoon it in?"

"Straight from the jar," Claire agreed.

That breakfast menu would be the easiest for him to handle. And based on the fact that he'd bravely rescued the crib prisoner without waking Claire, Griff certainly deserved a chance to succeed with his first foray into baby feeding.

Especially deserving after last night, she decided, her reminiscent smile hidden by the pillow.

"THAT COLOR'S GOOD ON YOU," she said, watching them from the doorway. Left alone upstairs, she'd finally decided she'd better check on them.

Griff hadn't opted for the state-of-the-art high chair against the wall. He was doing it the old-fashioned way— baby held securely in his lap, left arm around her middle, spoon in his right hand and a goodly portion of cereal on them both. Gardner had reached the stage where her hunger had been satisfied enough to allow her to be creative.

"It's called rice and bananas," Griff said, looking up.

Gardner's mouth made a couple of futile attempts to capture the elusive bite on the spoon he was holding. Griff's attention was rather flatteringly directed on the length of leg exposed under the short silk robe Claire was wearing, however, instead of on what he was doing. After another openmouthed lunge toward the spoon, Gardner finally gave up and batted at it with her hand, sending more cereal to join the splatters on the table and on her father.

"Did you taste it?" Claire asked, watching him guiltily stuff what remained on the spoon into Gardner's mouth.

"Was I supposed to?" he asked, looking up again.

"I can't ever resist. It's all pretty yucky, if you ask me."

"I've always preferred my bananas flambéd in brandy," he said. And then he smiled at her.

Griff Cabot's smile had always made her knees weak. Right now, coming at her from over their daughter's head, with an endearing splotch of rice cereal on his dark, bewhiskered cheek, she thought it was the most sexually devastating thing she had ever seen.

"Will you marry us?" she said softly.

The silence that followed her question was too long, broken only by Gardner's monosyllabic chant and the slap of her palms against the oak table.

"Nothing's changed about who I am, Claire," Griff said, the smile gone, replaced by the same sternness of expression with which he had dealt with all the setbacks of the last two weeks. "Or about what I've done. And, as much as I wish I could, I can't guarantee it won't ever touch your lives again."

She thought about the truth of what he said. About Gardner. But somehow, seeing them together, seeing Griff hold the baby she knew he would give his life to protect, she knew how right this was. And therefore, she also knew how wrong she had been before.

"I know," she whispered. "But...*I've* changed, Griff. At least in thinking the world is black-and-white. Thinking that I'm right about it all, and that you're wrong. Nothing is ever that simple. And there are no guarantees for anyone that evil won't touch their lives.''

She hesitated, thinking how to phrase the hard lessons she had learned this last year. And then she decided that what was in her heart was best said exactly as she felt it.

''I just know that if it ever threatens her again, I want you here. Protecting us.''

Standing guard over those we love, Griff thought.

That had been the standard under which his team had operated. Something that the world would perhaps never understand about what they did. Something Claire had never believed. But never before had the meaning of those simple words been so real to him. Or so personal. And so damn right.

''If you're sure, Claire, that this is what you want,'' he said. ''If you're sure, then yes.''

She smiled, the strain that had grown around her lips as she waited easing. Her eyes touched briefly on Gardner's face and then came back up to his.

''I don't think I've ever been as sure about anything in my entire life,'' she said softly. ''Except maybe a political position or two,'' she added, her tone teasing, her smile widening as he reciprocated it. ''But we can discuss those later.''

''Or agree to disagree about them,'' he said, his tone lightened to match hers.

Her eyes were again on their daughter. ''Especially since we've got all the important stuff sorted out.''

Griff nodded, feeling his throat tighten unexpectedly. Just as he had seen Claire do last night, he cupped his big hand around Gardner's head and pulled it near enough to kiss the top, pressing his lips for the first time against the shining softness of his daughter's hair.

Standing guard. Today and for the rest of my life, he promised silently. *Always, standing guard.*

Epilogue

"I need the practice," Tyler Stewart Hawkins said. She reached to take a squirming Gardner from Kathleen Cross's capable arms and settled the baby on her hip, one chubby leg resting atop the small bulge of her pregnancy.

"Well, *I* certainly don't," Kathleen said, laughing. She smoothed her hand over the baby's head, and then looked up to smile at Hawk's wife, whom she had met for the first time today.

The party that celebrated Griff Cabot and Claire Heywood's wedding had been small and intimate, but there had been no doubting the joy the guests had taken in this union. The living room of the Maryland house had been transformed by hundreds of roses, the scent of which filled the room.

Claire had been radiant when she had entered on her father's arm. Her eyes hadn't left Griff's face as he waited by the windows that looked out on the sleeping garden, except once, to touch briefly, smilingly, on Monty Gardner, who was serving as Griff's best man. Perhaps either of the other two men in attendance might have had a better claim to that role, but neither had objected to Griff's choice of the old man.

The bonds of their friendship, forged in danger and commitment—to each other and to the missions they had undertaken—were too strong to need any such outward confirmation. Despite the fact that the team they'd once belonged to no longer existed, the ties that bound them surely did.

"I wonder what they're talking about," Tyler asked, her famous violet eyes focused on the three men, who were visible through the open door of Griff's study.

"The good old days, I hope," Kathleen suggested lightly as her gaze followed Tyler's.

Then, almost unconsciously, it was redirected to her children, who were being entertained by the story Rose Connor was telling. Her broad face was beaming, her hands gesturing enthusiastically, and Meg and Jamie were listening with the rapt attention they usually reserved for when Jordan read to them.

Safe, Kathleen thought. The need to know that they were, no matter the situation, would always be in the back of her mind. She couldn't imagine how Claire Heywood had endured having her baby stolen.

With that thought, her eyes sought and found the bride, elegant in a winter-white wool suit. Claire seemed so beautifully serene as she saw to the needs of her guests, as much at home in this huge house as Griff himself. And just a little intimidating, Kathleen thought in amusement. She had felt that same sense of awe when Jordan introduced her to Griff.

Of course, considering the respect Jordan had for his former boss, Cabot had already achieved near-legendary status in her mind, long before she'd met him. Her gaze returned to the room where the three men were talking. At least Hawk and Jordan, standing before a huge desk, were talking. Griff, seated behind it, seemed to be merely listening. He was, however, giving whatever they were saying the same serious attention he had devoted to Jamie's meandering narrative about his new puppy.

Finding that Griff was warm and down to earth enough to listen to an excited two-year-old's disjointed story had been a pleasant surprise. But then this entire day had been surprising, Kathleen thought. She had expected the ghost of Jake Holt's betrayal to overshadow the joy of this wedding, but it hadn't. Probably because everyone was determined it wouldn't.

"It looks as if they might be up to no good."

Surprised, Kathleen turned to find Claire Cross standing at her elbow, her eyes, like Kathleen's and Tyler's, focused on the meeting in Griff's study.

"What do you think it means?" Tyler asked, shifting Gardner into a more comfortable position on her slender hip.

"Why don't we ask them?" Claire suggested, including Gardner in the smile she directed at Tyler. "After all, I think the three of us have a vested interest. Don't you?"

"You lead the way," Kathleen suggested, smiling. "After all, you're the one who's married to the boss."

Belatedly, she wondered if Claire might be offended by that teasing comment. When Claire laughed instead, Kathleen decided that she just might like this woman, whose face she had seen dozen of times on her television screen, as much as she liked Tyler, whose face was, she realized, equally famous.

"That position as the boss's wife is still a little new for me to feel totally confident of my reception, but somehow…" she paused, her eyes finding Griff again "…somehow I don't think he'll throw me out. At least, maybe not today." And still smiling, she lead the way to the room where the men they loved were talking.

GRIFF SPOTTED THEM FIRST, his smile at Claire probably warning Hawk and Jordan that their conclave was about to be invaded. Not that she believed he would really mind this very feminine invasion.

Especially when Gardner reached for him, almost lunging out of Tyler's arms as soon as she spotted him.

"Obviously a daddy's girl," Kathleen said, smiling at Griff as he took his daughter. Then her eyes shifted to Jordan's face, and she added, "I have one of those."

Jordan returned her smile, holding her eyes, the unspoken communication obvious. And seeing it might have been what prompted Hawk to put his arm around Tyler's spreading waistline, pulling her firmly against his side.

"We were wondering what you three were up to," Claire said.

The silence that followed her comment lasted too long, and it was Jordan who answered it.

"Hawk and I were offering Griff an employment opportunity," he said, his tone amused, because they all knew Cabot's financial resources.

"An employment opportunity?" Claire repeated carefully.

"We're offering Griff a job," Hawk said. "Since we've found out that he's not really dead. Just unemployed."

"Like us," Jordan added.

"A job doing what?" Claire asked.

"Standing guard," Hawk said softly, his tone free of amusement. "It's what we're good at."

"You don't mean..." Claire hesitated, trying to imagine exactly what he did mean.

"Going private," Jordan said, clarifying what they'd been thinking. "Providing protection for people who have problems like the three of us have had recently. We think there may be others from the team who might be interested in something like this as well."

"After all," Griff said softly, his eyes on Claire's face, "we have the skills."

It was what he had told her before. And he had offered to use those skills on her behalf even before he had known the truth about Gardner's birth.

To find and retrieve what was lost or stolen. To guard and protect the innocent. Like their daughter. Like Jamie and Meg Sorrel. Like Kathleen, and Tyler Stewart.

The skills these men possessed had been acquired on a very different battlefield. They had proven, however, that what they had learned in that war could be adapted to the kinds of missions the three of them had undertaken during the last six months. Protecting lives rather than destroying.

"We'd like to use them for other battles," Griff said, echoing her own thoughts. "To fight other wars."

"There isn't any other war," Claire said softly, and saw by the sudden pain in his eyes that he hadn't understood. And so she clarified it. After all, this was one of the things she still needed to say to him.

"It's all the same war," she said, her eyes leaving his to touch on the faces of the men and women who had gathered today to celebrate their union. "A war against evil—the same evil you've always fought. And if people like you don't choose to fight that war...then eventually evil will win."

The silence in the small circle of friends was profound and complete. No one knew better than these six people about the reality of that evil. It had touched each of their lives.

"And it must not," Claire said softly, her eyes coming back to Griff's. "It must never be allowed to win. Not even one small battle. Not if any one of you can prevent it."

"I take it then I have your permission," Griff said after a moment, smiling at her.

She wondered if she could really bear to let him face the dangers this kind of enterprise would involve. Then Gardner's hand touched Griff's mouth, and smiling, he put his lips against her fingers, a father's kiss.

"*And* my blessing," she said softly, letting him go to be again what he had always been. A good, strong man fighting evil. And it had taken her too long to realize that.

"And mine," Kathleen said, watching the same interplay between father and daughter. "I know what it's like to live in fear. If the three of you can do for someone else what Jordan did for me and for my children—our children," she corrected, smiling again into Jordan's eyes, "then you must."

Tyler's fingers were unconsciously spread, almost protectively, over the baby she carried, and her eyes had found Hawk's face. She studied the rugged features and then drew a deep breath.

"In all honesty..." she began and, wide violet eyes still focused on her husband, she hesitated, as if reluctant to say aloud what she felt.

And they were all waiting, Claire realized. Silently waiting, breathing suspended.

"In all honesty, Hawk's not too handy around the house. I've been a little disappointed in that," she said apologetically, speaking to Hawk before she turned back to face the others. "But I can tell you from personal experience," she continued, the corners of her beautiful mouth tilting, "he's hell on wheels at protecting people."

Hawk was the first to laugh, the sound of his laughter unexpected, rich and free. The others joined in as soon as they understood that Tyler had given her permission, as well.

"To the future," Claire said, her eyes on Gardner's face. Then she lifted them to her husband. "And to your new team."

"Something new, rising from the ashes of the old," Griff said softly.

He was right, Claire thought. They had all risen from the ashes of their pasts. Hawk, who according to the CIA no longer even existed. Jordan, who had been transformed into someone else. And Griff... Griff, who had literally come back from the dead.

"Like the mythical phoenix," she said, "born from the fire that destroys it."

"The Phoenix Brotherhood," Griff said.

And they knew, just as he had, that it was exactly right.

* * * * *

Don't miss these upcoming titles by Gayle Wilson.
LADY SARAH'S SON,
a November release from Harlequin Historicals,
will be on the shelves in October.
EACH PRECIOUS HOUR,
a December release from Harlequin Intrigue,
will be on sale in November.

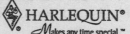

Looking For More Romance?

Visit Romance.net

Check in daily for these and other exciting features:

Hot off the press

View all current titles, and purchase them on-line.

What do the stars have in store for you?

Horoscope

Hot deals

Exclusive offers available only at Romance.net

Plus, don't miss our interactive quizzes, contests and bonus gifts.

PWEB

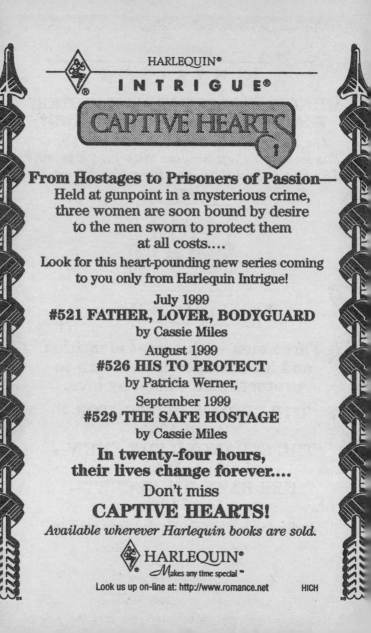

COMING NEXT MONTH

#521 FATHER, LOVER, BODYGUARD by Cassie Miles
Captive Hearts
Amanda Fielding remembered nothing of the robbery or blow to the
head that caused her partial amnesia. When she woke in the hospital,
she gazed into the dark, sexy eyes of Dr. David Haines—her former
lover. David swore to protect her from the danger stalking her—and
she knew she'd finally have to tell him about their baby...

#522 WANTED: COWBOY by Kelsey Roberts
The Rose Tattoo
Barbara Prather ranted on about Cade Landry, her cowboy
protector—but she couldn't seem to get enough of him! As the
only witness to a murder, Barbara had an assassin on her trail. Cade
kidnapped her to save her life—but was his interest professional...or
personal?

#523 HER EYEWITNESS by Rita Herron
Blinded in the line of duty, police officer Collin Cash had a transplant
to regain his sight—and woke to a vision of murder. The dead man's
widow stood accused—and only Collin could prove her innocence.
When Sydney Green discovered Collin's identity, would she accept
his help...and his heart?

#524 THE BRIDE'S SECRET by Adrianne Lee
Nikki Navarro would do anything to find the family she'd never
known—even take on Chris Conrad, the dark and sexy owner of
Wedding House. Nikki was the spitting image of the bride whose
portrait graced the master suite—and only Chris could protect her
from someone determined she would never know if she was, in fact,
the bride's secret...

Look us up on-line at: http://www.romance.net

In July 1999 Harlequin Superromance®
brings you *The Lyon Legacy*—a
brand-new 3-in-1 book from popular
authors Peg Sutherland, Roz Denny Fox
& Ruth Jean Dale

3 stories for the price of 1!

Join us as we celebrate
Harlequin's 50th Anniversary!

Look for these other
Harlequin Superromance®
titles wherever books are sold July 1999:

A COP'S GOOD NAME (#846)
by Linda Markowiak

THE MAN FROM HIGH MOUNTAIN (#848)
by Kay David

HER OWN RANGER (#849)
by Anne Marie Duquette

SAFE HAVEN (#850)
by Evelyn A. Crowe

JESSIE'S FATHER (#851)
by C. J. Carmichael